PRAISE FOR : S

"A touching, funny tale of a Chinese American underachiever's unlikely journey into standup comedy while also navigating the duties and obligations of society and his traditional family. The comic yet poignant acts that make up the life of Sirius Lee will both entertain and haunt you."
Cheryl Lu-Lien Tan, author of Sarong Party Girls

"An epistolary novel with a devastating sense of humor that will break your heart and captures that space between a rock and hard place of being Asian American in search of unconditional love. Self-centered outcast, precocious megastar Sirius Lee (Hor Luk Lee) shares his life lessons with his daughter, making himself known to her with courage and candor in an appeal that will make you nod with recognition and laugh in that way that only the sharpest comedians can make you laugh, with tears in your eyes."
Jimin Han, author of A Small Revolution

"Leland Cheuk's wacky and wondrous novel follows Sirius Lee, the ultimate anti-hero, an Asian American comedian who overcomes all odds to become a star. With brio and humor, Sirius fights prejudice, substance abuse, and his own worst instincts, always striving for a world bigger than his own. By the last page, he was so real to me that I longed to turn on the TV and watch the legendary comedy special that gives the novel its name."
Kirstin Chen, author of Bury What We Cannot Take

"Leland Cheuk's *No Good Very Bad Asian* tears the tarp from the Asian American experience and exposes its deepest desires and fears. It articulates perfectly the amusements that make the entire room uncomfortable. Cringing never felt so good."
Ed Lin, author of 99 Ways to Die

"... a darkly hilarious story that turns the immigrant sage on its head...Cheuk manages to imagine twisted, hilarious worlds that seem to ring with a prescient knowledge of our time and our culture."

The Rumpus
on *The Misadventures of Sulliver Pong*

"... at once heartwarming and wrenching, examining heritage, immigrant life, and injustice in America with bite and comedic verve."

The Millions
on *The Misadventures of Sulliver Pong*

"We're big admirers of Leland Cheuk's fiction, which blends innovative forms with psychological acuity."

Vol. 1 Brooklyn

"... uproarious and wildly, sometimes even inappropriately, entertaining."

The Collagist
on *The Misadventures of Sulliver Pong*

"[Cheuk] upends striver stories and stereotypes of Asian American men in the ultimate dysfunctional family story."

Elliott Bay Book Company
on *The Misadventures of Sulliver Pong*

"... Cheuk exposes truths Chinese American immigrants faced in a transitory culture."

The Good Men Project
on *The Misadventures of Sulliver Pong*

"Leland Cheuk is far and away one of my favorite emerging American writers. His wry wit and acutely observant social humor are always perfectly calibrated to remain humanist and empathetic, never veering into the snarky easiness of self-satisfied hipster irony. His is a shrewd and highly compassionate imagination of a kind that makes you want to not only read him, but to reread him."

Kris Saknussemm, author of Zanesville
on *Letters from Dinosaurs*

"Daring enough to slay the Model Minority myth, upend tired tropes, and inject a much needed dose of humor and irreverence, Leland Cheuk is the writer Asian American lit has been waiting for."

Shawna Yang Ryan, author of Green Island
on *Letters from Dinosaurs*

". . . brims with Vonnegut-flavored humor and Delillo-esque commentary as it sends up Asian American struggles and father-son rivalries. This is the hilarious and assured debut of a wise and wacky new talent."

Laurie Foos, author of The Blue Girl
on *The Misadventures of Sulliver Pong*

"As sneakily addictive as a game of Pong (which was named, we're told, after the narrator's dad), this zany zip-line of a novel takes the piss out of the Asian American 'good immigrant' story. Full of charming antiheroes making comically bad choices, the story dazzles us with its absurdity, which makes its eventual wisdom--about lineage, ethnicity, and the meaning of family--all the more wonderfully surprising."

Michael Lowenthal, author of The Paternity Test
on *The Misadventures of Sulliver Pong*

NO GOOD VERY BAD ASIAN

a novel by

Leland Cheuk

C&R Press
Conscious & Responsible

Cover design by Laura Catherine Brown
Photo credit by Lisa Kristel

Copyright ©2019 by Leland Cheuk

Library of Congress Cataloging-in-Publication Data

ISBN 978-1-936196-99-9
LCCN 2018956126

C&R Press
Conscious & Responsible
crpress.org

For special discounted bulk purchases, please contact:
C&R Press sales@crpress.org or SPD Distribution
Contact books@crpress.org to book events, readings and author signings

For Jess

and to the dream chasers

OUR PLAN

To my dear Maryann,

Our plan is going to seem rather unorthodox. Today is your seventh birthday (happy, happy)! I'm writing to you from a remote-controlled reclining desk that seems to have a mind of its own. When I *want* to sit up, it lays me down. When I want to lie down, it stands me up. This desk is just one of many things that haven't worked out as I'd hoped.

Back to the aforementioned plan. First and foremost, I need you to keep our correspondence top secret. Whatever you do, please don't tell your mom. Second, do not under any circumstances read past the first few pages of this letter until you're eighteen. A lot of what I'm going to tell you is inappropriate for kids.

Oh, who am I kidding? It's not like I'll be able to stop you anyhow. If your mother and her divorce attorney have their way, I'll never see you again. As it is, you and I haven't seen each other in a year. If we met up tomorrow, I wonder if you'd even recognize me.

Last time I saw you, we were still living in New York City. I cooked your favorite meal (spaghetti with tomato sauce, butter, and a sprinkle of pepper). You were sullen and smelled of Froot Loops. You wore that ridiculous red wool dress with white elbow length gloves that your mom insisted on buying from Jacadi Paris. You looked like you were dressed as Jackie Kennedy for Halloween.

"All you need is the pillbox hat," I quipped.

You didn't laugh.

I could never make you laugh.

That's what I do: make people laugh. You can look it up. I was the eighth comedian ever to sell out Madison Square Garden. Most of us are so big that people know us by just one name. Eddie. Louis. Dice. Dane. Rock. Aziz. And me, Sirius. I was one of the fucking best; ask anyone. Excuse my language— the delete key on this laptop is broken and I can't go backward and correct mistakes, a sad situation that closely resembles life.

I think about you all the time. I see you everywhere in the city even though you're not here anymore. I see you as your future self, going to middle school, wearing a uniform. I see you jogging in Central Park, your ponytail swaying, your gait springy. I see you having drinks in bars with friends. I see you in restaurants, gazing lovingly into the eyes of your partner, tea lights flickering over your face. Seeing you hurts.

They say time heals all wounds but who are *they* anyway? *They* are incorrect. I've discovered that the wound doesn't hurt much more than a paper cut at first, but it gets worse over time and now I'm typing this pain out to you because if I don't, I'll burst and no one here wants to scrape pieces of me off the walls.

The odds are not good that I'll see you again. That's why I'm going to:

1. Write down everything you might want to know about me.
2. Give you my side of the story about what happened between me and your mother.
3. Impart whatever wisdom I may have gleaned from my drunken slalom through the ill-kept roads of Life.

Our situation is not ideal, but it's the best I can do because your mother is determined to keep you as far away from me as possible, while attributing it to her "new career" (as if being arm candy for a Russian oil magnate is a job). I apologize for speaking so coarsely about her. It's the missing delete key, I swear. It's my fault she wants nothing to do with me.

Please accept these pages from my manager Sarah and don't involve the militarized security force at your way-too-expensive prep school.

You are about to get your father, live and uncensored.

Love always,
Dad

GOD'S VOMIT

Never in my wildest dreams did I imagine becoming a successful anything, let alone a comedian. I fully expected to be a huge disappointment.

Life's first disappointment was my name. My real name isn't Sirius. My Chinese name is pronounced "whore." Hor Luk Lee.

I was born in America.

Your grandparents saw *Sixteen Candles*. They were quite familiar with Long Duk Dong.

They named me Hor anyway.

It was my dad's idea: he wanted to keep me as Chinese as possible. For much of my childhood, I remember him as a yellow version of a Black Panther. He wanted me to learn *Teochew hua*, understand every little Chinese tradition, and eat only South Chinese cuisine (even those lotus seed mooncakes that taste like sand and a sprinkle of piss).

You know what his name is?

John.

One of my earliest memories was of my dad having a conference with my kindergarten teacher Mrs. Jarmuschki. Mrs. J was my first crush. (God rest your pants suits, Mrs. J.) She was also sixty.

As a kid, I had bowel control problems (foreshadowing events in adulthood). In Mrs. J's classroom after school, my dad had to squeeze into one of those kiddie desks and explain my accidents.

Even though he had cleaned me up on many an occasion, my dad denied the existence of my loose bowels like they were Iranian nukes. "Why you don't think it someone else, eh, Mrs. Ja-moose-ski?" he said. "Why you think it my son? Is it because he Chinese?"

Mrs. J rolled her eyes. "Of course not," she said. "Half the class is Chinese."

"Does that make you angry?"

"You're being ridiculous," replied Mrs. J, who glanced at me apologetically.

"You white women are all the same," my dad said. "I will report you to principal."

Mrs. J planted elbows on desk. Her palms met like she was in prayer. "Listen, Mr. Lee," she said. "Your son smells like God's vomit."

I let out an embarrassed laugh, which turned into an uncontrollable fit of giggles. The more I thought about what she said, the funnier it became. Wouldn't God's vomit smell like flowers made of soap and glow like cartoon gold? Mrs. J and my dad both stared at me like I'd been possessed.

That was the first time I remember laughter making me feel better about myself.

I didn't have a happy childhood. I don't know what to do around people who have a love-love relationship with their families. When folks talk about how nostalgic they are for their upbringing, I expect someone to cue a laugh track.

I grew up in Alhambra, California, near Pasadena, in San Gabriel Valley. There are lots of Chinese people there. By "lots," I mean when people talk about "white flight," San

Gabriel Valley is *From Where The Whites Flee* (that might be a children's book). The Chinese there aren't very assimilated. My parents knew millionaires who'd been in America for three or four decades and didn't speak or read a word of English. Most of the kids I grew up with in my neighborhood never left the Valley. They had thick accents despite being American-born. They lived with their parents well into their thirties. When they married and had babies, they lived with their moms and dads, their grandparents, their spouses, and their brood in the same house—the ultimate Yellow Panther achievement! The America outside San Gabriel Valley—where it was okay to be gay, where every black person wasn't a likely criminal, where women didn't have to take a back seat to men—might as well have been Mars.

My parents owned and worked at a round-the-clock liquor store near Hollywood. Mom, Dad, his parents, and I lived in a tiny two-bedroom apartment, where I slept on a sofa every night (Yellow Panther bonus points!). To this day, I have trouble sleeping in real beds.

Mom and Dad argued a lot. My mom didn't like the way my dad spent his days, and my dad didn't like being questioned. When he wasn't working, he loitered at a Vietnamese deli where they served banh mi, sweet coffee, and gambling addiction. Whenever my mom mentioned condensed milk, we all knew she meant baccarat.

My grandma and mom hated each other. Grandma took my dad's side on everything. If Dad wanted to gamble a little bit after a hard day's work, put it all on red! If my mom had a problem with it, get a second job!

Grandma was often horrified by what American schools taught us. In first grade, around Thanksgiving, the teacher made us make Puritan hats out of black construction paper, with the buckle cut out of white cardboard. White is the color of death for the Chinese, and Grandma couldn't have that. She took a red ballpoint pen and colored in the buckle so I wouldn't risk being suddenly struck down by the Chinese gods. I cried and cried and told her that I'd be ridiculed nonstop, but she just kept scratching away that evil color, steadfast and uncaring. I had to wear the defaced hat to school, and sure enough, the white kids called me "ricepicker," "boat monkey," "refugee," and many, many other names.

"Why didn't you listen to me?" I wailed when I came home.

"Why would we?" she said. "You're just a child."

I wasn't a shy kid. I enjoyed standing in front of class and reading things aloud. But I started noticing that whenever students were asked to speak, white kids were picked first. In second grade, I got sick of it. While Matt Pohle read his book report on Richard Nixon in front of the chalkboard, I stood at my desk and began reading my paper about Amelia Earhart aloud. I was kept after school. When my mom came to get me, she asked what the hell I was thinking.

"The white kids always talk first," I said.

"Why do you want to talk?" she said. "You're not that smart anyway. Stay quiet. Study."

The next day, I was walking around a corner on the way to class, and Matt Pohle tripped me. I fell so hard that I landed on my chin, and my front teeth cut my lower lip.

"Chinny-Chinny Chinese," he said, strutting off like an action hero back to his group of white friends.

The next year I sat next to Matt Pohle and noticed that he had a Yoda action figure in his open front desk. When he went to sharpen his pencil, I stole the little green Jedi and left that day tickled that Matt was blubbering to the teacher about it.

I wouldn't get away with my crime so easily. The next day, our teacher, Ms. Yu, pulled me aside and asked if I'd taken Yoda. I denied it, of course. When Grandpa came to walk me home from school, Ms. Yu was waiting. In Mandarin, she asked him to ask me whether I'd five-fingered the figure. Grandpa just stared at me, arms akimbo, waiting.

He was balding and long-faced with those big bags under his eyes framed by thick dark-rimmed specs and shaggy gray brows. He looked so much like the personification of honesty I couldn't lie to him. I took the figure out of my backpack, returned it to the teacher, and apologized. Grandpa walked me home in silence. But as we turned onto the street where our apartment complex stood, he said, "If you wanted the toy, I could have bought it for you."

"I didn't even want it," I said. I told him I stole it to get back at Matt Pohle because he had tripped me and called me Chinny-Chinny Chinese.

Grandpa's expression was placid. "They are free to be who they are," he said. "But we have to be better than them. Understand?"

Our apartment was so small that I could hear it whenever my dad tried to get frisky with my mom, usually on Sundays when the liquor store was closed. He didn't succeed often, thank God. As for the times he did? Let's just say it didn't sound like he was any good. I was nine when I realized what they were doing.

Once, on the drive home from the grocery store, my mom and I were in our pickup truck at a stoplight, and in the car beside us was a white couple making out.

"*Ai-yuh*," Mom said, disgusted. "Don't watch! White people are always having sex. They look at each other and that's it! They can't control themselves! There's something wrong with Americans. Always having sex like animals! Your dad learns from them. Always wanting to fool around!"

I did my best to tune her out as she went on and on.

She did not like sex. This, she made clear.

In fourth grade, I noticed that I only found white girls attractive. I used to watch every last re-run of *My Two Dads* because I wanted to marry a girl like Nicole. Something was wrong with me. My class was almost two-thirds Chinese by then, and I didn't think about any of the Chinese girls in the same way I thought about the white ones.

I liked this girl named Courtney. She had blue eyes, freckles, and long, wavy auburn hair, and she wore these print maxi dresses that made her look like a seventies love child. I liked her mainly because in addition to finding her cute, she was the one white girl in class who was shorter than me.

Because I liked her, I attacked her mercilessly in four square. One day, after eliminating her yet again with a barrage of corner shots, she pushed me in the chest and shouted, "Why do you keep picking on me?"

We were talking! I was so excited. "I'm sorry," I said, steeling my jaw. "But I'm trying to make you better."

"You're so mean."

"No, I'm not," I said. "I like you, and I want to be your friend."

Courtney lowered her eyes and shook her head. "I'm not going to be friends with you," she said. "You look like a Lego."

A Lego! Little, yellow. With C-shaped hands?

"Well, your freckles make you look dirty!" was the best retort I could manage.

Courtney started wailing and ran to the teacher on recess duty. There would be no recess for me for two days.

Now that I'm older, I know the way I saw Courtney and the way she saw me were a result of a malfunctioning in our brains. I put her on this pedestal, and she looked down upon me because of the color of my skin, because of the different ways we dressed, because she was a girl and I a boy. It was all subconscious and it happened before we could do anything about it. Soon, people will look at you in ways that you don't want to be seen, Maryann. Maybe they'll wonder "where you're from." Maybe they'll be eyeing your prep-school uniform and thinking about how much money your family has. Maybe they'll be gawping at your height, your weight, the size and shape of your body parts. Their gaze might make you feel worth less than the next person, unwanted. You might not want to be seen at all—maybe you'll just want to be free, like the Matt Pohles of the world.

The mindless way we look upon each other is a disease and it has many names. Some call it racism. Or sexism. Or classism. I call it zombie-ism. There's no cure, no doctors to help, and we all suffer from it from time to time. All you can do is be aware that what a zombie sees isn't real.

As I reached puberty, the Lee women agreed on one thing: something had to be done about my face. Mom hated the way I looked. I was chubby. My hair stuck up from multiple cowlicks. My acne was so bad that my mom got tears in her eyes when she stared at me too long.

She spent the little money we had dragging me to dermatologists, who did painful extractions and made me a lab hamster for Accutane and Retin-A. My mom would often say that no one would want to marry me unless I lost some weight and did a better job of washing my face. (Now that your mom has left me, my mother has resurrected this talking point.)

Grandma distrusted American medicine so she kept flushing my pills down the drain. She preferred to scrub my face with natural products Chinese people could vouch for. Chrysanthemum tea, warm water and ginger, and lotus root soup. They fought over me like I was a Middle Eastern oil field. With them buffing my face like a truck, it was a miracle I didn't reflect sunlight.

My future was the only thing everyone in the Lee Council could bond over. From the time I was in middle school to when I left home, entire dinners were spent debating what I should do when I grew up.

"Once he's old enough to work at the store, I'll teach him how to succeed in business," my dad said. "*Een-vess-mun!*" That's how he pronounced the word "investment."

"Doctor," Grandma said.

"Lawyer," Mom said.

Dad slapped the dining table. "C-E-O!" He thrust a finger skyward with each letter.

My grandpa was a quiet man who absorbed, with a sublime and distant grin, every one of my grandma's insults ("rice bucket," "deficient brain," and my personal favorite: "professional airplane hitter"—a euphemism for chronic masturbator). Sometimes he'd just say, "Suffer today so you can have a better future. That's what we do." He glared accusingly at Dad and Grandma. "For generations and generations, that's what we have done."

Dinners were when the adult Lees shared their hands-on love for the family business. They loved port wine. They went through a case a week. By the time I was in junior high, I knew from watching afternoon soaps that people didn't drink port before dinner, and they certainly didn't go through a bottle per person in one sitting. My mom was the only member of our family who limited herself to a few sips because she had to drive my dad to his 8:00 p.m. to 6:00 a.m. shift at Lee's Liquors. She was usually home and in bed by nine because she had to get up before dawn to work the 6:00 a.m. to 2:00 p.m. shift before her brother relieved her.

Eventually, I informed her that port was a dessert wine.

"What do you know about wine?" she snapped.

"That's why it's sweet."

"I don't know who taught you that," she said. "It's sweet because it's good."

"And you're only supposed to drink it from a small glass," I said. "Not giant plastic cups from 7-Eleven like you do."

My mom was speechless for what seemed like a full minute. "We drink it because it is healthy for adults. Even the whites think so."

When they weren't planning my future, my family would make up stories about why America was the way it was.

On why Mexico was poor: Dad concluded that no one could make big money selling tacos.

On Bill Clinton's affair with Monica Lewinsky, Mom said that his infidelity showed that the president was born smart because naturally intelligent men deserved multiple wives, as exemplified by her grandfather, who had four wives and happened to be a scientist.

On the Oklahoma City bombing, Grandma asserted that Jesus was, in fact, a living white man in hiding, sent from God to control American terrorists via telepathy.

Even Fox News would have called my family's nightly hot takes total nonsense.

Sometimes, after the rest of the Lees went to bed, I'd sneak out of our apartment and walk a mile to the South Pasadena metro station. I'd watch the light rail trains go by and fantasize about stepping in front of one. I knew from an early age that I was growing up in a pile of bullshit and that I could never be happy in that home. I learned how families were supposed to behave not from my own but from watching sitcoms. We were supposed to love each other no matter what. You were supposed to learn useful lessons from your parents. Home was supposed to be the one place on Earth where you could do no wrong.

There were nights on that platform when I'd close my eyes and step close enough to the tracks to feel the whoosh on my face as the train passed. But when I imagined my parents screaming and crying over my dead body, I couldn't bear it, so I'd step back.

I'm glad I didn't have the balls to do it. Otherwise, I wouldn't have achieved my lifelong dream of becoming a comedian.

And, of course, I wouldn't have had you.

When I was twelve, the old Chinese lady in the apartment next door croaked, and it turned out that she was a hoarder. Our landlord hired a team of Mexicans to clear her tiny apartment, and in the hallway, I discovered that the woman had a treasure trove of used VHS tapes, including *Rant in E-Minor* by Bill Hicks and Eddie Murphy's *Raw*. She was one of those ladies who went around collecting aluminum cans to recycle. Who knew she was into the funny (and Eddie Murphy's endless bits about the nature of a lady's private parts)? Life is a self-published mystery.

I stole those tapes, and when I watched Hicks, in that black suit jacket and turtleneck, being smarter and funnier than everyone else, doing that bit ripping parents for thinking their babies were special even though children came from millions upon millions of sperm, I laughed harder than I'd ever laughed.

I started stealing from my mom's wallet to buy standup CDs from the Tower Records near home, and then I'd sneak them into the house in my baggy shorts like a prisoner hiding a shank so my family wouldn't ask me any unwanted questions. Late at night, I'd plug headphones into an old Discman and listen to *Strategic Grill Locations* by Mitch Hedberg or *Bigger and Blacker* by Chris Rock. My living room/bedroom transformed into an imaginary comedy club where I wasn't a chubby, pimply teen suffocated by his family anymore. I was just another person in the audience.

There's this Hedberg joke about a talk show featuring an inspirational story about a lady on TV born without arms. "They said, 'Lola does not know the meaning of the word "can't."' And that to me was kinda worse in a way," Hedberg said. "Not only does she not have arms, but she doesn't understand simple contractions." For a solid year, I listened to that joke over and over, and every time, it made me laugh until tears fell.

Comedians spoke truths I couldn't speak at home, and people laughed and felt okay about their disappointing lives. I felt okay about my disappointing life.

Comedy saved me.

THE FAMILY RAZZMATAZZ

My junior high school was even more Chinese than my middle school and as competitive as a televised death match. We had no arts classes: no drama, no music, no shop. But there were five different algebra courses. English and history were made incredibly easy (all fill-in-the-blank tests, no essays), as if the faculty was annoyed that it had to include those subjects at all. Teachers openly encouraged us to read Cliffs Notes instead of actual books. I don't know why they didn't just keep the school open on weekends because most of the kids met again for Saturday Mandarin school and extra math tutoring at Kumon learning centers anyway. I was terrible at math and science. I barely graduated seventh grade, and my parents began to worry that I was community college-bound.

My father took out a second mortgage on the liquor store and enrolled me in a private prep school in the Hollywood Hills because he thought I had a better chance of competing academically against white kids. Marsden High in Guernica Beach was one of the top-ranked (richest, whitest) schools in Southern California. It was also where MTV filmed the reality show, *The Family Razzmatazz*, the one about the drug-fried comedian Johnny Razzmatazz, who came up in the eighties with Bill Hicks and Sam Kinison.

Guernica Beach was the center of the reality-shows-for-teens universe at the time. The success of *The Family Razzmatazz* spawned a show about a group of Marsden High kids named *The Beach*, the success of which begot *Hearstwood*, about Marsden's rival high school. Guernica Beach churned out throngs of new D-list celebrities like Stephanie Bold, Laura Castelli, Elizabeth Haymon, their Mervyn's fashion lines, failed singing careers, underbaked chick-lit novels, and beefy white boyfriends, who parlayed their high school 'ships into thousands of nights of underaged bottle service and at least a half decade of worry-free unemployment or a thirty-season run as a regular on MTV's *The Challenge*.

The summer before freshman year, I rented the first season of *The Family Razzmatazz* to see what high school was going to be like. Johnny Razzmatazz's daughter Veronica was a sophomore and all her friends were white. Like Aryan white. Like Veronica-was-the-only-brunette white. There were no minorities on screen, not even in the background. They didn't even have black kids on the basketball team. Kids were being dropped off in four-wheeled bejeweled boulders of German engineering. I knew I'd look poor when my dad rolled up in our '79 Dodge Adventurer with its flatbed packed with boxes of liquor. I was the only kid in school who slept on a couch in a living room, didn't own a cell phone, and wore T-shirts, sweatpants, and sneakers my mom bought from the super cheap street markets of Kowloon on her annual trips back to the homeland.

The first few months at Marsden sucked. In San Gabriel Valley, I was one of many Hors. At Marsden, I might as well have worn fishnet stockings and a sandwich board reading "Suck For A Buck." Almost everyone who knew my name relished the opportunity to say it as many times as possible with a snicker.

At gym class, I was picked last for mixed softball, after giggling quadruplet girls. I figured I'd be the last dude chosen, but four times, the captains went with the frail, likely bulimic Mylars (who didn't even wear closed-toed shoes) before me.

Then, as pitcher, one of the quadruplets started chucking soft-balls overhand at me. Everyone laughed as I dodged and skipped in place like I was in a hip-hop dance class.

There was the time Robert Childs, a curly-haired jock, punted a fresh pile of dog shit at me, splattering me square in the face. Then he showed his friends what he'd done and encour-aged them to take their shots. Literally shit-faced, I still have never run so fast in my life.

One of the first people at Marsden who didn't bully me was Veronica. It was the year 2000, and she was living her sloppy, awkward adolescence in front of America. Her hair was wild and frizzy, and she had braces, a round face with her dad's wide jaw. A lot of students were anxious to grab seats near her on the off chance she was being filmed. I happened to be early to the first day of German class when Veronica took the open seat in front of me. She was wearing a bright yellow jacket with huge lapels and a black Daniel Johnston "Hi, How Are You?" tee with ripped jeans. She just looked so . . . cool. Way too cool for me.

While my mind searched for something witty to say to Veronica, our teacher wrote conjugations on the blackboard. *Ich bin. Du bist. Sie sind.* She was in her fifties, white-blonde, and fresh off the U-boat. Her hair was aerosol-sprayed so brittle and obscenely high, you could see through it. Her married name was Jackson.

"I hear Frau Jackson likes black guys," I blurted under my breath.

Veronica looked at me like I'd farted.

"Ten bucks says Herr Jackson is five-four and wears track suits."

Veronica turned just enough for me to see her smile. I happened to be five-four. Thanks to my mother's latest bargain shopping extravaganza in Hong Kong, I was also wearing a track suit.

"Excuse me!" Frau Jackson barked. Veronica and I straightened. Frau Jackson's face turned colors as she stomped to her desk and fingered her seating chart. "Pay attention, *Hor*," she said.

The class cracked up when they heard my name.

Hor Luk Lee kills for the first time!

By the end of the semester, Veronica and I were friends. We would talk over the phone, usually after the show aired. In one episode, Sherry, Veronica's mother, berated her for never being home for the dinner their Mexican cook (who never said anything on camera) had so thoughtfully prepared. To make an example of Veronica, her mom prepared a plate, set it in front of her, then promptly fed it to the family's yapping, shitting Pomeranians. Johnny sat there expressionless. With his sunglasses on, you couldn't tell whether he was asleep or not.

"The show's her idea," Veronica told me. "She's been planning my future. She doesn't think I can think for myself."

I said I knew how she felt.

Veronica was the first girl to pay any attention to me, so it was only a matter of time before I developed a mad crush. My mom walked in on me in the bathroom, jerking off, with my German notebook in the sink. I was running a finger over the big loopy letters of a note Veronica had written me (how deeply she imprinted the pages; oh, the way she dotted her "i's" with hearts). Luckily, my back was turned.

"I'm studying in here!" I cried out, hands up in faux outrage.

"Okay, okay," my mom said, shutting the door. "What are you studying so hard that you need to study in the bathroom?"

I got an after school job at a drugstore near Marsden formerly known as Rite Aid formerly known as PayLess formerly known as Thrifty. Because of the store's proximity to Hollywood, I regularly saw D-list celebrities from my post at checkout counter four.

I saw Eddie Griffin, Tom Green, and David Spade around the time he was in *Joe Dirt*. One night, Johnny Razzmatazz was in the store, perusing a *Maxim*. He looked like he'd been left behind by his motorcycle club. He wore calf-high boots and that ridiculous leather jacket with a billion zippers. He had this gigantic gut and a ragged, badly receded hairline. He wore sunglasses after sundown and an unlit cigarette dangled from his lips.

At first, I thought Johnny was alone, but then I saw he was with a black lady wearing an ass-high skirt—a hooker. A cameraman and a boom mic operator trailed them from aisle to aisle. I tried to exchange a knowing look with Ivey, my party-school-bound co-worker with the nose stud, but she just yawned. Johnny put the magazine back on the shelf and staggered red-faced toward my counter. He was buying antacid and a box of condoms. I straightened as the cameras appeared, preparing for my television debut. Then the cameraman said:

"Johnny, can you take aisle three?"

He muttered inaudibly and did as told. Ivey brushed her short dark bangs with her fingers and artfully showed off her wrist tattoo to the lens. The cameraman circled and when he saw that I was in the shot, he moved behind me and filmed Ivey and Johnny from over my shoulder.

"Are you Johnny Razzmatazz?" Ivey asked.

He croaked the high-pitched catchphrase that made him famous: "Why 'ello 'ello!"

Even though Veronica and I were friendly in class, we didn't speak outside of German 1. Whenever she and her pack of Brads, Darrens, and Stephanies strutted into the drugstore, I would wait outside to see if she'd acknowledge me in front of her white friends.

She never did.

During class, I finally raised the courage to invite myself over to Veronica's place to do German homework. She looked at me like I was Joe Rogan on *Fear Factor* asking her to eat a hundred-year-old egg. (They happen to be delicious! Don't know why white folks freak out about it.)

"What's wrong?" I asked. "You don't have people like me up at the ranch?"

"Don't make this a race thing."

"Do you have any friends who aren't white?"

She smacked me on the arm.

Frau Jackson let out a sharp warning cry. "No hitting!" she shouted, hitting her desk with an open palm.

After I successfully race-shamed Veronica into hanging out with me, she drove me up to her house in a Mercedes convertible. She was a year older and had just gotten her learner's permit and was driving everywhere without a parent in tow anyway. The mansion had iron gates with a nameplate reading "RAZZMATAZZ!!!" in gold cursive. When they opened, the left gate took the "RAZZMAT", leaving the right one with the "AZZ!!!" The house was a salmon-colored Spanish-style place with a large driveway that swooped down the side of a hill overlooking the L.A. basin. Parked were several large black busses and white vans crowned with satellite dishes—the crew from MTV.

We entered the house through giant double doors. The inside was cold and silent and smelled of wet dog. The walls were crammed with rich-person clutter. Big mirrors with curlicued frames. Oversized clocks. Pastel-colored paintings of kids on beaches.

Veronica hung her backpack on a coat rack that was made of marble and shaped like a giant burning bush. "We all love days off from the show," she said. "My mom gets her nails done and takes the dogs to their spa treatments."

The dogs got spa treatments.

On the living room floor, Johnny Razzmatazz sat cross-legged in sweatpants and a T-shirt. He had his sunglasses on, so I couldn't tell if he was sleeping sitting up or staring at the empty handle of whiskey on the coffee table. I followed Veronica through the house, on tiptoes.

"Why 'ello, 'ello," he said, startling me.

"Hey, Dad," Veronica said.

"Who are you?"

"Your daughter."

"I fucking know that," Johnny said. "Who's he?"

"This is Hor."

"Your name is Hor," he stated to confirm.

"Yes, sir," I chirped. "I'm a huge fan of the show."

"What are you a fan of?" he asked. "Of me sitting on me arse playing a doped-up vegetable? You a fan of me sitting on me arse, eh?" He wobbled skyward like a sail. He smelled of soil and towered over me.

"You a fan of me now?"

I thought he might even take a swing.

Veronica rolled her eyes. "Mom's going to be home soon." Her voice was calm, like she was the parent.

"Fuck her," Johnny muttered. "Fuck a whore!" Laughing hoarsely, he staggered into his den and pulled the double doors shut. Then we watched Johnny go out onto a patio that overlooked their prairie of a backyard.

"He's safest outside, believe it or not," Veronica said. "The fences are too high to climb."

The garage door roared, and soon, two galloping dogs entered the house, followed by a short-haired, wide-faced woman. Sherry Razzmatazz. She was wearing so much eye makeup that she looked like a lemur. The Pomeranians began jumping at my crotch, and Sherry did nothing to stop them. Instead, she eyed me, blinking and silent, like she was trying to remember whether she had ordered takeout. Her gaze swooped wildly left and right around the house, then past her daughter, and out the window at Johnny.

"What's he doing?" she asked with a British accent.

Veronica shrugged and said nothing, suddenly sullen and shrunken.

I wasn't sure exactly what to do about these furry beasts barking and nipping at my nethers.

"Mick! Bianca! Down!" Veronica said to no effect.

Finally, I kneed one of the dogs hard enough that it flew in the air like a soccer ball that Sherry caught. She glared at me.

"Come here, Mick," Sherry said. The dog stopped attacking me and heeled quietly beside Sherry's very expensive-looking, gold-buckled high-heeled boots.

"Guess the spa didn't relax them," I said.

Sherry continued to glare at me.

"Hor, this is my mom," Veronica said.

"I told you to call me 'Sherry,'" she replied.

Veronica closed her eyes and sighed.

"Nice to meet you, Mrs. Razzmatazz," I said, holding out my palm.

"I said 'Sherry,'" she repeated, her handshake limp to the point of impalpability. She glanced outside again at Johnny, who was punching the air like he was training for kung fu. Sherry shook her head and huffed.

"I'll be upstairs," she said. "I have a call-in with Ricki Lake at four."

Veronica made a throaty noise in acknowledgement.

Sherry put Bianca down, and the trio scurried past us and up the staircase into a golden supernova of sunlight coming from giant windows.

While Veronica and I did homework at the dining table, I was distracted by the sound and sight of Johnny shooting clay pigeons. I couldn't see who was pulling the shells. He cussed loudly and colorfully when he missed ("fucky cunt burgers twat shit on a cock!"). Johnny caught me eyeing him and beckoned.

"Aye, you!" he shouted.

"Better get out there," Veronica said, without looking up from her workbook.

"He's not going to shoot me, is he?"

Veronica shrugged.

"Bruce Lee!" Johnny yelled. "Come on out! I need gunpowder! Now!"

I went outside and joined him in the sun. "I was busy 'tossing universes in my underpants,'" I said, quoting Bill Hicks.

Johnny looked down at me. "You're way too young to have seen that."

"You can watch a lot of stuff on the internet now," I explained, as if he didn't know.

Mufflers hung around Johnny's neck, and his long shadow shielded me. He rested the barrel of his shotgun on the ground.

"Ever fire a gun?"

I shook my head.

"Mr. Razzmatazz!" a woman called out from a distance. "It is very hot!"

"Hold on, Janet!" Johnny shouted. To me, he muttered, "Janet, my ass. Esmeralda's her fucking name."

I laughed.

"You like Bill Hicks?"

"Yeah."

"He gave me my start."

"I know. I watch the show."

"Have you seen my stuff?"

"No."

His shoulders sagged and he faced the ground. "My memory's shot," he said, sighing. "Can't even do ten minutes anymore."

"Maybe it's the drugs."

He frowned at me. "You think you're a funny little prick, don't you?"

"I didn't mean—"

He released an open-mouthed, chest-rocking laugh and smacked my shoulder hard enough to stagger me. "It's good to be a prick!" he bellowed. "Especially in comedy!"

"Mr. Razzmatazz!" Janet/Esmeralda shouted again.

"Okay, okay, *por favor!*" Johnny handed me earplugs. After I put them in, he gave me the gun, which was heavy in my hands. I raised the barrel and peeked one-eyed through the sight like people do in the movies. Johnny fished two shells out of his pocket.

"What's your name again?" he asked, sounding far away.

I told him.

He helped me load the gun before putting on his mufflers. Then he fixed his hands softly on my shoulders.

I flinched. I couldn't remember the last time anyone had touched me with affection.

"Easy, Hor," Johnny said. "I'm not going to hurt you." He raised my arms toward the sky. "This is what you do."

MY HOROSCOPIC
DISADVANTAGES

While I began hobnobbing with reality TV stars, my mom started hobnobbing with the Chinese horoscope. She became a devoted fan of the popular Chinese radio show *Master Ming's Suan Ming Hour* after meeting Master Ming in person at the Chinese New Year Festival in nearby Monterey Park. Master Ming had billboard ads all over San Gabriel Valley and was a local celebrity who was especially popular with the ladies because he was a handsome man in his early forties who claimed to have learned his craft from several generations of acclaimed fortune-tellers in China. He also wore a round hat and a mandarin robe like he was still in the 1800s.

After reading Master Ming's fortune-telling books, the pages of which were printed on the thinnest of gray pulp, my mom relayed what she claimed were the zodiac's predictions for each family member. At best, the future would be tragic and, at worst, apocalyptic. My dad was born on a year of the Dragon, and according to my mom's horoscope readings, because September 2001 was a bad month for Dragons (as were January through August and October through December), she told my dad to brace himself for a car accident. Nothing ever happened, of course. Because fortune-telling is Chinese for bullshit.

Poor health was in my zodiac forecast, so Mom did all kinds of things to head off the storm of ailments coming to Hor Town. She checked the level of coating on my tongue daily. She changed her cooking based on whatever the Chinese newspapers claimed was healthy. She boiled herbs and forced me to drink bowls of those rancid, tar-like concoctions. When she picked me up from school, she'd have me hold these white crystal balls and point them in whatever direction the day's horoscope said bad luck was coming from. I'd be sitting in the passenger seat, staring at a compass in my lap and waving my arms with those balls in hand like an air traffic controller. I started hoping we'd get in an accident.

"Master Ming is so good that he predicted 9/11," my mom insisted one night at dinner.

"*Choy!* Crazy," my dad said, shaking his head.

"Jesus knew about 9/11," my grandma said. "Jesus made them do it."

My dad was particularly drunk that night, and his eyes went around the dinner table, and I could see him wondering how he could possibly be related to us. He stared at my mom and me with a creased brow, and then he just got up, throttled his bottle of port wine, and left without a word while my mom asked repeatedly where he was going.

She waited for him, expecting to drive him to the night shift at the store. Eight p.m. came and went, and she left for Hollywood without him and worked that night with my uncle.

My dad didn't return until after midnight. I pretended to be asleep while he stumbled through the living room, knocking over one of the plastic tea cups on our Buddhist altar.

He was sniffling. He had been crying.

"Dad?" I asked. "Are you okay?"

"Go back to sleep," he said. "I wish you'd just . . . "

I waited for him to finish, but he didn't. "What?" I asked.

"I wish you'd just go back to sleep," he muttered, before disappearing into the bedroom.

He brought home a scent that I'd become quite familiar with. The scent of cold, the scent of wood chip, the scent of rail.

I might not have been the only one in the family to make that walk to the train tracks.

When I wasn't at the drugstore, I spent weekday afternoons at the Razzmatazz mansion. One day while I was over, doing homework with Veronica, Johnny was running on a newly installed treadmill in the living room when he began shouting my name repeatedly.

The cameraman looked at the boom mic operator. "What did you say, Johnny? You want a whore?" asked the cameraman. "Like, now?"

Johnny stepped off the treadmill, panting. "Get the fuck out," he snarled. "I'm done. Okay? Done."

The crew lowered their equipment and escaped into the garage, where Sherry was telling the director that she wanted to go to Cartier and Tiffany's that afternoon. The boom mic operator groaned.

"Stepped in dog shit again," he said while the cameraman laughed.

Sherry shrieked, "Janet! The dogs, for God's sake!"

Veronica dropped her pencil on her notebook and tipped her head back, opening her mouth. "How many Hail Mary's do I have to say to end this show?" she said.

"Hor!" Johnny shouted. "Can you write something down for me?"

I went into the den and rummaged through the desk drawers, which were filled with a bizarre assortment of items including a Bowie knife, bags and bags of microwavable popcorn, and a

James Brown doll. I finally found a notebook and pen in the center slide-out drawer.

He told me an expletive-laced bit about his life being so boring that he found himself wanking to a woman on a reality show only to realize that she was his wife and the reality show was his own.

I read the bit back to him and added a little playacting, puffing my chest and jabbing my right hand like I'd seen Johnny do in YouTube videos of his old performances. He didn't laugh. His expression was very serious.

"Might be something there," Johnny said with a shrug. He removed his sunglasses and toweled off his face. "You're funny when you cuss. You just don't look like someone with a dirty mouth."

"What do I look like?"

He gazed down upon me. That was the first time I'd seen him without his sunglasses on. His eyes were dollar-bill green against that pale face and smoke-yellowed smile.

"You look like a nice kid," he said. "Polite. Well-behaved."

I hated that he thought that about me. I wanted to be like him. I wanted to be like Chris Rock. I wanted to be a truth-teller. I wanted to be a star.

"Do you want to be my assistant?" he asked.

Of course, I instantly agreed. Despite his drugged-out TV persona, he had never stopped writing. He had shoeboxes of mini-cassette tapes that needed to be transcribed.

When I told my mom I wanted to work two jobs: shifts at the drugstore and at the Razzmatazz house, she was dead set against it.

"Master Ming says you will not be lucky this year. Who is this man?"

"A comedian."

"What's that?"

"A funny man."

"Does he take drugs?"

"I don't know," I lied.

"Those white people take drugs!" she exclaimed. "This is a bad luck time for you! A bad luck time!"

I told my mom I couldn't live my life based on her horoscope readings. She stopped washing dishes and faced me. For once, she looked me in the eye.

"Why doesn't anyone listen to me in this family?"

She was right. It wasn't just me who disregarded her. We all did. I felt guilt about it. Still do. Ignoring women is part of the Chinese culture, part of my family. My dad was the boss. Chinese people don't ignore women like Americans do. They don't do it politely and then feel ashamed after the fact when someone writes about it on the internet. Chinese people are like Nike. They *just do it.* And then they claim that the Chinese way of doing everything is the best way. They've got the zombie-eye disease and they're *proud* of it. I tell you because you should know the type of culture you come from, Maryann. Don't even spend an extra split-second waiting for someone to listen to you if they don't hear you the first time. My mom should've left my dad and our shitty family long ago. If you want a better life, never wait for permission. You make it happen. *You* just do it.

"This is what I want to do," I said. "Please? He's on TV. He's famous."

"TV? No way, Jose!" she said in English, before adding in Mandarin that I shouldn't see so many people because "Your skin is so bad and you are so ugly!"

My jaw clenched and I tried not to cry. "Mom," I said. "Stop it."

She shrugged and looked away when even she saw that she had hurt my feelings. "Ask your grandparents," she said, turning back to her dishes.

That was her way of ending the conversation. She knew I wouldn't ask them. *They were too Chinese.* I was losing my ability to speak Mandarin altogether. My mom asked my grandparents whether I should work the second job. She recapped (again) my horoscopic disadvantages. My grandparents were sitting as far from each other as possible on the living room sofa.

"What does his dad say?" my grandma asked.

"Who cares?" my mom said. "He's never here!"

"Hor must work at the liquor store," said my grandma. "A son must learn from his daddy."

That set off another argument between my mom and grandma about whether my dad was out "drinking condensed milk" again. As usual, my grandpa remained silent, reading his newspaper.

Because Johnny couldn't work a computer (or TV or microwave), one of my only school-worthy skills became useful: I had good handwriting. Every so often, while I was transcribing Johnny's jokes, I got an idea for one of my own, and I'd jot it down in a second notebook that I took home.

I enjoyed the work so much that I even preferred it to hanging out with Veronica. I couldn't wait to get through my German homework so I could retire to Johnny's den to dive into the world of jokes. (That's the way you'll feel when you find your passion—that one thing you do best that means the most to you. The rest of your life and everyone in it will suddenly feel like background music.)

One afternoon, Johnny walked in and saw me writing in two notebooks and asked what the second one was for.

"They're my jokes," I told him.

"You write jokes? Then tell me one."

"'I had an unhappy childhood,'" I read. "'And I'm still having an unhappy childhood.'"

Johnny raised a brow, but didn't laugh. "That's very Hedberg," he said.

"It is?"

"Yeah, he has that joke: 'I used to do drugs, I still do, but I used to, too.'"

My chest puffed a little. Johnny was comparing me to Mitch Hedberg!

"Can't do it," he said. "It's so close you're almost stealing the joke, and that's a no-no."

I felt myself shrinking. "I didn't mean to."

"That's okay," Johnny said. "You have good writing instincts. Keep doing it and the good jokes will come."

I nodded and saluted him like a sailor. "Aye-aye!"

"So tell me," he said, putting a hand on my shoulder. "Why is your childhood so unhappy?"

I told Johnny about my mom's growing obsession with the Chinese horoscope.

"Why don't you try having a point of view about her superstitions? Tell us how absurd you think she is and why. Do an act-out or an imitation. Write it all out. Then categorize everything into a premise, a setup, and a punch. Pick one of each, put them together, and you have a joke."

Johnny explained what all those terms meant—the basics of joke construction. A premise is the topic, the way a comic sets expectations with an audience. A setup leads them a little further along those expectations. Then the goal of the punch is to surprise, subverting what the audience expects. Later that day, I read one of my new jokes to Johnny:

My mom lives her life by fortune cookie. She uses the Chinese horoscope to make big life decisions. I told her she should have used it before marrying Dad.

Johnny managed a single, barely audible snort. "Try it out in front of an audience," he said. "That's the only way you'll know if it works."

"How do I do that?"

"You can do it with me." Johnny said he could book a night at a club in West Hollywood named The Funny Bone. "Do five minutes before I go up."

I immediately felt an urge to pee. I was in disbelief. A chance to do what my heroes did on those CDs? A chance to speak truths? A chance to make people laugh?

"No way," I said. "I'll be so bad."

"I'm just as scared as you are," he said. "I haven't been on stage in ten years. What's the worst thing that can happen? We bomb and then we'll get up and try it again."

On the night of the performance, I told my mom I had to work at the drugstore, and Johnny picked me up there and drove us to the club. He wore what he always wore on TV: the leather jacket, the sunglasses, the spiked hair, and the cologne that smelled of bubblegum and cigarette smoke—the persona of The Sleaze. I wore one of my knockoff velour sweatsuits. Only years later did I realize that The Funny Bone was an underwhelming imitation of The World Famous Comedy Store, where every big star from John Belushi to Robin Williams had once performed. Outside, The Funny Bone had its own wall of performers, but it was just a chalkboard of names no one recognized, faded and erasable. Johnny had chosen the club because it was a D-list one in the city—low pressure, perfect for working on material.

"You ready?" Johnny asked in the green room, which was painted the color of puke. There was no door or curtain. We were right next to the stage and faced straight out into the crowd.

I was more nervous than I had ever been or ever would be. I could feel my heart drumming all the way in my balls. But I told Johnny I was cool.

"Then what's with your knee?"

It was going up and down like I was stomping grapes.

Johnny ordered a Tanqueray and tonic. One of the waitresses soon returned with the drink—clear with a lime—and placed it on an end table.

"Drink up," he said. "Go ahead. It'll relax you."

My first taste of liquor was a good one. Too good. To this day, I remember my buds prickling, my saliva like soda. Bittersweet.

A balding man with a brown goatee walked in, and Johnny gave him a big hug. He introduced himself as Maury Polivakis, Johnny's manager.

"Who's the kid?" he asked.

"The feature," Johnny said.

"How old is he?" Maury glimpsed my drink. "You're going to get me arrested!"

He scrutinized me like I was a broken appliance, like he was my mom. He pinched my oversized sweatshirt and shook his head. "You know the crowd paid money tonight, right?" he said to Johnny.

"It would be shitty if they didn't get to see my very best," he said, grinning.

Maury rolled his eyes. "Still a fucking asshole." He asked for my name.

"Hor Luk Lee."

"Whore Luckily?" he said. "Do you think you're a pornstar or something?"

"Maybe we should come up with something better," Johnny said.

"Seriously," Maury said.

Johnny took his sunglasses off and looked me up and down. "Seriously," he repeated. "Sirius Lee."

Maury raised a brow.

I spoke my new name aloud. I sounded like an American for the first time.

Before I went on stage, Johnny grabbed my arm and whispered, "Remember that no one expects you to be funny unless you take off your shirt or buck your teeth or something. In fact, no one even expects you to be interesting. So anything remotely surprising is going to get a laugh."

"Good to know that the bar is so much lower for me."

Johnny shrugged. "You people are shorter."

I didn't laugh.

"I'm just kidding!" he said. "So sensitive." He pushed me out of the green room.

On stage, the lights were hotter than I expected. My mouth was dry. I was sweating profusely. There was a long moment of silence before I pulled the mic out of the stand with a thump and slowly untangled the cord. The room was huge and smelled of stale armpits. It was a quarter full even though there were about forty people. Of the crowd, I saw mostly silhouettes, scattered in groups of six to eight. In front of the stage, there was a man whose eyes were closed and legs were splayed like he had been knocked out cold. I tried to remember my set. Blank. Not a word appeared. For a few long seconds, I was sure I was going to die out there. A woman loudly sucked her drink like she wanted to make sure she got the liquor before the ice did. That's when I remembered my first joke.

"My mom is very superstitious," I began, my voice sounding lower-pitched than usual, like someone older. "She's like super into feng shui. So much so that when she had me, she made sure her vagina was pointed east."

A few chuckles.

"My dad is pretty nuts too," I said. "He thinks I'm going to be a C-E-O. He thinks that See-Eo is a word in the dictionary that means: 'guy who funds his gambling addiction.'"

To my surprise, that got a big, rolling laugh. It was like nothing I'd ever experienced. I felt like I was levitating. Like another person inside me had started speaking for the first time. People were looking up to me, listening, waiting for what I would say next. I was being heard.

I've been chasing that feeling ever since.

EATING RIBS
WITH THE FAMILY LEE

To keep my parents at bay, I told them I had joined an SAT study group on nights I was actually at the comedy club. On weekends, out of guilt, I volunteered at Lee's Liquors.

Your grandfather ran the store as if it was his own reality show. He got his share of Hollywood douchebag types coming by in their BMW convertibles to pick up liquor on their way home to coke parties, and my dad would entertain them as if he were the sommelier of their ridiculous vices. He shopped at the *Miami Vice* rack at Marshalls. He always (always!) came to work wearing a white cotton blazer, a pink polo, khakis, and penny loafers without socks. Sometimes he'd even wear sunglasses inside the store at night, like Johnny.

With his thick accent, my dad would ask customers what kind of event they were shopping for.

"I'm looking to get fucked up," this white dude in his twenties once said.

"Yes, but what kind fuck up? You want easy fuck up? You want hard fuck up where you wake up with head hurt in morning?"

"I just wanna chill."

"You don't have big belly," my father said, even though the guy, in fact, had a sizable one. "You're not big belly beer man. And you're no cheap wine guy. I think you like whiskey. You like whiskey?"

My father wouldn't stop his foreign charm assault until the customer bought at least one bottle of the priciest whiskey.

He was so happy when I worked at the store that he tried to cram in as much teaching as possible about the ways of the business. He taught me how to spot a shoplifter in the concave security mirrors and how to give change in small bills to encourage tipping. His knowledge about wines and spirits was prodigious, even if he didn't know when to drink port.

"Wine in box, cheap," my father said in English. "The more expensive wine, high on shelf. Many wine from California, just as good as France or Germany, but because Europe far away, people buy far away wine for more money. Same thing for liquor." He held up a bottle of Ginebra San Miguel. "People buy from places they want to go. We sell holiday and vacation."

My father showed me the ledgers and the safe in the back filled with clean stacks of cash. "I put some money in bank for your college," he said. "But sometime it good to have money in your hand." He got up on a chair, reached for the top shelf, and pulled down a handgun with a lock over the trigger.

"Protections," my father said.

I was surprised he had a gun. He never talked about it at home. This was the first time he'd exposed me to the dangers of his job. This was why he worked the night shift instead of my mother. It made me feel guilty for feeling suffocated and I reminded myself to show him more respect. Like my grandfather had said, he was suffering the present for a better future.

He returned the gun to its hiding place. "Your grades are only okay." He looked around for my backpack. "Where are your books?"

"I thought we were working."

"You need to stop worrying about work. You study. Stop working at that drugstore!" His face reddened with exasperation as my hand absently rummaged through a jar of Reese's Pieces on the counter. My father walked back behind the register. He unscrewed his bottle of port wine and poured some into a Dixie cup. He glanced around the store like he was lording over a dealership of luxury cars.

"Don't worry," he said. "Someday, all this yours."

Thanks to Johnny, I got a chance to do my five a few times a week, and then the five turned into ten, and the ten turned into fifteen, and so on. On some nights, I bombed and bombed hard. I remember doing this aimless ten-minute bit that was an act-out from the perspective of the abused pie in the movie *American Pie*, and there was an audience member who shook his head and moaned "that's awful" after each one of my failed punch lines. Once, in a crowd full of black people in what comedians call "an urban room," I unwisely referred to the mic stand as a thin black man, knocked it over, shouted that I was police, and got booed off stage. When I look back at old videos of my performances, I cringe. In the early days, if I bombed on a couple of jokes in a row, I could see the fear practically glowing from my eyes. I used to try to blow through my set as quickly as possible. If a joke didn't work, I moved onto the next one as fast as an auctioneer and made a mental note never to tell the joke again. One night, in front of a packed house of 150, I told a joke about my living in a town with so many Chinese people, it needed a One Child Policy for every child, and it bombed so badly that I forgot my last few jokes and slunk off the stage a minute earlier than planned.

In the green room, as the emcee tried to rally the crowd into giving me one last round of applause, I winced at Johnny and apologized.

"Don't give up on that joke," Johnny said. "Next time, just stand there until they get it."

"Really?"

The emcee began to introduce Johnny. "As opposed to what?" Johnny asked. "Fake-ly?"

So the next night, I waited until the crowd digested the joke (admittedly, a bit of a thinker) and didn't let the silence spook me. Eventually, a decent-sized laugh came.

On the drive home, Johnny said, "Remember they're on your time, not vice versa."

He then pointed out that I spoke too fast on stage and stood very stiffly in one place like a contestant in a spelling bee.

"And don't run over your laughs," Johnny said. "You tend to start your next joke while they're still laughing. You should wait until every last person is quiet. Milk the laugh."

I wished I had my notebook to write everything down.

"Next time a joke bombs, do some crowd work," Johnny said. "Pick someone in the audience and say something like, 'well, this guy didn't get it.' And then make fun of the look on his face. Crowd work can get the audience on your side again."

"What if I just keep bombing?"

"You keep working," Johnny said. "It's like riding a bull. You can't get off and get on again. It's your job to hold on until you're thrown off."

"I'm too chubby for the bull."

Johnny smiled. "When you first start out, the most important thing to remember is that you are enough. Over time, that you will become a separate you called your persona. And when you get to my age, you'll be so sick of that you, you'll wish you died young."

Here was a famous comedian with almost three decades of experience telling me I was enough. He never said I was fat or my face was ugly and would scare people. He never conde-scended, never said, "Do it my way or else!" Johnny was the parent I wished I had. That Johnny was the parent I wish I could be for you.

One afternoon, I was at the Razzmatazz house and Veronica said, "Don't take this the wrong way," which encourages one to take whatever follows the wrong way. "Do you shop for your own clothes?"

I felt like the kindergartner that smelled of God's vomit again. I told her I didn't have the cash.

"You don't have your own credit card?!" Veronica exclaimed.

She drove me to the mall. We went into an American Apparel, and she offered to buy me a pair of dark jeans, a T-shirt, and a jacket that made me look like the performer that I'd become. I felt like a better person with the right clothes on, but I wasn't comfortable spending her money, so I told her that I would come back and buy them myself (though I knew I never would).

"Let me do this for you, Hor," she said. "Let this be 'I'm sorry' for not having you over sooner. Besides, this is fun! Isn't this fun?"

Fun? For a fourteen-year-old boy who'd never had a girl-friend, this was a fun monsoon! A twenty-four-hour roller-coaster ride and a lifetime supply of cotton candy!

We had so much fun that she bought me a week's worth of shirts, shorts, and pants that I balled up and stuffed in my backpack to hide from my parents. And when they dropped me off at school, I'd dart straight into a bathroom and change into my wrinkled but new outfits.

Like magic, my bullies vanished.

Robert Childs picked me for his softball team before the quadruplet Mylars. He even invited me to kick dog shit on a Latino kid after gym class. For the record, I did not partake. And I don't know why Robert enjoyed kicking dog shit so much.

Even though I still wasn't hanging out with Veronica's Brads, Darrens, and Stephanies, she and I would walk together to German class, and I could feel the other kids sizing me up and wondering how I'd gotten into Veronica's reality TV circle. Suddenly, students were coming up to me after school trying to be my friend.

"What are they like?" my new friend Landon asked. He was chubby like me, but only in the torso; his limbs were bird-like. He also had a receding hairline that made him look fifty.

What were they like? I thought of Sherry and the dogs, Veronica and her homework, Johnny and his treadmill, and struggled to find an appropriate reply.

"Just a normal American family," I said.

My grades halfway through sophomore year were horrible; I was shaming Asians all across America. My dad found out I'd missed the PSAT, the preview of the standardized test for college admission. He'd heard from one of his Vietnamese deli friends, whose kid had gotten a perfect score.

"Unaccept!" my dad shouted in English.

He glared at my mom, who was cooking. "How come you don't know about this?"

"How come you don't know?" my mom retorted.

My dad slammed a fist on the dining table. "Don't talk to me that way."

My eyes bore an imaginary hole in the ground.

"You have too many friends," he said to me. "You need focus."

But I was happy, maybe for the first time. In comedy, I'd found the first thing I was good at. At school, I was liked—the funny, round Asian kid. I didn't want to lose that feeling.

"I'm happy the way I am," I muttered.

"What?"

"I am enough," I said, louder.

My dad began to laugh. "Happy? Why are you happy?"

"Because I have friends."

Now both my parents were laughing. "Friends are useless," my dad said.

"When you make money, you will get all the friends you want," my mom said. "Look at Master Ming. He's rich and has all the friends in the world."

My dad rolled his eyes. My grandmother entered the living room, glanced at us, and without knowing what we were talking about, said, "Your dad is right."

"Is that why our family has no friends?" I asked.

My parents glared at me. My grandfather, who was reading a newspaper, turned the page and chuckled.

I swear I saw him smirking at me.

I apologized and promised to be a better Hor Luk Lee. But I had no intention of getting better at anything other than comedy. I quit the drugstore. As his new material got stronger, Johnny and I would work six or seven hours straight five days a week. He would pick me up from school and drive us to open mics at Ha Ha Café, UCB Theatre, and Hollywood Hotel. He feasted on the attention of young comics. Sometimes, mics would stop altogether so everyone could pose for photos with him. Only the fact that Johnny had to drive me home stopped him from letting everyone buy him drinks. The comics would come up to me after sets and pat me on the head and pinch my cheeks—especially the female comics, when, as a joke, I'd ask them out on dates.

MTV asked for a signed parental waiver so my face could be shown on future episodes. I didn't even try to get a signature from my parents, knowing how they'd react. I just signed for them and officially became a minor character on *The Family Razzmatazz*.

That's when things got crazy at Marsden. My social calendar became packed. Even Veronica's Brads, Darrens, and Stephanies allowed me to lunch with them. We cruised out to Melrose in Veronica's convertible and I was superexcited to see what these shiny cool white kids did for lunch. (I had to ride bitch, of course.)

We stopped for fancy cupcakes. That's it! For lunch! I was starving.

"Can we, like, stop by In-N-Out on the way back to school?" I asked. I had never been to an In-N-Out, so I was curious.

"No way," Veronica said. "That stuff is so bad for you. And they're like totally evil Christians. Haven't you seen the Bible verses on the bottom of the soda cups?"

"I'm more of a McDonald's guy anyway," I said, trying to play it off.

Veronica and her friends groaned.

That was the last time we lunched.

Even the Mylars wanted to be my best friends. They would drag me over to their lunch circle on a patch of grass near the track, and ask me for advice on which boys to like.

I held forth, trying out material on them. "You've got to play the long game," I said once. "Date the ugliest guy because chances are when he grows up, he's going to be the richest."

Veronica bought me a pair of sunglasses for my fifteenth birthday, and I wore them everywhere, even in class. I began chewing gum at all times because I thought it was cool and I didn't think I could get away with smoking cigarettes with the Lee Council breathing down my neck.

One day, Principal Payne called me into his office. I thought I was in trouble until I saw the photos in frames on the wall. Mr. Payne and Johnny, Mr. Payne and Sherry, Mr. Payne and Veronica, and even Mr. Payne and Mick and Bianca. The assistant principal, Ms. St. Claire, who was six-foot-four and smelled of Play-Doh, stood by Mr. Payne's desk, holding a digital camera. Mr. Payne self-consciously patted his stiff, salt-and-pepper hair, as he looked at his reflection in the glass of his framed photograph with Johnny.

"We're so glad you're here, Lee," Principal Payne said, putting his arm around me. He always called me by my last name for some reason. He beamed for the camera.

"You two look so cool," Ms. St. Claire gushed, staring into the viewfinder.

When the cameras were around, Johnny refused to show up as his doddering, stoned character anymore. He stopped wearing leather and spiking his hair. He lost twenty pounds and intentionally dressed in oversized sweatshirts, jeans, and sneakers like Joe Soccer Dad.

"Come on, Johnny," the show producer said, following him from the den, then into the hall, and on into the master bedroom. "Don't be like this." The producer was a short, balding, and scrawny fellow with a blond mustache like Hulk Hogan and a drinking problem.

"You think I wake up with my hair done and my sunglasses on?" Johnny shouted. "You think I wear leather chaps to sleep? I'm at home! This is my home!"

"You can be home after we get this scene," the producer said.

In the living room, one of the production assistants, toting a scrim, sighed loudly. A cameraman abandoned his station and flopped facedown on the couch. Veronica and I sat at the dining table, trying to concentrate on our homework.

The producer emerged from the bedroom, shoulders bowed, nipping from a flask. He gripped the banister and shouted upstairs for Sherry.

She and the dogs came traipsing down, passing the crew without even looking at them, before marching into the bedroom.

"Again?" she shouted. "Again?"

"We talked about this!" Johnny bellowed. "One season and then the comeback! It's been three!"

"Comeback from what?" Sherry retorted. "Comeback from making seventy-five bucks a night at Crackers and then coming home and passing out on top of me and pissing yourself?"

Ratings were down a quarter in season three. Fans wanted to watch drugged-out, absent father Johnny, not an average, working adult and his short, acne-faced Kimosabe.

The dogs began yapping. I noticed Veronica's hands were shaking, her face reddening.

"We agreed!" Johnny shouted.

"I'm surprised you even fucking remember anything we talk about!"

The resounding crash of a large object hitting the floor.

"My torchéres!" Sherry screamed.

Veronica shut her notebook and fled up to her room.

Doors slammed upstairs and downstairs. Sherry appeared in the kitchen and apologized to the crew and asked that they take a one-hour break. She regarded me with suspicion. While she stood in front of a giant mirror in the hallway, plucking the grays out of her sleep-mangled ruby-dyed pixie cut, Sherry asked me what my parents did for a living. When I answered the liquor business, she said, "No wonder Johnny loves you."

"But he's sober," I said. He hadn't touched a drink in months.

"Well, maybe you should help him change that."

I was galled into silence.

"I'm just kidding," she said. "John's not the only comedian in the family."

Veronica came out to many of our shows. After gigs, she and I would wait in the green room while Johnny mingled with fellow comics and the well-adjusted folks who hang around fellow comics such as alcoholics, drug dealers, and disgruntled, fame-hungry waiters and waitresses. We would make up games to kill the time.

Our favorite was Name That Place. One of us would act out a destination we'd want to travel to, and the other would have to guess it. At a club named The Laughing Owl, we sat on one of the nastiest couches in the history of man. I did a bad frown-mouthed imitation of Robert DeNiro to illustrate my desire to move to New York. Veronica guessed Israel, Italy, and Korea before I finally told her the answer.

"That's where Chris Rock came up," I mansplained. "He would hang out at Catch a Rising Star on the Upper East Side for twelve hours waiting for stage time." I had read that in a profile about him in *Ebony Magazine*, which I'd plucked from the newsstand at the drugstore during an especially slow night. I didn't even know where the Upper East Side was.

"There's a Chinatown in Manhattan, you know," Veronica pointed out.

"Gee, thanks for the info," I cracked. "So you think just because I'm Chinese I like to go to Chinatown?"

"I'm just saying," Veronica said. "God, everything has always got to be about race with you! Are we going to play this game or not?"

I let it go, knowing I couldn't stop her. That's the thing about saying racist shit: I don't bristle because I'm overly sensitive. I bristle because I'm tired of the clichés and annoyed that white people aren't as tired of them as I am.

Veronica charaded a mustachioed man. I guessed Libya, Iran, and Iraq before she said, "Paris."

"I've always wanted to go somewhere that was the opposite of L.A.," she said. "Paris seems like that place."

"Yeah, they, like, respect creativity and art and life and culture and stuff, don't they?"

"I don't even think they watch TV over there."

"That's ridiculous!" I said. "Of course they watch TV."

"No, I think they only make films about really old men dating teenaged girls."

"They're too good to call a film just another fucking movie."

"You're right," she said. "Maybe my dreams are stupid."

I paled. "I never said that."

"Don't worry," Veronica said. "I'm not mad at you."

"I didn't think you were mad at me."

"Yeah, you did," she said. "You should have seen your face. You became as white as my friends."

I laughed. "That's pretty funny."

"My dad's not the only comedian in the family."

"Your mom said the same thing."

Veronica's smile disappeared. "I can't wait to get out of that fucking house. I just want to be free. I can't breathe in that place. I just want to break out and be me, you know?"

I put a hand on her leg, which was covered by a long summer dress. "You'll get out, for sure," I said. "If Johnny gets out, you'll get out."

Veronica moved her leg out of my hand. "You're optimistic. I like that about you."

Later, when I was home, back on my shitty sofa bed, I lay awake, remembering the feeling of the bulb of her knee against my palm.

By summer 2001, after several months of performing, while driving me home, Johnny said, "I'm going on the road. I want you to come with me."

My parents would not allow this. "A Chinese army will overrun your house," I said. "We have a billion people in San Gabriel Valley alone! You won't stand a chance."

"Why don't you invite me over for dinner? I'll ask them politely. You people are all polite, right?"

Johnny? In our cramped apartment? That sounded like a horrific idea. I told him so. "Have you been to Chinatown? Do those ladies seem polite to you?"

He chuckled. "You should write that down. There's a joke there."

"They don't really know that I'm working for you."

"Hmm," Johnny said, drumming his gnarled fingers on the steering wheel. "Will you be at the liquor store?"

The next time I did my shift at Lee's Liquors, Johnny pulled up in his Maserati.

"Why 'ello, 'ello," he said when he entered.

"What can I help?" my dad said in English.

I came out from behind the counter.

"So this is the famous Lee's Liquors, eh?" Johnny said, examining a bag of pretzels dangling from our sale display of assorted snacks near past due.

My dad looked at me. "You know him?"

"He's a TV star," I said. "The Dad of one of my friends."

"Your son is a very funny and very smart young man."

My dad was puzzled. He didn't imagine me as particularly funny or smart.

"I'm looking for a bottle of wine for dinner tomorrow night," Johnny said.

"What kind dinner?"

"One where we eat?" Johnny said.

I snorted, but my dad's expression was unchanged. He walked Johnny to the wine shelves.

"My family and I haven't had a dinner together in months," Johnny said. "We've been so busy. I've been preparing for my tour."

"What is tour?"

"Shows, lots of shows, all around the country."

My father still didn't appear to understand.

"Would you like to come over for dinner, Mr. Lee?" Johnny asked. "Your son is a good friend to my daughter. We really feel he's part of our family. We'd like to meet you and your wife and Hor's grandparents."

My father frowned. He was upset Johnny knew so much about us. "Oh, uh, my wife, she no speak English very well."

"People say I don't speak English very well, either," Johnny said.

"Can we, Dad? Their house is really cool."

"I insist," Johnny said. "We won't be filming tomorrow if that's what you're concerned about."

"Let me ask wife," my dad muttered, before remembering to put on his customer-friendly smile.

At home, at the dinner table, sitting in front of a half bottle of port, my dad wasn't smiling.

"Who is this man?" he asked in Mandarin.

I told him again.

"What does he want with you?"

"He wants me to work for him."

"How much will he pay you?"

"Ten bucks an hour."

"I can pay more."

"It's not about money."

"Do we not give you everything you ask for?" he said. "We give you things so that you will have a better life. America is not interested in people like you. Do you see a lot of Chinese on TV? We deliver food. This is not our country."

"Americans will bring you to church so you can worship Jesus and you know what those priests do to those boys?" my mom said. "They're gay, you know. All of them. You can't believe in their God. I knew this was going to be a bad luck year for you."

"You have to worship all the gods, even Jesus," my grandma said. She wore a rosary, a cross, and a jade Buddha around her neck. "Just in case."

My mom rolled her eyes. "Don't listen to her," she said to me.

My grandma foisted her cross in my face. "Jesus."

"Johnny wants me to go on tour with him," I said, backing away from Silver Christ. "All across the U.S. This summer. I'm going."

"Go where?" my mom asked.

"On shows," I said. "To perform. Like in a theater."

"Why would anyone want to see you?"

"You're not going," my dad said.

"Are you with that man's daughter?" my grandma asked. She told my parents there was an American girl who frequently phoned me.

"Cheers to Hor's American girlfriend!" my grandpa said, raising his cup.

My mom said that if I was with an American girl, she had to be blind.

My dad took another huge swill of port and his face turned a much darker shade of red.

He began to tear into a short rib with his teeth. "White women are lousy in bed," he said while chewing.

My grandma nodded and laughed. "Listen to your father. White women are lousy in bed."

My mom cussed under her breath and blinked back tears.

How my father knew about the ways of white women in bed, I had no idea. Hot with rage, I blurted, "You're an amateur alcoholic, Dad."

"Why do you keep using words we don't understand?" he said, talking with his mouth full. He ate like he only chewed with his tongue and the roof of his mouth. A puree was visible. I wiped one of my dad's meaty splatters from my arm.

"I hope you don't eat pussy like you eat ribs."

My dad slapped me. My mom gasped and cried out, "You're not really doing this, are you?"

"How dare he speak to me like that?" he shouted at my mom. "Are you teaching him to speak to me like that? I'm his Daddy!"

My grandma pointed a finger at me. "What did you say? What did you say?"

"You're not my dad," I said. "You're a joke."

He raised a leg and kicked me over in my chair. "Useless, fat, ugly abortion," he said. "I should have sent you back to China. Then you'd know what a hard life is."

I lay on the ground, feet in the air like a flicked-aside roach. My mom, my grandma, and my grandpa just sat there, silent, afraid of my dad.

I had nowhere to go. I couldn't even run into my own room. All I could do was lie there. I saw myself one day becoming my grandpa, planted quietly and passively in his place, letting God-knows-what in his head rot him from the inside. I went to the bathroom as if nothing had happened. I shut the door with a soft click. Then I let myself breathe. My face burned and my breathing became panting and my panting became something I couldn't name. Noise emerged from my gaping mouth, a cross between groaning and sobbing.

You can't hide what you're ashamed of forever. I'm ashamed of my family. I'm ashamed of being Chinese. We're polite. We're well-behaved. We tell white people what they want to hear. We smile and nod and pretend we're natives on someone's exotic vacation. We can be so much better than that. We should be able to chase the most improbable dreams and scale the highest heights, but we settle. We cower and refuse to believe that America can be our country, too. My parents settled. I settled. You don't have to, Maryann. You can be the best at whatever you do. Not just the best you can be, but the best, period.

That night, I packed a few things in my backpack and called Veronica and asked her to pick me up. I waited until everyone was asleep before I snuck out the front door.

To this day, I travel light. I've spent a lifetime on the road. My apartment in Manhattan often feels as foreign to me as a Double-Tree in Kansas City. I've been running from home ever since.

The next morning, after spending the night at The Razzmatazzes, my parents were waiting for me at the entrance to Marsden High with Principal Payne and Ms. St. Claire.

"Oh shit," Veronica said, as we walked toward them from the parking lot.

"Get to class, Veronica," Principal Payne said. "The hair and makeup folks are waiting."

Ms. St. Claire held my shoulders tight so I wouldn't run. Veronica eyed my parents like they were extraterrestials as she disappeared into the building.

"Where have you been sleeping, Lee?" Principal Payne asked.

"On a sofa bed."

"Very funny," Principal Payne said. "Save it for the cameras."

"My son kidnap," my dad said.

"Mr. Lee, let me do the talking." Principal Payne stooped over me. His eyelids looked heavy. "What's going on between you and your parents?"

"I'm going on Johnny Razzmatazz's comeback tour. I'll be performing. I'll come back to school in the fall." I tried not to look at my mom, who was crying.

Principal Payne looked surprised. "Wow," he said. "Congratulations! I didn't know you did standup. I've always wanted to try it. So brave."

"That is so cool," Ms. St. Claire said. "You're so lucky."

"Yeah, it's like a total dream come true," I said, blushing. "Johnny has been coaching me. I'm excited. Happy. I feel like this is a once-in-a-lifetime opportunity, you know?"

"I have to admit, I'm jealous of you, Lee," Principal Payne said. "I wish I had chased my dream, instead of . . . " His voice trailed off. "Anyhow, I'm excited for you."

Judging by the way my parents' eyes were bouncing between the principal, Ms. St. Claire, and myself, my mom and dad had no idea what we were talking about.

"That man take my son," my dad said. "*Ee-lee-gull!*" He jabbed his finger with each syllable.

"Mr. Lee, it seems that something truly wonderful is happening to your son," Principal Payne said. "MTV has been so generous to Marsden. I have a meeting today with the architects of the brand new football stadium that the show has funded. Groundbreaking starts next week. A rising tide raises all ships. That's why I am so excited for you and your family, Mr. Lee."

My father eyed Principal Payne with an uncomprehending expression. "Come home," my dad said to me in Mandarin.

My mom repeated the same words.

I'd never seen my parents stand next to each other. I'd never even seen a wedding photo. I'd never seen them happy.

"Do something," my mom said to my dad.

He just stood there, blinking, clenching and re-clenching his fists. Principal Payne glanced at his watch, then at the sea of white kids flowing into the building. The first bell rang.

"Tell him to call the police," my mom said in Mandarin.

"No," Dad said.

"Why not?"

"Be quiet!" he hissed.

My mom began saying my name repeatedly between sobs. At the time, I didn't care why my dad wasn't pressing charges or physically forcing me to come home. I just wanted to be free. I was willing to do anything to go on Johnny's tour. I would have hopped in a white Ford Bronco and tried to get away, even though I couldn't drive. Only years later did I learn why my dad didn't do more to keep me.

Principal Payne side-eyed my mom, not knowing why she was so sad about my big showbiz break. "Well, Mr. and Mrs. Lee, it was good meeting you," he said, shaking their hands. "Good luck with everything. And thank you for being part of the Marsden and MTV family. Now if you'll excuse me."

As he headed back toward the building, Principal Payne wandered to a parked Porsche SUV in the drop-off circle, stuck his head in the passenger-side window, and exchanged chitchat with a richer, whiter parent. Ms. St. Claire waved to my mom and dad as the last bell rang. My mom smacked my dad's back repeatedly and stomped her feet like a child in a tantrum. When Ms. St. Claire turned to head back into the school, I practically ran away from all of them, toward my first class. I did not look back. But I can still see my parents standing there—permanently imprinted in my memories—staring dumbfounded, not knowing why I was leaving or how to make me return.

JOHNNY'S GEERTS

About three years ago, I took you to a playground at Brooklyn Bridge Park on an unusually mild December day. There's a section called Swing Valley with sets for toddlers of various ages connected by rubberized walkways and nestled in a fortress of hedges. Like almost every kid activity in that part of Brooklyn, you're never the only parent with a bright idea, so Swing Valley was crowded that day and you soon had to wait your turn.

Your grandpa on your mother's side is white so you're light-skinned and big-eyed. You barely look like me at all. You're more beautiful than I ever imagined my kid could be. You were queued up, and this boy was taking his sweet time on a swing while his dad was playing with his smartphone. I walked a few strides away to text someone, and out of the corner of my eye, you caught the swing-hogger and shoved him out of the seat. He landed with a thud on the soft rubber and started bawling like the wimpiest four-year-old ever. The dad (a balding white guy) shot back into the scene before I arrived, lifting his son by the armpits. He looked me in the face and asked, "Where's her parent?"

"I am."

The white guy glanced at you and then at me again. "Oh."

"Is that kid yours?" I asked. "I mean, he has hair."

He blinked, circulating my words through his spacious, airy noggin. "You should tell her not to touch other kids."

I told you to apologize to his son.

"No," you said calmly.

"Come on, M," I said. "Do the right thing."

"You gotta watch your kid, man," the dad said.

"I heard you the first time, Young Willard Scott, okay?" I snapped.

"I don't even know who that is," he replied.

As we walked out of Swing Valley, you said, "I hate myself and I'm a bad person."

Man, it fucking hurt to hear you say that. My parents brought me up to hate myself and think I was a bad person. The last thing I wanted was for you to feel the same way. And there you were, beating yourself up for the problems me and your mother were having.

I tried to be a good parent. Often, I think that you became so quiet towards me because I suffocated you with affection. You probably don't remember this, but your mother used to tell me to give you space because just the sight of you made me want to hug and kiss you like I hadn't been hugged and kissed as a child. I wanted you to smile and laugh with me, for me. Those were my only expectations of you. But you rarely expressed joy in my presence. And you'd turn to your mother for everything. I envied the way you smiled and laughed with her and how you two talked freely like old friends. I wondered if it was because you looked more like her than me. I wonder now if you knew I was failing to make your mom happy before I did.

I've been thinking about how my dad must have felt when I brought some multimillionaire TV star into his store to show off that he could piss away his largesse over and over and get rewarded with TV shows and comedy tours while my dad had to work seventy hours a week for peanuts and stare into the face of an ingrate son threatening to drop out of school and leave home. If you did that to me, I might have kicked your ass over in a chair too! (Okay, maybe not.)

I don't think I ever expressed joy in front of my dad, either. I'm sure he wanted me to. Every parent does.

I wish I could have dealt with your grandparents differently back then. Maybe I should have done comedy *and* kept up with school. Maybe I could've shown them more appreciation somehow. But my feelings were real and intense, and I wasn't smart enough then to realize those feelings could be temporary. I've had numerous opportunities since to confess my regrets to them, but I've been too prideful. Now, it feels like the moment has passed. Even if I wrote what I felt, they wouldn't be able to read it.

I believe we get second and third and fourth and fifteenth chances in life. But we often fail to recognize when those chances are happening.

Back to 2001. Johnny's comeback tour took us across the country for six months. I never did go back to Marsden. Opting to save money because they were getting ready to pull the plug on *The Family Razzmatazz*, MTV didn't send a crew with us. Instead, every few weeks, there'd be a couple of random local contract dudes backstage getting footage of our performances, but we weren't being followed 24/7 like we were in L.A., which freed Johnny up . . . to be Johnny again.

We were in Chicago on a wintry night after a show. Johnny took me to comic Ari Demerol's apartment. They started snorting meth. (Very bad stuff, M.) The first time I saw the white powder getting corralled into lines by Johnny's Amex Black Card, I was afraid I might get addicted just by being near the stuff.

Ari asked if I wanted any, and Johnny said no before I could answer.

"He's too young!" he said. "Get him some bourbon instead."
#johnnyfatherfigure!

Eventually, I got plastered and passed out on the couch
while Johnny and Ari were trying to top each other with one
bizarre premise and punch after another involving the horrible
misfortunes of unwitting dwarves. The next day, when I woke,
the two of them were gone.

Fifteen years old and I was alone in a stranger's apartment in
the middle of winter in a new city. I learned a few life lessons
that day:

1. Californians don't know what winter jackets are.
2. Not having a cell phone sucks.
3. So does having no cash, especially after you've spent the
    few bucks Johnny gave you on Kit Kats and Red Vines.

From a stranger, I found out I was way out by O'Hare
Airport. Our hotel was downtown. With nothing on me but
my first hangover and the room keycard, I walked at least ten
miles on a zero-degree day with a wind chill of twenty below.

We still had another show that night. Backstage, Johnny
made it seem like I had left too soon. "We were getting you
breakfast," he said.

"I didn't know they scrambled meth with eggs," I replied.

On stage that night, I said, "I hang out with druggies, but
I don't do drugs. It's like watching a foreign movie without
subtitles. Why can't these people stop blinking and tripping
over furniture? Why are they cleaning shit? What I'm trying to
say is: I hate foreign films."

I thought I had killed.

When I rejoined Johnny backstage, he was downing a
fifth of Jim Beam. As he was introduced by the emcee, he was
swaying so badly I thought he was going to go facedown at my
feet. Then his name was called, and he faced the stage, plucked

the lapels of his leather jacket, and smoothed back his hair. He adjusted his sunglasses and looked at me.

"Watch me crush," he said.

He did an hour and a half and had the crowd laughing so hard, they were gasping for air and trying not to pee themselves.

I had most definitely not killed.

I celebrated my sixteenth birthday backstage at a club named Hack City in Lancaster, Pennsylvania. I performed with a now-famous comedian who shall remain nameless. Let's call him Geert. Geert plays arenas, stars in big rom-coms, and employs a huge staff that carefully manages his brand. But back then, he was just another road comic like Johnny. Geert confessed to needing massive amounts of Paxil to stay straight, and he had a tendency to forget his dosage, which would cause him to randomly fly off the handle. We were smoking cigarettes outside the club, and he was talking about wanting to have a bunch of kids so he could name them all after comic book heroes. (You couldn't really talk to Geert because he was always trying out his next bit on you.) A big rig's headlights appeared in the distance, and, mid-sentence, Geert ran out onto the icy road and stood there, hands on hips like he was Superman. The truck screeched to a halt and came within a few feet of jackknif-ing and making Geert road beef.

We stood there in shock while he sauntered back into the club as if nothing had happened. When one of the other comics asked what he was thinking, Geert grabbed him by the collar and threw him into a foursome of middle-aged ladies, who were enjoying bright red cocktails until the bright red part spilled all over them.

The people in Johnny's entourage were all Geerts.

I learned quickly that being on a comedy tour wasn't the best place for a teenager. If I was suffocated at home with the Lee Council, I was just treading water with Johnny's Geerts. Every night I was on a bus or a plane to the next place, meeting the next group of Geerts, each eager to show me their particular strain of Crazy. After just a few weeks, Crazy didn't seem at all crazy anymore. There was a comic in Cleveland who said he preferred to go on early because he wanted to be home with his wife.

We all stared at him like he was crazy!

Veronica and I kept in touch over the phone. She said she wished she could be out there with us. Sherry was pushing singing lessons because she wanted Veronica to have an album out by the end of the year while the reality show was still on the air.

"Run away like I did," I suggested. Run away with me, I meant.

Veronica laughed. "I'm not you, Hor."

If she truly wanted to drop out of school and the reality show, she would have. But in Guernica Beach, at Marsden High, Veronica was somebody. On the road with us, there would be no Brads, Darrens, and Stephanies telling her how perfect and famous she was. There would be no Sherry Razzmatazz seeing multiplatform, global stardom in Veronica's future. She would just be another one of Johnny's Geerts.

"I thought you wanted to be free," I said.

Veronica sighed. "I do, but I can't leave Marsden," she said. "Do you know who these parents are?" She began to list the job titles of her friends' moms and dads. President of Sony Records. Vice President of Universal Studios. A-list actors.

"They matter," said Veronica.

I tried to call my parents at least once a week. My dad was never there. As for my mom, she spent most of our limited phone time reaming me.

"You think I didn't want to do things for myself?" she asked. "I used to be good at drawing and singing. Chinese people don't do that here. White people do. Chinese people cannot be selfish like Americans."

"Chasing my dream isn't selfish," I said. "It's living."

"For yourself," she said. "When you are old, you will realize what a waste of time living for yourself is. You will understand how alone you are."

Sometimes, she'd give me my horoscope according to the teachings of Master Ming. She'd ask how we were getting from one city to the next, and if I told her we were boarding a bus, she'd say Master Ming predicted I'd get in a bus accident. If I said plane, she'd say Master Ming predicted a plane crash. She'd ask me to send photos of myself home so she could see how many pimples I had and how coated my tongue was. She'd take those photos and see a traditional Chinese doctor and then during the next phone call, she'd implore me to eat more corn, more dates, more blueberries, and asked where she could send them.

"By the time it gets here, I'll be gone," I said.

"You always say that."

"What do you mean?"

"You always say you'll be gone," she said, her voice breaking.

Sadness took my breath. I told myself not to cry. All the horoscopes and the homeopathic remedies were her ways of telling me that she loved me. I knew she'd never actually say the words or hug me or do anything to ensure that I was happy or emotionally healthy. She loved me like a possession—a plant or a car—that could only be enjoyed when I was within arm's reach, sitting on a shelf for her to dust, manicure, de-barnacle of acne, and so forth. That I could talk and feel and think for myself, well, those were obstacles to how she preferred to love me. The only way I could satisfactorily show her that I loved her was to be home and by her side and obeying her commands, like Sherry's Pomeranians.

I tried to love you differently. I tried to tell you "I love you" as much as possible. One time you even replied, "I know, Dad," all annoyed. Do you remember? For a second, I was hurt, and then I thought about my childhood and realized that I had just accomplished something special as a parent. You knew that I loved you; you could, at the very least, take that for granted.

I like to say that, even though I never went to college, getting up night after night in 500- to 1,000-seat theaters was like majoring in standup. The laughs in those venues were so much bigger. The sound would come at you in waves, from the balcony and rafters, and lift you up. On stage, you felt like a Hulk version of yourself.

My stage time slowed and sped up at the same time. On the good nights, the jokes I told seemed to happen in slow motion. When I saw the light telling me that my twenty minutes were up, I didn't feel like wrapping up my set. I wished I could be there for hours more—forever, even.

Knowing that I had to get up every night and deliver, I wrote new jokes all day, and I'd work them into my act. Some of them, I still use. Like this one:

Ever notice that racists are usually only good at one thing: being racists? Like what else has David Duke done with his life? Nothing. Other than get lots of plastic surgery.

Or:

With its elderly flight attendants, flying has become like a nursing home in reverse. The patients have to take care of you.

Or:

I went to a very posh, very expensive high school. I miss it. It's where I came of age. I entered a boy and exited a white boy.

If comedy were wine, my dad would probably say: some jokes are like the finest bottles. They'll last long after you're dead.

I started noticing that there were always a few auto-graph-seekers waiting outside for me after shows. A lot of them were older versions of me. Nerdy, chubby dudes. Asian. Johnny told me it was the reality show. MTV was showing clips from our performances.

"You're so inspiring," said a Japanese American fan.

Was he talking about me? It was as if he'd said I was sexy. Impossible! I signed his Johnny Razzmatazz Why 'Ello ' Ello Tour tee with a white marker. "Inspiring? Like R. Kelly's 'I Believe I Can Fly'?"

"I feel like I can relate to you," he said.

I thanked him and returned his shirt.

"I wish I was good at something," he said, eyes downcast.

"Hey," I told him. "If you can see it, then you can do it . . . there's nothing to it."

"Not really," he said. "I'm just a programmer."

"I believe I can code," I sang, putting my arm around him and clenching my fists. "I believe I can touch the code. I think about it every night and day. Spread my code and fly away." I admit I was a bit tipsy.

He smiled but refused to play along. "You're making fun of me, aren't you?"

"You and R. Kelly, yes."

"Only a few people get to do what they love, you know?" he said, pushing me away. "The rest of us are still trying to find out what that thing is."

"I'm just messing around, man," I said. "For a guy who came to a comedy show, you're awfully serious."

His face got really red and angry. "I was trying to tell you that you give us hope and we need it, you idiot!"

Now I felt bad. "Well, I appreciate it," I told him. I looked around for something to give him. Finding nothing within reach, I held up my white marker. "Want my pen?"

On the last night of the tour, Johnny took a bunch of us to Scores in New York City. While our fellow comics got private room lap dances, Johnny and I stood outside in the purple light, drinking whiskey. He mussed my hair, which I'd started scrunching and spiking like him. He fixed his bleary eyes upon me. I could see the green of them behind his Ray-Bans.

"Do you want to stay?" he asked.

"What do you mean?"

"Here," he said. "In New York. With me. I'm done with the show. And with Sherry."

He had filed for divorce that morning.

Only then did it dawn on me that I couldn't go back to San Gabriel Valley if I wanted to continue to be Sirius Lee. If I returned, Johnny wouldn't be in L.A. to take me to comedy clubs, which meant I'd go back to Marsden and finish up high school and try to get into college so I could become the doctor, the lawyer, the CEO that the Lee Council wanted. Johnny was making me an offer: standup or bust.

"Of course I want to stay," I said.

Johnny held me to his broad, sweaty chest, and I held him back.

"That's good," he said. "That's good, son."

After I told my mom I wasn't coming home, she began to cry.

"Master Ming told me this would happen. I don't know why my luck is so bad. What did we ever do to you to make you run so far away? We did nothing but care for you and worry about you and give you the best life. The best life!" Her voice was quaking and plaintive at first, before gradually rising into an ear-splitting rage.

"I hope you fail," she went on. "And when you fail, don't come running back home because we won't want you, okay? You go be selfish and do what you want. And we'll do what we want. We'll be fine without you. I'm already glad I don't have to worry about you anymore! I never thought I'd give birth to such a snake person! When I first saw you, I wished I had a girl because I knew a boy would be disobedient! I wish I had a girl instead of you. I wish you were never born!"

That hurt. My parents made it clear that if I didn't accept their sacrifices and become the person they wanted me to be, they didn't want me. To this day, they have never said they missed me.

Johnny and I moved into a loft in SoHo. He assigned me a corner of the flat and got a big screen television and a Play-Station to keep me occupied while he hooked up with pretty much every one of his exes from the past thirty years. When he wasn't storming around the place yelling on the phone at Sherry or her lawyers or bedding someone on his end of the loft, he was back on the sauce again and on every drug imaginable.

When Veronica found out we weren't coming back, she was shocked. "I thought I was Dad's favorite," she said.

One of the things I've learned from my time with comedians is that we're among the most self-absorbed people on the planet. The truth about standup is: you're just doing it for yourself. Comedy ain't a service. You ain't joining the Peace Corps. You don't care about the audience. You suck up their laughter like a vampire drinks blood. You consume their joy to feel better about yourself. I was like Johnny and Veronica now. I was entitled to attention. When I stepped on stage, I expected to be heard. *I was my favorite; Johnny was his.*

I quickly gained thirty pounds because all I ate was pizza, and military-grade weed flowed from the faucets. I advised those who dared to visit that to lounge in our bean bag chairs was to invite a staph infection. Suffice it to say, I drew the line at cleaning up Johnny's puke. Our place was such a flophouse that it encouraged me to go out and do drop-ins all night and clean up in a Starbucks or McDonald's like a homeless dude until Johnny was sober enough to call a maid.

I'll be the first to admit that I don't know much about life. Whole chunks of it escape your view when you drop out of school and leave home at fifteen. Here are a few things I didn't know until well into my twenties:

1. April fifteenth is the national tax deadline.
2. You need to understand compound interest rates before buying an apartment.
3. "Dry clean only" doesn't mean that you can only put it in the dryer once.
4. Credit cards have to be paid back every once in awhile.
5. Having a bank account and knowing how to get to your money without someone else's assistance is helpful.

The Village Z Comedy Club on MacDougal Street was where I really lived, where I grew up. It was a few doors down from the more famous Comedy Cellar. The club had seen better days and had the yellowed newspaper clippings and wall memorabilia to prove it. There were articles about Brett Butler, Damon Wayans, and Richard Klein, and a placard claiming that Woody Allen used to perform there.

The place had the worst bathroom I'd ever seen. It was like walking into a shallow pond. Every part of the toilet was broken. The fill valve, the handle, the flapper. There was even a crack in the tank. And it was never repaired.

The owner was in his sixties, and he wore a hot pink tie, a suit the color of dog diarrhea, and his hair in a gray ponytail. He always appeared to have had a rough night. His shirt was often untucked, his collar folded into his neck. His name was Dan Van Pido, and the comics called him Pidofile.

Before the shows, he was usually curled over the bar, counting out the register. Judging by the paltry height of the stacks, the club didn't do well financially. Like Chris Rock's early days at Catch A Rising Star, I'd hang out from the time Village Z opened until after closing, doing odd jobs like waitering the open mics, taking tickets for the early shows, or barking on the street. I got on stage after headliners like Sarah Silverman, Todd Barry, and Louis C.K. I was one of the comics who performed for those who wanted to stick around for half-price drinks and the free aftershow. We were the sad, funeral procession of amateur, "up-and-coming" comics desperate to get five to ten minutes of stage time.

Pidofile was protective of me because I was so young.

"Are you sleeping?" he'd ask hoarsely, his face a terrarium of stubble. "You look like a fucking burnt-out, alcoholic detective."

I told him he didn't look much better.

"My wife kicked me out of the apartment," he said. "Tried to bring the girlfriend home again." He did standup in the 1970s and 1980s and knew Johnny well.

"You need to establish your own thing," he warned. "Johnny's not a great guy to count on."

I was finding that out on my own. Johnny would disappear for weeks on end without telling me where he went. Only after he returned would he reveal that he was doing dates on the road. Once he disappeared for three months to work on a cruise ship.

I was lonely. I was never with anyone my age. The other comics would talk about things I knew nothing about: your first kiss, losing your virginity, living in college dorms, getting your heart broken, working shitty day jobs that made you question whether you were born to be a desk drone. I just nodded and smiled and pretended to understand.

But I got to meet all the greats. Seinfeld. Margaret Cho. Attell. Maria Bamford. I especially loved Greg Giraldo.

Whenever he'd drop in, I would tell him that he was my second favorite comedian of all-time next to Chris Rock and he'd tell me to go fuck myself. I laughed so hard I cried when I first saw that bit he did on America needing big SUVs to haul their fat fucking kids up hills. He never recognized me or remembered that I was a comic. He always thought I was just another kid coming to see a show. One night, a few years later, after I'd become more established, I asked to take a photo with him. His eyes were bloodshot and his face was sweaty even though he hadn't gone on stage yet. His wife was waiting for him by the exit. He told me he liked my material and to keep working. The next day, I walked around town with a big goofy smile thinking about what he'd said. By the end of the week, he was dead. I was nauseous for weeks after; I couldn't perform. We all knew he had a problem with substances. But so many of us had those same problems. His death should have warned me. Johnny and his Geerts should have warned me. Pidofile was trying to warn me. But I ignored them all.

My photo with Greg Giraldo still hangs in my living room. I named you after his wife Mary-ann, who, at a benefit concert Jerry Seinfeld threw for the Giraldo family, told me that Greg once said he was sure I'd become a star.

When I was eighteen, I signed with my first real manager. The person handing you this pile of pages: Sarah Coleman. Before I signed, I wanted to meet her in person so I visited the agency office and informed the twiggy, young white male receptionist with a walrus mustache that I was there to see Sarah.

Twiggy fingered the speakerphone. "Mr. Sirius Lee is here to see you." With a smirk, he added, "Seriously."

"Send him in," Sarah said.

"Sure thing." He disconnected. "Please take a seat."

"She just said, 'Send him in.'"

The man's lips separated like an opening vacuum seal. He swigged bottled water and tucked his longish hair behind an ear. I repeated myself. He patted his armrests as if to show me what a seat looked like.

Puzzled, I sat. The receptionist vacated his post, humming some pop song by a Mickey Mouse club star whose name I can't recall. (The chorus was "Wet Your Love In Me.") After a few additional awkward moments alone, I began to wander the mostly empty and silent cubicle rows. Reading the name-plates, I eventually discovered Sarah's corner office. She rose from her desk and gripped my hand hard and pumped my arm like a well lever. She was in her late thirties and dressed in men's slacks and dress shoes, a cream-colored starched shirt, and a silver tie. Her dark hair was short and slicked back, gleaming like the finish of a new car. Her jaw was square, her cheek-bones high, and she had dark, liquid eyes resembling wet rocks. She was not white; her ethnicity was difficult to place. Her desk was so neat and paper-free it appeared she didn't work. Hanging shelves boasted framed photos of her posing with the likes of Tom Cruise, Samuel L. Jackson, and Charlize Theron. Concert posters surrounded us. Led Zeppelin, Rolling Stone, Sheryl Crow, and U2. There were no comedians.

"Did you get lost?" Sarah asked.

"Well, your receptionist—"

"Talked your ear off, huh?" she said. "Happens to me all the time. Interesting guy. Sings Yiddish folk songs in a Cuban disco jazz ensemble. Keeps inviting me to go all the way out to Queens to see him play. No can do. I have a wife and kids!" Her laugh only moved the lower reaches of her chin, like a ventriloquist's dummy. "Please, have a seat."

I did as told.

"Look, I've heard great things about you from Dan, and you're so young you're a greenfield," Sarah said. "I have big shit planned for you. Sitcoms. The movies. Book deals."

"And comedy albums?"

"Sure, why not?" she said. "But you know and I know that the money isn't in selling comedy CDs."

"But that's what I do."

She reclined in her leather chair and pointed a finger at me. She held it there long enough without speaking for me to look over my shoulder.

"You're going to be an actor," she said finally.

"I am?"

She pointed to her posters. "You want to be up there, don't you?"

"Only Sam Jackson."

"You so gangsta!" she exclaimed.

My eyes bulged with surprise.

"No more headlining the fucking Banana Peel in Morristown on a Wednesday night," she said. "Extend your brand. Our relationship is going to be like a marriage. One partner is always pushing you to do more than you're willing to do on your own."

"I don't really know what you're talking about," I told her. "I'm only eighteen, and I've never even been on a date."

"I love comedy," she went on. "Long commute on the Metro-North. I read comedian memoirs all the time. *Born Standing Up. Too Fat to Fish* by Artie Lange. The Lenny Bruce one with the long title I can't remember right now. That one is my all-time favorite."

"If it's your favorite, why can't you remember the title?"

She shrugged, palms up. "Because it's too fucking long. When you do your book, the title has got to be short."

"Do you *do* a book?"

Her gaze descended upon me for the first time. "You're a natural wordsmith, you know that?"

I informed her I hadn't even finished high school.

"Neither did I," she said. "I ran away from home because my parents were super Christian. They didn't like my gayness. But like you, I focused on achieving my dream, and now, I'm here."

I wanted to be like Sarah when I got to her age. Slick, together, and different. She engaged with the world on her terms. There appeared to be nothing she couldn't have, no matter how unusual she chose to be. When I imagine you as a grown-up, I often imagine that you'll be like her.

"You know the key to getting up there?" she asked, gesturing toward her posters again. "It's not talent. It's dumb luck. There are hundreds and thousands of Tom Cruises and Charlize Therons and U2s, but they're going to die forgotten. Why? Because they didn't have the luck, and once they realized they wouldn't have the luck, they stopped showing up. They quit. I started with a lot of people just like me. But as the years went by, they looked up at the partners of the agency and said, 'Wow, they're all straight, middle-aged white guys and I'm not one of them.' One by one, they dropped out. I stayed. And now, I'm here. Do you understand what I'm getting at?"

At the time, I wasn't entirely sure what she was saying applied to me, but I nodded anyway. Now, of course, I know she was speaking truth to power.

"Coleman Client Rule One is: show up and do your job," she said. "Whatever that job is. When I call, you say 'Yes.' Okay?"

"Isn't that two rules?"

Ignoring me, she added, "Wanna know Coleman Client Rule Two?"

"Okay."

"I hate it when clients call. I call you."

After *The Family Razzmatazz* was finally canceled, Veronica decided to visit colleges in New York. Johnny got so excited he purchased a full living room set. He had it delivered before she arrived, as if his addictions were a stain on the floor that a couch could hide.

I hadn't seen her in over three years. When she came to the loft, she was dressed in tight white jeans and a dark down jacket with a fur-lined collar from a brand so lux that it might have even given a Kardashian sticker shock. Her hair was dyed ruby red. She hugged and kissed me on both cheeks. I told her Johnny was out grocery shopping. The truth was he had called from a hotel room in Secaucus to report that he was nursing the hangover of the century and a sprained ankle from playing a sport I'd never heard of named dance tennis.

"You look great," she said. She was lying. I had gone from chubby to unquestionably fat.

"No, you look great," I said.

She didn't deny it.

"Can I get you anything?" I asked.

"Do you have sparkling water?"

In the fridge, there were rows and rows of beer bottles. "No sparkling," I said. "Want tap?"

She said she was fine.

I made myself a drink. Jameson's on the rocks. One in the afternoon. Calmed the nerves. Veronica walked around, inspecting. She must have seen what I saw: the lack of anything a functional adult might have in a home. No photos. No books. No shelves. No wall hangings.

She eyed my glass and the bottle on the kitchen counter. "Do you miss me?"

During every phone conversation we'd had since I left home, she would ask whether I missed her. I usually answered "*Natürlich*." But now that she was in front of me, I didn't want to give her the attention she craved.

"My dad's out getting trashed, isn't he?"

"No."

"Don't lie to me."

"Last night, he got trashed. Right now, he's hungover."

Veronica didn't even crack a smile. "Am I the only one that worries about him?"

I drank up. What did Veronica do about her worrying? Nothing. She was just as selfish as I was. Maybe that's why I was still in love with her: she and I were made for each other.

Johnny didn't come back. He didn't call. He didn't appear until the morning of Veronica's flight home. She and I spent her entire visit together. On the last night, we went out to a hidden club near Chinatown. We were underage so I expected to be turned away by the fedora-wearing bouncer. But once Veronica showed her California ID and said that her father was Johnny Razzmatazz, we were let in.

We got a table and were brought a bottle of Dom Pérignon. Free, just because Veronica was a celebrity. From a bejeweled case, she fished out an electric cigarette that lit with a twist. In the dimness and the red lights, our glasses of champagne looked orange. We clinked and drank. The club was pumping some very loud song sung by a frantic and brooding white guy. Veronica wore glittery lip gloss that made her mouth shine like the skin of a supermarket apple.

"We're all grown-up now," she said, behind a vapor puff.

"I thought we'd get more privileges for being grown-up," I said. "Like free rollercoaster rides or all the best candy and ice cream."

Veronica laughed. I had forgotten what her laugh sounded like. A series of chirps. I liked the way she sounded. I liked the way she smelled. Like Swedish Fish. I couldn't believe we were out on the town together. This was the first time we had been in public since we went shopping for my first performing outfit.

"I've seen your videos on YouTube," she said. "You're incredible. I'm so proud of you."

A billion times, people would come up to me after shows and say I was funny. I never blushed. But when Veronica complimented me, I turned bright red and tingled all over.

"Your dad taught me everything I know," I said. Johnny certainly did; I was so used to drinking whiskey that I downed champagne like it was water.

She nodded at one of the booths. Five white kids. Three girls in absurdly revealing dresses and two guys in blazers. They looked straight out of a high school stage production of *American Psycho*.

"They want to take our picture," Veronica said.

"They want to take yours."

One of the girls snapped a shot of the two of us. That photo would later appear on *PerezHilton.com*, and for months, the gossip columnists speculated that Veronica Razzmatazz was dating me, even though her publicist kept saying we were only friends. I started seeing bigger crowds at my shows. People came to clubs specifically to watch me. Then someone from *Live On Air*, CBS's new Sunday night competitor to *Saturday Night Live*, contacted Sarah. A few months later, on my nineteenth birthday, I auditioned to join the cast.

THE FEATURED INTERN

O kay, maybe not the cast.

I joined *LOA* as what they called a "featured intern" in 2005. That's below the permanent cast (repertory players). They did an open call for comedians of color because that was the year the show hired Annie Gemellino, Stuart Stevens, Bill Dreyer, and Andy Maynard, so someone at CBS suggested to Slade Turnham, the executive producer, that they actually consider some non-Anglos to balance the cast out. I was one of them, along with my buddies Archimedes Jones, Frye Johns, and Jesus Iglesias.

The featured intern auditions were the same as the ones for the regular cast. You did your stuff on that stage in Studio 58 (the one they made to look like an entrance to Port Authority), except Slade yawned throughout and pocket-combed his voluminous white hair and none of the stars of the cast were there. You had three minutes before the next guy came out, and there were about twenty of us, and you were occasionally interrupted by one of the writers trying to get to Slade. He upped and left during my audition. Then afterward, we were lined up like Jews, and a white lady picked a few of us. It was all over in under an hour. Oddly enough, I never saw that lady again.

On my first day at work, Slade stood on the stage at Studio 58, holding a sheet of notes with quaking hands, and led a meeting with all of us to make sure we were on the same page about his strengths and weaknesses and the goals of the higher-ups at the network.

"My background is in sports," he said. "I don't really know comedy. So I'm expecting you guys to tell me what's funny. Look at me as your manager, like in baseball, or your coach. I'm here to help you perform on the field."

Sitting in the theater seats, we were silent and stunned, realizing that we might have made a major career misstep.

"My boss tells me that the ratings for *SNL* have been sliding for years, and according to Development and Programming, the research is telling us that viewers want to laugh on Sunday nights instead of Saturdays," Slade said, with a nervous chuckle. "So what we want here is to duplicate *SNL*. Except on Sundays."

The shoulders of all the cast members sagged at once.

"But we can't be the exact same show," Annie Gemellino said. "Can we?"

Slade blinked at us and scratched his nose with his pinky. I began searching for lifeboats.

"We have a lot of great intelligence on what NBC is doing," said Slade. "We hired many of you because you look like some of the comedians they hired."

The cast stirred, many of them groaning. "Who am *I* supposed to be?" Annie asked.

"You look like a woman they've just hired named Kristen Wiig," Slade said. "Bill, you look like Bill Hader. Andy, you're a lot like Andy Samberg." He said all this like we were the stupid ones.

"Slade, we have to be distinct in some way!" Stuart Stevens said.

"We can be more live," I joked.

The room went quiet. Annie nodded. "Yeah, none of that 'taped in front of a live studio audience' bullshit!" she said. "We go live, every time!"

The cast began to chant "Live, every time!" like a bunch of comedian baboons.

Slade straightened and beamed, relieved to have avoided a full-on cast mutiny. "I can take it up the chain and see what they think. But I think it's a great idea."

The higher-ups loved it. And so we were *Live On Air*, just like *Saturday Night Live*, but on Sundays . . . and *live-r.*

That first season, the featured interns just did printer runs, grabbing the sketches off the HP and sprinting them to the writers and the cast. Occasionally, they would have a role for a comic of color that wasn't taken up by Ayana Johnson or Jamal Thompson, and we'd get to participate in table reads and dress rehearsals. I only got in a few sketches:

1. I was the security guard in Annie Gemellino's first sketch as the Walmart Lady who's way too enthusiastic about her job.
2. I was one of the backup dancers doing jumping jacks in a spacesuit in Andy Maynard's viral rap video "When I Push Your Head Down, It Means I Love You."
3. I was the guy who delivered takeout to Stuart Stevens's gluten-intolerant wheat tycoon in the recurring soap opera spoof *Kansas*.

The cast partied a lot. Being on the show got us free booze, drugs, and entry into any club in New York we wanted. A few of us would hit the town at two in the morning, party until closing time, and then come back to Studio 58 to write all night. Featured interns didn't have to show up to work until late morning, so if the club kicked us out, we drank in the street. A little pizza for breakfast and a nap and we were good to go. Ah, to be nineteen again.

Archimedes and I were sitting on the curb outside Ed Sullivan Theater at 5:00 a.m., drinking St. Ides out of a paper bag. He was pissed off we weren't in more sketches. I told him to be patient.

"Naw, man," he said. "We're brown dudes. That's just about the lowest of the low. We're always going to be a half step up from being an extra. Look at Jamal." Jamal played all the black celebrities as well as every Middle Eastern or Indian character. Everyone from Denzel Washington to Shaq. Everyone from Gandhi to Saddam Hussein. "Ayana gets hers because she's a woman and light-skinned. Fuck this. I'm just still here because my management would drop my ass if I quit. The show isn't even funny."

"That's not true."

"Honestly, I've never even watched *SNL*," he said. "That shit's only funny to white people. I auditioned for *MADtv*, but they didn't want me."

"We'll get our chance," I said. I believed that. I expected to get my shot. I was going to be the first Chinese American superstar comedian. There wasn't a doubt in my mind.

Archimedes laughed and shook his head. He was gap-toothed like Eddie and skinny like Rock.

"Is that what Johnny Razzmatazz tells you?" he asked. "Because it was probably true for him because he's white. If you're white and on the fringes, you can have a career. Johnny can be the 'next' Sam Kinison. But if you tried to be an Asian Johnny or a Black Dice Clay? No way. Because we don't look like them. We have to be twice as good to get half the opportunities."

I chewed on that for awhile, remembering what my grandfather had said when I was a kid. *We have to be better than them. You'll have to be better than them, M.*

"I don't know if that's true," I said.

"How come I know how the world works and you don't?" he asked between sips of beer. "You're supposed to be smart."

It was Archimedes, not Johnny, who introduced me to cocaine. Things had gone especially poorly that night during dress. I was blamed for costumes getting lost or queue cards being incorrect, I can't remember which. At the club, I was feeling so down Archimedes hooked me up out of pity. "Just a little bump so you don't get addicted," he said, dusting the back of my closed fist before emptying his rocket sniffer into his nose while a waitress waited patiently for our drink order. Let's just say I wasn't the best at my intern duties. A little bit of coke actually made me do better. I felt looser, funnier, more vocal, more focused. At first, I thought the yeyo was great, and I wondered why Johnny hadn't introduced me to it sooner.

I began to take a little coke every afternoon like a normal person takes a shot of espresso. I felt like I needed it to keep up with the schedule. Fifteen hours a day, six days a week. I had to get through those boring early-in-the-week writers room meetings where I didn't get to do anything. I might as well have been working an office job. I barely had any time to work on my own material. On Mondays (the worst of nights to work a comedy club because the crowds are predominantly made up of non-English-speaking tourists), I had to get on stage at Village Z just to feel like a comedian again.

Occasionally, I would feel courageous enough to suggest a joke or a premise to one of the writers. Once, I suggested that I play a short, fat superhero bad at his job while Bill Dreyer could be my hunchbacked sidekick on a leash. The writer told me it was a funny idea, but when it came time to pitch Slade, somehow I became the one on the leash and Bill Dreyer became Arend, his recurring flamboyantly gay horse carriage tour operator character. I noticed that when the white guy was the butt of the joke, the response from Slade and the writers would be tepid. Almost all of the writers were white. I learned that if I made myself the butt of the joke, writers were more likely to pitch my idea.

When we were away from Studio 58, Archimedes, of course, would remind me that this was exactly the sort of shit he was railing against. Jamal would tell me my idea just wasn't funny enough and then go on to say that he'd never seen a really funny Asian before, and I'd get pissed but I'd let it go, and then the next week, the same shit would happen again, and it would eat at me.

Archimedes and I weren't the only ones to feel uncomfortable. Frye and Jesus quit midseason. And Archimedes got himself fired after he showed up high to dress and called Slade a kike.

By the end of 2005, I was the last of the featured interns and got promoted to permanent cast member. Like Sarah had advised, I kept showing up.

Veronica chose NYU and moved east. When she started school, she and I hung out a lot because she didn't know anybody. Without her Brads, Darrens, and Stephanies, she was uncomfortable in New York City. Too crowded. Too many tall buildings. Too cold. She missed her car. She spent three nights a week with Johnny and me, crashing on our couch. We were her safety blanket.

Of the two of us, I was the TV star now. She started looking at me differently. When we would go to the movies, she'd put a head on my shoulder in the theater. When we were out on the street, she'd take the crook of my arm.

I couldn't fucking believe it; I had a chance!

On one early winter night, after a karaoke outing with a few of Veronica's dormmates, as we were walking back through Washington Square Park toward my apartment, laughing over how poorly we rapped Nelly's "Country Grammar," I snaked an arm around her waist, and before I knew it, we were exchanging wet, bitter kisses in the lightly falling snow.

Even though they say love overcomes petty things like the color and complexion of your skin, I'll always be a little shocked that white, famous, rich Veronica was taken with no good Asian me.

Just like back in Guernica Beach, she loved to go shopping for me. She'd cut classes so she could dress me up at all the high-end boutiques in SoHo. She'd routinely drop $1,000 on a jacket I'd wear once or $500 on a pair of fitted jeans that I needed Spanx to get into.

"You need to lose, like, thirty pounds," she said. When she noticed the stung look on my face, she added. "For health reasons."

She had me keep a food log and started stocking my fridge with fruits and vegetables.

"But 'I don't like fruit! I don't like it!'" I said, quoting the Dave Attell punch line.

Veronica stared at me, not getting my reference, but Johnny laughed heartily until he started smokers-coughing.

"Just try to have an orange with your pizza from now on," Veronica said, shaking her head.

I did. And I started eating broccoli and spinach too, even though I hated them. I didn't lose much weight, maybe a few pounds, but I did become so regular, I began to incorporate bathroom stops into my daily commute to Studio 58 in Midtown.

Veronica made Johnny and I promise to stay substance-free in her presence. He became a different person around her. It was as if the two of them watching rented movies and eating delivered pizza was the high Johnny had been chasing all along. He was home more often, did comedy less, and never touched a drink when she was around.

It was during those nights as a threesome, as an almost-family, that I realized that Johnny had no paternal feelings toward me. He'd get on Veronica about keeping up with her studies, but never ask me about how my comedy was going or how things were on *LOA*. He and Veronica would play checkers for hours, laughing and talking trash to each other, never inviting me into their game. We'd have dinner, and while I put the dirty plates in the dishwasher, Johnny would look over at Veronica and say "Checkers?" and it was assumed that I'd retire to the living room to play console games.

Back in Los Angeles, I had mistakenly assumed that he would look after me as a father might. But in his mind, I was just another amateur comic hanger-on in his entourage, just another Geert who happened to be his non-rent-paying SoHo loftmate. I was hurt; I had been used, like Chinese labor, to get his career going again. But I kept my feelings inside and reminded myself that I should have been grateful to Johnny for giving me my start, like I should have been grateful to my parents for immigrating to America. Whether or not my hurt was justified, I wished for more from him. I wished for what he gave to his daughter.

Once Veronica moved out of the dorms and into her own apartment, I moved in with her. After living with Johnny, living with someone who cared about my behavior was a shock. I was used to doing whatever I wanted, whenever I wanted. *What do you mean I can't play video games until six in the morning and then complain when you ask me to have breakfast with you?*

I gave Veronica whatever she asked for. We were having sex! When you're twenty and having sex regularly for the first time, you're pretty much willing to do anything to keep this new natural resource plentiful. One day, you'll discover this amazing fossil fuel of the soul for yourself, and you'll be so lucky, because I won't be in your vicinity to threaten your future partner with murder.

Whenever it was business time, Veronica's eyes were squeezed shut, and she insisted on turning off all lights and covering any reflective surfaces.

In bed one night, I asked her why we had to go through all the extra arrangements.

She eyed the ceiling for some time before answering, "I don't like the way I look."

Why the hesitation? This was a person who took two hours in the bathroom to get ready for school. Many of the rooms at the Razzmatazz villa had numerous mirrors, and when Veronica would pass them, she'd stop to check her face. She would watch episodes of *The Family Razzmatazz* after they aired to make sure MTV showed her best angles. Was she lying to me so she wouldn't hurt my feelings? I felt like an asshole for doubting her, especially since I also hated the way I looked, but I couldn't help but wonder if she secretly found me unattractive.

(M, I'm going to pause here and let you catch your breath a little. I know this is probably a lot more than you want to know about your dad's love life. I've pulled a "My Mom," except I like sex. I apologize in advance, but like time, words only move in one direction.)

I wanted to spend every waking minute with Veronica. I was her first, too. She told me she knew there were others who wanted her, but she didn't feel safe with anyone else.

"It's not in you to mistreat me," she said, in my arms. "I know you won't cheat on me like Dad cheated on Mom. You respect me."

She told me repeatedly I was the sweetest, nicest guy she'd ever met. She kept saying I could not possibly treat her better. In the fog of first love, I remember being so pleased with myself. *I'm killing this boyfriend game*, I thought. (It was only later that I'd realized that sweet and nice were traits Veronica settled for.)

She came to most of my standup shows. We dined in Michelin-starred restaurants where celebrity chefs rushed up after our meals to take photos with us. Before long, Veronica collected her new set of Brads, Darrens, and Stephanies at NYU, and we got invited to the Hamptons with other rich and successful friends. We were at this party where truckloads of pizza were delivered, people hurled midgets into the pool, and the band Everclear played for three hours until the lead singer became so hoarse that he complained that he was about to cough up blood because the host (some Saudi prince) refused to let the band stop. (A security detail surrounded the stage to keep them from leaving.) Ninety-five percent of the people at these parties were white. I would choose twenty folks at random and count the Caucasians. Quite often, I got to nineteen. Somehow, little Chinese Hor from Alhambra, California had gained access to the life of the gossip girls and the one percenters.

Maryann, when you fall in love for the first time, you'll probably want to control your feelings. But know that the stronger and deeper they are, the less you'll be able to handle or even explain them.

When Veronica and I weren't together, I was outrageously jealous. There wasn't a six-foot man between the ages of twenty and ninety in New York that I didn't imagine enrapturing my girlfriend. I once flew into a rage when I met her after one of her classes and saw her pushing her septuagenarian English professor around in a wheelchair. ("His dick still works!" I insisted.) I'd start these fights just to reassure myself that she cared enough about our relationship to cry over it.

I was blind to other women. Believe it or not, I had opportunities. (Thanks, two-drink minimums!) One night at Village Z, this German coed came up behind me at the bar after the show, wrapped her arms around my belly, and whispered in my ear that she had a thing for Japanese guys.

But after my spots at the clubs or long nights at Studio 58, I literally ached to rush home to do nothing more than sit on a couch and watch a late night movie with Veronica.

Johnny took a dim view of my relationship with his daughter. "Like incest," he said to me one night in her apartment, bottle of whiskey in hand, 11:00 a.m., while Veronica was in class.

"If I'm not good enough for her, you should just say so."

"If that's what you think, I'm not going to stop you thinking it."

"You're a fucking asshole, Johnny."

He nodded vigorously at my assessment.

"You know I've been in love with her since high school," I said. "At least you can be happy for us."

Johnny was tickled by the word "us." "What you two have isn't love," he said. "It's sympathy confusion. If I wasn't here to get her heart gushing warm family thoughts, she'd never even consider you."

"I guess I should thank you for being such a good matchmaker."

He tottered toward me, his arms stretched forward like Frankenstein's. He put his hands on my shoulders, fumbling with them as if he were trying to figure out what shoulders were used for.

"You should find a nice Asian girl," he said.

I didn't talk to Johnny for weeks after that. I told Veronica what he had said. Of course, she implored me not to take him seriously because he had been drinking, and she gave Johnny a talking-to.

"Do you love me?" I asked while we walked hand-in-hand on a ninety-degree day in Washington Square Park, not far from where we'd had our first kiss.

She paused before blurting a fluty "Sure!"

"Because I love you."

She released my hand. "Oh, Hor." When she called me Hor, she was talking to the nerdy fourteen-year-old from Alhambra that she was buddies with. When she called me Sirius, I was the rising star standup she was dating. In bed, she called me Sirius. When we were out at night, I was Sirius. During the day and around her friends? Sirius. Around Johnny? I was always Hor.

After I started talking to him again, Johnny went out of his way to treat me like a future son-in-law. He kept referring to Veronica and me as "V-Hor." He talked about some million-dollar home in New Jersey he wanted to buy for the three of us after Veronica graduated. He even called me "son."

You know what he didn't do? Apologize.

There I was, this chubby Asian dude who wore retro T-shirts extolling the coolness of video games and phallic innuendo, hanging out with Veronica's squad of Anglo Aberzombies. It didn't feel right. I didn't fit in.

One of her friends was named Gage. Gay Gage, I liked to call him. Because I like accurate nicknames. We were at this house party, which sounded fun, but in reality, it was a debutante ball held at some twenty-year-old's gigantic Upper West Side apartment. By day, the place probably belonged to a charming vampire. Black light and emo tunes throbbed, and high-heeled cigarette girls handed out acid tabs and ecstasy.

Gay Gage came up to Veronica and me, and I could tell he was tweaking on something. (His nose was twitching like the velveteen rabbit.) He pecked Veronica on the cheek and told her how beautiful she looked.

To me, he said, "Nice vest." I was wearing a blazer. He patted my belly. Veronica didn't hear him and had started schmoozing someone else.

"Thanks, Gay," I said.

Gage squinted. "What did you call me?"

"Gay."

"My name is Gage."

"I know your name."

"Then why don't you use it?"

"Sure, Gay Gage."

He rolled his eyes. "I have no idea what V sees in you. She could do so much better. There are guys lining up for her at school. They think you're her gay best friend. Nobody watches *Dead On Air.* I heard you're barely even on the show. I've never thought you were funny."

"I never thought you were heterosexual either."

"Prick."

"Used asshole."

Veronica finished chatting up her many admirers and rejoined us. "What's up, boys?"

"Gage was just telling me how popular you are."

I didn't tell Veronica about the other things Gage had said. Because deep down, I knew them to be true. She could do better. Johnny knew she could do better. The tabloids knew she could do better. You could tell from the way other guys looked at her. Veronica would dance with her friends, while I'd watch in a corner, quietly sipping seltzer water, having long since given up talking to people since the music was so loud. I pretended to enjoy myself, but I just wanted to be home, making love to Veronica. She and I were doomed from the start. I was only the nice-nerd way station to the smorgasbord of pricks and assholes that awaited her.

We almost lasted a year. One day, Veronica said that she was dropping out of college and moving to Paris to record an album with a middle-aged music producer named Guy. Sherry Razzmatazz had introduced them. Veronica had been telling me she chose NYU to get away from her mother and to escape a showbiz future. Now, she was saying she hated studying and missed "music being a part of my DNA," like I was some celebrity reporter.

I'm not easily moved to tears, but when she told me we were over, I wept.

"Please stop, Hor," she said. "Don't make this hard. You know exactly what this is like. I just want to chase my dream without anything holding me back."

"I'm holding you back?"

"I told you to stop it with the neediness," she said. "You'll always be my favorite."

Desperate, I asked, "What about keeping your father clean?"

"Daddy is *so* supportive," she said. "He knows better than anyone that the industry is only getting more competitive. My window is closing. I don't want to be like you on the sidelines at *LOA*. I have to do something positive for my future."

It occurred to me that Veronica might have been trying me out all along. Seeing what it'd be like to be with a childhood buddy, the little boy she used to dress like a doll. Before adding me to her permanent cast of Brads, Darrens, and Stephanies.

I had been Veronica's featured intern.

SHOW BUSINESS IS LIKE
FINE DINING

My grandfather was in and out of the hospital for several months in 2007 with recurring bouts of pneumonia. After my second season on *LOA*, I flew back to Los Angeles to spend the summer with him. I visited just about everyday.

"You actually took time to see us," my father said at the hospital. "Are you out of work?" I didn't think he knew I was on a TV show. I had no clue what he thought I did all day.

"I'm here to help," I said.

"Now you want to help?" my mother said.

"Are you going to be like this all the time?" I asked. "I want us to have a regular relationship."

"Family means something different to you," she said. "You are like American. In America, family means you come back once a year or when someone gets sick. To Chinese people, family means more."

To them, family meant I owed them my life. If my happiness came at the cost of their definition of family, well, I had no right to want for myself in the first place.

Ever since I was your age, Maryann, I've had this anxiety, this feeling that I was destined to accomplish something lasting and great, but I didn't have much time to do so. For as long as I can remember, since even before my nighttime walks to the South Pasadena light rail station, I've had the sense that I would die young. I don't know where this feeling comes from. Maybe because growing old seems so unimaginably far away when you're a kid that you tell yourself ridiculous things like "I'm going to be the world's biggest star by the time I'm twenty-one" or "I'm going to go out in my prime instead of withering away in a nursing home." I wasn't about to hand my precious time over to my parents, no matter what I owed them. And I'm going to tell you this because I'm not going to get a chance to do so later: you don't owe me or your mother a goddamn thing. You only owe it to yourself to be your version of exceptional, whatever that may mean.

My grandfather hardly recognized me because I'd gained so much weight since Veronica left me. My mother made sure he didn't miss it though.

"Look, *Yeh-yeh*, look how fat Hor has become," she said. "He's become fat because he has no family in New York and all he eats is hamburgers and pizza because he would rather die than have a family."

Your grandmother wasn't exactly wrong.

"Exercise is very important," my grandfather said. "You don't want to end up like me."

"Hor just runs away," my mother went on. "Maybe I should have been on more bed rest when I was pregnant. Then he would be smarter and wouldn't run so far away from the family."

"Looks like he's too fat to run," my father said. "Fat like white man, but not so tall."

"Are you done?" I asked.

My mother paused. "You are so fat," she added.

After my parents left the room, my grandfather asked what my life was like in New York. He even asked if I was happy.

"I am," I said, even though my heart was as thoroughly broken as my Mandarin.

"Your father told me you had a girlfriend."

That surprised me. I didn't tell him about Veronica. Had he actually read the English-language tabloids? "We broke up."

"You should probably have a few more girlfriends before you settle down," my grandfather said. "What do you do for work?"

"I make people laugh. I'm on TV."

"How come we never watch you?"

"Ask Dad. I've been on a show for a year."

My grandfather seemed to sense my disappointment, my anger. "Your father's been very busy."

"Drinking condensed milk?"

"He's trying to find a buyer for the store."

This, I did not know.

"My hospital bills are a burden."

I had assumed that my mother was still working at Lee's Liquor, but that wasn't the case. She had started doing nails in El Monte and horoscope readings from one of Master Ming's many new storefronts in San Gabriel Valley. All this just multiplied my guilt. Here I was, living an expensive life in New York while my parents were struggling more than ever. I had to do something. I showed up at Lee's Liquors to offer my father money. The store looked much smaller than I remembered. The wood paneling and dim lighting made the place dated and dungeon-like. My father looked like he had aged much more than the five years since I had left home. His hair was uniformly gray now, hands liver-spotted, and the bags under his eyes were puffed and prominent. He'd started to resemble my grandfather by the time I was in grade school, but now he looked just like him; they could have been brothers. I asked if he wanted help with his finances.

"No," he said, without hesitation, as if he had expected the question.

"But the medical bills."

"Taken care of."

"How?"

"None of your business."

"I'm doing well," I said. "I can help. You know this."

"Take Grandma for a walk," he said. "That's how you can help."

I sighed and felt like I was exhaling pure exhaustion. "Fine. The offer stands. Call me if you need anything."

"You're too late, Hor."

My father asked me to help him unload the flatbed. He said the Mexican he had hired had just stopped showing up (probably because my dad hadn't paid him). While he handed me boxes of wine to load on a dolly, he told me that my grandfather's medical bills weren't the only problem—he owed a lot of money to some guy named Mr. Ngu for "the women" and was also on a serious losing streak with the cards. His words were faraway and half stuck in his throat, his gaze filmy.

"Very big loss this time," he said in English.

He had fallen behind on his mortgage payments. The bank was about to repossess Lee's Liquors.

He told me that back when I left home, he didn't ask Principal Payne to call the police on Johnny because he was afraid they would find out about his taste for the illegal gambling houses and brothels in the Little Saigon part of Westminster in Orange County.

I began sending big checks to my father's P.O. box so my mother wouldn't know he needed help. I started to feel an increased urgency about my career. I was still lowest on the totem pole at *LOA*, by far the youngest in the cast and categorically awful at pitching ideas.

Tuesdays would come around, and I'd sit there with my Moleskine notebook just like the rest of the writers. Everyone else seemed to have dozens of great sketch premises, and the loudest and most aggressive were heard. Comics were blurting out ideas with the speed of an auctioneer. The pitches would all blur together: Chewbacca comes out of the closet to Han Solo, a rogue Dunkin Donuts employee insists on selling the donut holes instead of the donut, a spoof of the movie *Pirates of the Carribean* where Johnny Depp's Captain Jack Sparrow suddenly loses his sea legs and spends most of the sketch vomiting. By the time I figured out that Chewbecca wasn't fucking Jack Sparrow into puking up donut holes, Slade would have decided yes or no to all of them and moved on.

My notebook usually had four or five ideas, and when I did pitch something, I did so with little confidence. Early on, I even raised my hand before speaking, which prompted weeks of ridicule. You know why else I was floundering? Everyone else was fucking good, and they worked harder and smarter than I did. The writers brought their best every week. Light, dark, nasty, horrific—there was no filter. I just wasn't keeping up. When I started, no one expected anything from a featured intern. Now they wanted hundreds of funny ideas on demand every week. The only reason I hadn't been fired already was because I wasn't white.

I missed standup. Since I had spent the summer in L.A., I had gone months without getting up on stage. I wasn't even writing jokes anymore because I was trying to create characters in the hopes I'd get in more sketches on *LOA*. I thought about quitting daily, but when I called Sarah and told her I wasn't happy, she said:

"You're kidding, right? You know your problem? When I ran away from home and I broke up with my first girlfriend, I knew I had to get my shit together. So I got my GED and enlisted in the Army. There, you learn the value of discipline and hard work. There, you learn the real definition of good and evil. Evil isn't 'oh my feelings are hurt because everyone around me is white.' Evil is fucking women and children getting killed and watching your buddies get blown in half by an IED."

"Mother of God, Sarah, you've overcome everything!"

"You tell jokes for a living, Sirius," she went on. "You're not curing cancer or colonizing Mars. So unless you have something better in the pipeline, like an action-comedy movie deal where you'd be the star, I suggest you go to work like any other adult would."

After one of the midseason episodes, one of the writers pulled me aside in the break room and wondered aloud whether I'd be better off sticking to standup.

"Not that I've seen your act lately," he added.

When I wasn't getting paddled at *LOA*, I was getting paddled in Hollywood. I auditioned for a part in a sci-fi action movie where there were hordes and hordes of short, fat, Asian-looking alien pirates threatening a planet of blonde and brown-haired dudes and dudesses. I auditioned for the leader of the alien group. They were named the Erfs. I got through one line ("The Erflings are far superior to the Earthlings.") before the casting director said, "Thanks!"

As a short, fat Asian, I didn't get the part for a guy in a short, fat Asian alien colony.

I would audition to play a doctor at least once a month, and I'd usually get rejected because I was too chubby ("not healthy-looking"). I went for a role as a Chinese restaurant owner in a sitcom and got rejected for not being fat enough. I auditioned to play a rapist on a crime show, only to be bounced for not looking "dangerous." I tried to get a part for a Buddhist monk, and they said my head was too big when I wore a bald cap. I lost a role as an accountant because my voice was too high. Almost always, a white actor was cast instead.

Frye Johns had parlayed his featured internship at *LOA* into permanent cast membership at *MADtv*, and he never hesitated to tell me how great it was, working with other comedians of color. He and I wrote a script and pitched a feature where I would play a delusional kid who thought he was deserving of an executive-level position at a major corporation. The film would be a mockumentary a la *Borat*. Every studio honcho took one look at me and said some variation of "I'm not sure you're ready to carry a movie."

One executive (who happened to be black) put it differently. "Show business is like fine dining," he said. "You start with a white plate. You put the protein on it, and the protein is the black people, but at a fine dining restaurant, you barely get any meat, and it's on a very, very big white plate. Occasionally, you have a garnish or a drizzle of sauce, and that's your Chinese, your Japanese, your Koreans, your Southeast Asians, your Indians, your Arabs or whatever. What's important is that the plate is white and the meat is black."

Ultimately, the film (*A Very Important Paul*) got made. They cast a nice Jewish kid named Turner Goldberg in his first role. The movie did well, and several years later, Goldberg starred in a couple of mega-blockbuster action movie trilogies involving CGI robots.

For our film, Frye and I got a writing credit, and I gave all the money to my dad. But I found out the hard way that Hollywood was not unlike Marsden High.

I was also failing at *LOA* because I was still heartbroken. Without Veronica around, I was boozing again, doing recreational cocaine so I could stay up all night and write screenplays, film treatments, and TV pilots that went nowhere. I was feeling so low, I remember calling Johnny just to hear a sympathetic voice. He was the closest I had to a caring family member. I was certain he was doing lots of drugs, too. I hadn't talked to him in at least three months. I complained about my career, how none of it was working out, and, instead of offering sympathy, Johnny laid into me.

"You know why things aren't working out for you?" he said. "Because you've lost your identity. What the fuck were you doing out there in Los Angeles? We left L.A. for a reason. I've seen you on *LOA*. You're not an actor. You're shit at sketch. You've got no improv background. You actually have to pay attention to other performers to make a sketch work. You're not a team player. You're a standup. When I tried improv, I hated that servicing shit. Standup is pure. Standup is a solo game, like golf or tennis. Pure standup is in New York City."

"Then what are you doing on the road so much?"

"They think I'm too old!" he raged. "I'm better than nine-ty-nine percent of those amateurs they put up at the Cellar. I'm better than you. Hell, I taught you."

"Maybe you are too old," I said. "I mean, what have you done lately, right?"

"Fuck you."

"It's a young man's game."

"Prick."

"It's good to be a prick, remember?"

"You should be thanking me." He was slurring his words. "You would never be on *LOA* if I didn't take you in, if I didn't lead you to the well."

"I worked for you," I said. "Your jokes didn't write themselves. We all know you couldn't remember them."

Johnny chuckled. "When my head is clear," he said, "I can remember."

"How's the Crazy Joker's in Gassburg, West Virginia?" I said. "Do they still serve five-dollar chicken fingers?"

Johnny hung up on me.

The following summer, my grandpa was in the hospital again, this time for mysterious fevers. Back to L.A., I went. I visited him one evening and he looked especially out of it. After I changed the television channel to a Chinese one, he seemed to liven up.

"Why don't you have a girlfriend yet?" he asked. He had forgotten that we had talked about Veronica.

"She left me."

"She probably wasn't good enough for you anyway."

I laughed hard even though he wasn't trying to be funny. I wanted to tell him that he was wrong, but I lacked the vocabulary.

"Your grandmother never loved me," he said. "In the beginning, I loved her. She was very beautiful. Above my class. Very outspoken. But then I learned that it is people with money and power who can afford to be outspoken. Her family thought I was beneath her because I wrote for newspapers. Many years later, she realized her family was right. There is no such thing as love from just one person. Love must be between two people. Otherwise, it is not love."

Then maybe you and I haven't loved, I wished I could say.

"You are here more than she is," my grandfather said.

I held his hand. It was tender with veins.

"Keep a high standard," he said, his head rising from the pillow. "Remember that. If you think small, your life will be small. Don't allow others to make you small. Even those who love you. *Especially* those who love you. Don't be like me. Never just be good enough. Understand?"

I nodded and insisted that he rest.

He released my hand and turned to the television, and together, in silence, we watched some dynastic Chinese costume drama featuring flying long-haired warrior men. He didn't so much as look at me for the rest of the evening.

I'll always remember my grandfather's advice. And it seems I'll always ignore it. After he went to sleep, seemingly comfortable, I drove to West Hollywood and was cocaine-cruising when my mom called from the hospital. My grandfather was gone.

Never just be good enough.

My grandfather was the only member of the family I admired. He didn't gamble away the family money, didn't visit brothels, didn't hit his wife or kid, and didn't try to keep my life small. When I think about him now, I wonder if we, the Lees, disappointed him. During all those nights at our fold-up dining table, when I was thinking that my grandfather's mind was elsewhere, I suspect he was quietly judging us.

At my grandfather's service, while the monks led chants, my dad, mom, and grandma were greeting people at the door, shaking hands, even chit-chatting with relatives they hadn't seen in a long time. They were sad, of course, but didn't cry. One might have mistaken them for hosts of a somber brunch.

Me? I'm ashamed to admit I didn't cry either. I paid my last respects, bending at the waist three times and putting the lit incense sticks into the sand-filled bowl like the rest of the two dozen or so Chinese folks. I stole a quick glance at my grandfather's black-and-white portrait from his younger days. He looked thirty-five in the photo, flat-lipped, but his eyes emanated a kindness that my other family members didn't have.

As I passed my grandfather's open oak casket, I looked down upon his sleeping face, framed by the dark round hat and the high red collar of his funeral robe. He looked like he was made of clay. I thought about my doughy body and how our physical selves all one day end up as sand and soil.

Love is a two-person thing; unrequited love doesn't exist. Don't allow the ones you love to keep your life small. My grandfather didn't say so directly, but he was telling me that I was right to leave home (at least, that's what I'd like to think), and my alienation was the cost of my escape, my freedom. His passing only made me more determined to make my mark in comedy and become a grown-up that my grandpa would have been proud of.

My parents treated me like a total stranger at the funeral. They didn't introduce me to any relatives, even while they were introducing distant relatives to each other. I wasn't a successful child who'd made something of himself. I wasn't their CEO, so I was irrelevant. Twice, I was asked by relatives whether I attended Pasadena City College.

Then one of my distant cousins came up to me and said he watched me on *LOA*.

"Oh cool!" I said, glad to finally get some acknowledgement for my success. I thanked him for watching and told him I very much appreciated it.

"So . . . um . . . why don't you play anything other than an idiot Asian extra?" he asked. "That commercial where you play a fat FOB who can't understand what a laxative does was just flat-out offensive."

"Gee, thanks for the fucking feedback on a day like this," I said.

He laughed and shrugged. "Hey, I just think Hollywood can do better, that's all."

"Good talking to you, Angry Asian Man," I said, walking away.

After the service, as I helped transport the shrine and all the offerings to the apartment, my mom said she wanted me to stay home for the post-burial service on the third and the seventh days.

"I'll think about it," I said, my eyes meeting the eyes of my grandfather in the enshrined photo.

"I'm not asking," she said. "I'm telling you. You have to be there."

"For what? So you can tell your friends how ashamed of me you are and what a bad son I am?"

My mom shook her head at me. "Selfish. Selfish. Selfish. You want to be the big star of your grandfather's funeral, eh? Would that make you feel good?"

"I just don't want to be here as your punching bag," I said. "This should be about his life, not mine, not ours."

My mother laughed. "Sure, sure, you're a big sufferer," she said, walking around me toward the bedroom. "Life is so hard for you here. So much sacrifice. It's like you have to eat from the trash. I don't know how you can stand to be around us."

My father and grandmother entered, she holding his forearm.

She shuffled past me into her room. "You stand like a white," she said to me with disgust, before shutting the door.

My father sat on the couch and looked up at me. Neither of us knew what to say to each other.

"Do you need anything?" I asked.

Without hesitation, he said, "I need you to send another check this month. I spent it all on the funeral."

Trust me when I say that, knowing the size of the checks I sent and the quality of the funeral home, there was zero chance that the funeral cost that much.

The next day, I boarded the first available flight to New York. I was disgusted with myself for practically celebrating, but I simply couldn't take being near The Lee Council for another minute.

For *LOA*, I came up with Naked-in-the-Club Man: a weirdo who tags along with hot chicks to get into the coolest clubs, and then when he gets in, starts dancing and taking off his clothes. Veronica and I had actually seen a guy like that once. There was a group of young women, all made up and squeezed into sequined dresses, on a warm fall night in the Meatpacking District. This dude wearing a suit walked up and asked the ladies whether they'd vouch for him. He was late to meet his friends inside, he said. The women shrugged and let him into the line.

Veronica, her friends, and I were standing behind them, and we could tell this guy did not have friends inside. The suit he wore was tatty and way too big on him; the sleeves were so long that you couldn't see his hands. From his red, darting eyes, it was clear he was on a Rite-Aid's worth of drugs. Eventually we ended up in the club and the first thing this dude did was start stripping. He didn't even get a drink. Let me tell you, he smelled like a country of taints. People backed away from him in all directions as he and his perspiring balls bounced around the dance floor. The thing was: nobody did anything about it. No one came to remove him. A few people even laughed and bought him drinks.

So that's how Naked-in-the-Club Man started. For the Standards and Practices folks, we changed it to Shirtless-in-the-Club Guy. So that was my first big character: Sirius the Shirtless-in-the-Club Guy. The first time I did it, the reaction was insane. Massive laughs. Even Slade, who never laughed at anything, couldn't stop guffawing about it at the after-party. ("I haven't seen a crowd that excited since the Miracle On Ice!")

Once Shirtless-in-the-Club Guy happened, the writers started writing for me for the first time. We came up with a lot of characters I was really proud of.

There was Toomer, the office worker who was living with a tumor on his face, and none of his co-workers wanted to call him by name because it would bring undue attention to said tumor.

There was Hop Chung, a version of my dad who owned a store and pretended to know everything about everything, but was wrong without exception.

There was Vern, Hollywood's Leading Premature Ejaculator, the guy the studios called when they needed someone to play a man with erectile dysfunction.

But they didn't hit like Shirtless-in-the-Club Guy, and Slade and the writers just kept ordering more Shirtless. They would shut down any other ideas I had. I'd find my other sketches slotted at five to one or cut for time at dress. I became a one-sketch wonder.

I started online dating, and there was this one person I saw for a little while. Her name was Splendid. She was a dead ringer for Veronica back at Marsden. Curly, frizzy, strawberry blonde hair. Pretty face and blue eyes. She was an aspiring actor who waitressed at a Jean Georges restaurant. We hung out on Monday mornings after *LOA* aired. Sometimes I took her to a club, or sometimes we just stayed in at my place and watched a rented movie.

When I'd tell her about my latest indignity at *LOA* or at the hands of my parents or Johnny, she'd just stroke the back of my head. I'd close my eyes and take a deep breath and imagine what it was like to have a family who sincerely cared about what I wanted. I imagined having someone who loved me and thought I was beautiful.

"My poor Sirius," she'd whisper in my ear. "My poor, poor Sirius. You're a good guy with a good heart."

I would weep. Was I good-hearted? I'm not religious, so I suppose you'll be my ultimate judge. I'd lie there in her lap, until I fell asleep. That was the best sleep. I didn't need pills or anything.

Splendid made me feel worth something.

For a few weeks, at least.

One morning, over breakfast in a diner, after I railed about Stuart Stevens stealing one of my ideas, Splendid just sighed and held up her hand. "Sirius, you've covered this already," she said. "Can we talk about something else?"

"Okay," I said. "What do you want to talk about?"

"How about me, for once?"

Had I been so self-absorbed? "Fine," I said. "Let's do it!"

Splendid waited for me to ask her something about herself. I wasn't sure where to start. We'd been dating for a month and

I didn't even know (or couldn't remember) where she was from originally, whether her parents were still alive, whether she had any siblings, et cetera, et cetera.

"Um, so . . ." I cleared my throat, buying time. "How have auditions been going?"

Splendid rolled her eyes and clucked her tongue. "Forget it."

Shortly after, she lost my phone number.

By the beginning of my fourth season on *LOA*, I would feel nauseous taking the R train up to Studio 58. (Okay, the nausea may have been caused by all the drugs I took.) Even though the show was doing reasonably well in the ratings, I just didn't want to be there anymore. I was never going to be treated like one of the stars. I was never going to be a Gemellino or Dreyer or Maynard. I was always going to be one of the colored boy interns who happened to be an Asian shirtless dude on TV every couple of weeks. I stopped attending read-throughs sober. I would smoke joints (sometimes even do coke) in front of everyone in the room.

Slade hated confrontation, so I channeled Archimedes Jones on his ass. Whenever he was in the room, I'd point out that I was one of the few colored cast members. No matter what sketch we were rehearsing I'd be a Chinese guy doing a Farrakhan impression. I was my dad's Yellow Panther. Let's just say that one week, during dress on Sunday, Arend the gay horse carriage tour operator couldn't get a word in edgewise while the cop I played did a monologue about how Slade liked to pretend that *LOA* was a sports team where everyone earned their starting spot because of talent, but his alleged meritocracy never had more than one or two spots for brown people, which pretty much implied that brown folks weren't as funny as whites.

Slade never looked angry or embarrassed. He just left, like he had better things to listen to. I think he knew how fucked-up *LOA* really was, like any pillar of unquestioned American greatness.

Archimedes was writing on *American Dad* out in L.A., and I called and told him about all the shit I was talking to Slade's face. He laughed so hard he could barely speak.

"I knew one day you'd become my nigga," he managed.

When they used me for Shirtless-in-the-Club Guy midseason, I basically fired myself by getting naked on live TV, ranting about a variety of topics including my theory that CBS was in on a global conspiracy to make sure the black guy running for president didn't win. Famous incident. No need for me to describe it. Look it up on YouTube.

I can't even remember all the stuff I was on. That whole week, I felt on the verge of getting fired. The writers thought it'd be funny for Shirtless-in-the-Club Guy to come down a chimney with a bottle of Ciroc and start dancing and stripping in front of a shocked family. I wasn't even shirtless in a club anymore. I was just shirtless, anywhere. While I ranted and raved and used every profanity I knew, I didn't get tackled by security or anything. I didn't get a "What the fuck are you doing?" Annie Gemellino, who was wearing an absurdly large and tousled red wig because she had, in the previous sketch, played Kathie Lee Gifford time-traveling to the year 2050 to resurrect a cryogenically frozen Regis, took me softly by the elbow and led me off stage. The studio audience was silent. The cast wouldn't look at me. They felt sorry for me.

I had chosen to leave home at fifteen to pursue this life and I was fucking overwhelmed. Would I have peace and sobriety if I had stayed in San Gabriel Valley, finished high school, went to a good college as my parents had planned? What if I lived a more normal life? Would the Lees love me then?

Johnny was right. I had lost my identity, like he had lost his when he became an inflatable, mute celebrity dad on a reality show.

I had, in my own way, become him.

NO GOOD VERY BAD ASIAN

Your biggest successes can come from your darkest times. That's the only way I can explain *No Good Very Bad Asian*. When the album first came out, it didn't sell. I couldn't even get an audience to buy more than two or three CDs after a show. One night, at Caroline's, I was especially wasted. I blanked on my first joke. I hadn't done that in years. So I started doing crowd work.

This smart-ass Korean dude in the front row asked, "When does the show start?"

Something about the look of this guy bugged me. He was tall, muscular, and good-looking, and he was with this China-doll girlfriend. Both were well-dressed prepsters, probably just out of business or medical school or some such boring life choice. The guy was the son my parents wished they had. No acne on that motherfucker.

"You double-parked outside in your rice racer?" I said. "Is that why you're in such a fucking hurry, you sellout math-major raisin dick?"

The crowd gasped. I was a little shocked myself, stir-frying assorted stereotypes like that. A few people laughed, thinking insult comedy was part of my act. The girl, for some reason, laughed hardest and loudest.

To the crowd, I said, "That's the best part about Asians. They're okay with *anything*. You can fucking tell this girl 'I'm going to send you back on the boat you came in on,' and she'll giggle and bat her eyes." The crowd loosed a shocked groan. Her boyfriend charged the stage and threw me to the ground before the bouncer escorted the couple out. They blistered me with obscenities as they left.

I haven't been invited back to Caroline's since.

Someone filmed the fight, posted it on the internet, it spread like HPV, and the album started selling. Then HBO called Sarah and asked me to do a special.

"Are you sure they want me?" I said.

"They said they wanted the 'bad Asian guy,'" Sarah said. "Is there another one I don't know about?"

The next thing I knew she was planning a massive North American tour for me. People came to see Sirius the Fallen TV Star insult the audience. If I just did material, I'd do okay. But if, at some point during the show, I ripped into someone, I would destroy.

And I ain't gonna lie. I usually picked on my fellow yellows.

Did I feel guilty? Absolutely. I had never gone after audience members personally before. And the stereotypes I used were so lazy. Small penises, dog eating, prostitutes, piano and violin lessons, bad driving, good at math. The easier the stereotype, the bigger the laugh. I hated how well they worked.

The crazy thing was: I was being *honest*. When I saw some middle-aged Asian lady at one of my shows, I saw my mom. When I saw some older Asian dude, I saw my dad. When I saw somebody my age, I saw the SAT-acing douchebag I could have been. That rage was truly inside me, waiting to be released on these poor Asians in my audiences. It was my zombie-eye disease again, M. My head was poisoned with self-loathing and the poison spread and made me hate those who looked like me.

I remembered that computer programmer fan of mine back when I was touring with Johnny. You're inspiring, he'd said.

What would he think of me now?

When I first started doing comedy in New York, I seemed to be the only Asian male comic in the clubs. But as the years went on, I noticed more and more of them. And for some reason, they all bothered me. I didn't think any of them were funny. Deep down, I wanted to be the only one. I wanted to keep the Asian dude standup spot in the American mind all to myself.

Some of those comics would even try to befriend me after shows. They'd buy me drinks and get me to talk shit about my time on *LOA*. If there was an Asian guy hanging out after a show at Village Z, I ducked out as soon as possible. One night, this Chinese dude named Leland surprised me. He popped out of the bathroom and practically latched onto the lapels of my jacket. *Where are you headed? Can I buy you a drink? You're my idol.* I told him I had to go. But he followed me like paparazzi. Finally, I relented and let him buy me a whiskey at a bar around the corner from my apartment.

"Did you see my set?" he asked.

I didn't and told him so.

"That's too bad because I thought I killed, but then Van Pido told me I only did okay," he said. "I've been doing this for seven years. What else do I have to do?"

"Tell me one of your jokes," I said.

"I'm on planes a lot," he said. "Last flight, I got an erection. What was I so turned on by? The guy next to me smelled like he'd been rolling around in a mass grave for a week. I decided to go to the back of the plane and walk around to get the blood flowing. But the aisles are so narrow now. I'm strafing left and strafing right, and I slap this kid in the face with my cock."

"That's the joke?"

"It killed!" he said. "That's my best joke."

"A joke about kid fucking is always going to be a tough sell," I said.

He whipped out his notebook and jotted down that hard-won piece of comedy wisdom.

I flagged down the bartender. "I think it's time for you to buy me that drink," I said to Leland.

He got me the double whiskey I asked for. Then he launched into another bit.

"I'm single now and I'm thinking about online dating," I said. "But studies say Asian males get the least interest. That's why my profile says I work for Match.com Customer Service."

I rolled my eyes. He wasn't terrible. If he were white, I would've told him to keep working. You can be a mediocre white guy comic and get your half-hour special to air at one in the morning on Comedy Central so you can cross that off your life list, quit comedy, and become an accountant for the rest of your life. But if you're a mediocre Asian guy comic, you'll be performing in cafés and colleges in front of Asian Studies students for free egg rolls until you become allergic to fried dough.

I looked him up and down. He was in his mid-thirties already. He was bespectacled and wore a bow tie and a short sleeve button-down like he was a Chinese Little Rascal. He had no chance. I wanted to put him out of his misery. So I downed my drink and said:

"No one cares about you. You don't have what I have. There's no more room on the boat. Sorry. That's just the way it is. Go be a doctor like your parents wanted. The only reason you get laughs at all is because no one expects a thing out of you other than 'yes, sir,' and 'thank you, ma'am' when you open your mouth. You should quit now because if it hasn't happened already, it won't."

His face crumpled like I'd just poured water on paper. His disappointment tickled me. Sounds terrible, but it's true. I walked out of that bar, onto the next one, savoring the look on Leland's face.

A month before the *No Good Very Bad Asian* tour, during one of the worst blizzards in New York history, Johnny buzzed my apartment at 4:00 a.m., wearing a trench over a wife beater and shorts. His lips were dried and cracked and his eyes were dark crystals. He was cradling a half-empty bottle of Wild Turkey. Dan Van Pido had told me recently that Johnny's management had dumped him and he had been begging for headliner spots at Village Z.

"I miss my daughter," Johnny said.

"She's in Paris."

"I fucking know that," he said, his teeth chattering. He stepped into my kitchen and poured me a glass of Wild Turkey. A crack on his lower lip was bleeding.

"No, thanks, man."

"Fuck you, you've still got a cocaine mustache!"

I wiped my nose. "It's late, Johnny."

"Did you know it was my birthday yesterday?"

I had no idea.

"Are you gonna have a drink with me or what?" he asked.

I prayed I wouldn't get HIV or herpes (if I didn't have it already). "Happy Birthday," I said, glass kissing bottle. That shit had my eyes watering.

"You're my only family left, Hor."

I don't remember what I said. I didn't even know how to respond.

"You know how many people called to wish me a happy birthday?"

"None?"

"Fuck off!" he said. He held up three fingers. "My dealer and my dentist's assistant. She was trying to schedule me for a cleaning."

"And the third?"

Johnny looked at his hand and lowered a finger.

"I didn't know dentists cleaned fake teeth," I said.

"I can't figure out if you're like a son to me or a second asshole."

"I don't remember birthdays," I said. "Besides, you're fucking old. Do you even want to be celebrating at your age?"

"Cocksucker," Johnny muttered. "You were never my friend. You just wanted to fuck my daughter."

"Don't be ridiculous. I wasn't good enough for her, remember?"

He drank long and hard from his bottle, his eyes shut.

"How did I fuck it all up?" he said, reeling from one end of the kitchen to the other like a boxer on the ropes. "I used to have everything I could want."

I felt no pity. I told him he was welcome to stay on my couch as long as he didn't mind me playing PlayStation.

"Who's opening for you?"

That was when I realized the true reason he was visiting. He wanted me to take him on tour.

"Pidofile told me," he said. "You're even doing MSG?"

I shrugged. "Yeah." Yeah, I'm that fucking big, I wanted to say.

"We could do it like old times, don't you think?"

The bitter part of me wanted to say no. But he had given me my start. He had helped me escape my family. He was family, almost.

"I'll see what I can do," I said.

We were on the road for a solid year. I hadn't done venues of that scale before. Everything from 3,000-seat theaters to arenas in big cities. I hadn't felt truly excited about my career since the early days at *LOA*. I did material from the album, but I also made fun of Asian people in the crowd, and we had a big screen overhead where they showed the sketches I'd been in on *LOA* and I *Mystery-Science-Theatered* the footage, joking about the absurdity of being on TV as a token colored guy. I must have used "Yeah, I was high for that" twenty to thirty times as a punch line. I couldn't believe that thousands of people were paying seventy-five dollars a pop to see my act. I was suddenly at the point in my career where I didn't even have to be that good to kill. When someone pays that much money to see you perform, they already think you're funny so whatever you say just confirms their biases. Lots of times I'd be halfway through a joke and the crowd would start laughing. It was surreal. I wasn't sure how it was all happening, but it was.

A few dates in, I noticed that Johnny wasn't having fun. While everyone else in the crew smoked weed and drank with me backstage, he moped around the post-show buffet like a toothless ghost.

After we sold out Madison Square Garden, I finally asked him what was wrong.

"I've never headlined MSG," he said.

"Now you're here."

"Yeah, but . . ." He sighed. "It's not the same."

"You should be happy," I said, putting hands on his shoulders. "*We're* here. *We're* doing this. I wouldn't have been able to get here without you."

Johnny's chuckle sounded like a grunt. "You're fucking right about that."

I shoved him in the chest. "Why do you have to be such a goddamn prick?"

"Comedy today, man," Johnny said, shaking his head. "You don't have to be good. You just have to be a color. You have to be oppressed. Talk shit about how white people are this and white people are that. Back in my day, I had to be better than Hicks. I had to kill more than Kinison. Now, guys like you just have to be yourself."

"I swear to God, I'm just trying to get good with you."

He shrugged. "I'm just being honest."

Johnny never told me he was proud of me. He never told me how much my act had grown. The more I accomplished, the more he pretended that my accomplishments didn't exist.

He was just like my parents.

Then there was the dreaded L.A. stop. I had a show at Staples Center, the biggest crowd I'd ever had. I stopped by Alhambra and gave my dad three tickets with backstage passes. I told him that it would mean a lot to me for the whole family to see me perform.

"You are getting fatter," my dad said.

I had indeed been putting on pounds at an alarming clip. The more successful I got, the more I performed, the more I traveled, the worse I ate. And I'd never exercised in my life.

"I still don't understand your job," he said.

"I've told you before," I said. "I'm a standup comedian. This is what I've always wanted to do. This is why I left home."

"People pay money to see you?"

"Surely they have the same thing in China."

He made a noise between a sigh and a grunt. I could tell he didn't want to come.

At Staples Center, I had one of the best performances of my life. I made fun of an entire Chinese tour group for an hour. ("How was the flight?" I asked. "Your kids didn't take a shit in the aisle, did they? You know the life jackets aren't complimentary winter wear, right?") Laughter buzzed in my ears for days afterward.

My family wasn't there.

You know who was?

Veronica.

It had been three years since she'd left me. She again looked like a new person. She had one of those jet-black pixie haircuts that looked like it cost a few hundred bucks. She wore a sleeveless blue cocktail dress that must have cost thousands with a diamond choker that likely cost thousands more. Her latest socialite look wasn't a complete surprise. I'd been following her transformation on the gossip sites.

She ran into Johnny's arms, squealing "Daddy!" He smiled for the first time in weeks. To me, Veronica said, as if shocked, "You've really done something, Hor."

Hor, her fourteen-year-old mascot.

Veronica launched into a long explanation about why she was in town. Meetings with her management. New reality show in the works. Recording sessions with producers. Whatever doubts she may have had about a showbiz life back when we were together had vanished.

"Nils is taking me to Ibiza," she said.

Who the fuck was Nils?

"Does he treat you well?" Johnny asked.

He never asked if I treated Veronica well. He *assumed* I did. While Johnny and Veronica talked, I searched for booze. I opened every cabinet and closet door and even looked in the rooms down the hall—not a drop. Johnny had kept the backstage dry. Why? Because he knew Veronica was coming. He must have been lying to her about being sober. I asked one of our assistants for a bottle of champagne. He stared up at me blankly. He was a dwarf.

"We've got that morning radio thing tomorrow," Johnny said.

That night, I fled the hotel in search of a high. I took the car service to a bodega named Bert's Everything Store. There was a Mexican guy behind the counter guarding tin bins full of rice, beans, menudo, and the like. I got a little bit of everything even though it was 3:00 a.m. and the food had been sitting out all day.

There I was, just five hours from the high point of my career, squatting on the curb of a two-lane road that dead-ended at a cement factory, making my driver wait while I inhaled a fifth of Jameson's with cold menudo, refried beans, and other fart-astic

Mexican classics—familyless and alone. Was this happiness? Was this "making it?"

Fucking Nils. Those terrible Veronica feelings returned with a vengeance. Fucking Nils. About halfway through the whiskey bottle, I dialed Veronica's U.S. number several times until she picked up.

"You're fucking Nils?!"

"Go to sleep, Hor," she said. "Call me when you're sober."

"Was I not Swedish enough for you?"

"Always making it a race thing," she said. "I have feelings for someone else. We're over. We've been over for a long time."

"It wasn't real," I said. "It was never real."

She hung up. I didn't make the morning show, ignoring Johnny's numerous calls. Hours later, I finally answered. My whiskey bottle was empty.

"Where the fuck are you?" Johnny asked.

I was in the middle of a dry concrete riverbed, staggering, forcing the black car to follow me. The traffic on the highways sounded like air conditioning. I had no idea where I was.

"I'm in fucking Sweden."

"Jesus, Hor," Johnny said. "You need to let her go."

"Why? Because I'm not good enough for her?"

"Stop being such a child."

"I am a child!" I screamed so loud that Sam Kinison would have been proud. "You fucking took me from my home when I was a child!"

Johnny let loose a full-bellied laugh. "Are you listening to yourself?"

"I know what you thought all along. You wanted her to be with some rich, white kid! You think I don't know?"

"This shit is all in your head," he said. "Trust me. I know when it's the shit in your head talking."

"Clean and white!" I shouted. "Nice and Aryan!"

"Tell me where you are."

"Where am I?" I asked the driver.

"Just hand him the phone, Hor," Johnny said.

"You know I wanted you to take me in, right?" I said. "You know I wanted you to be my dad."

Johnny was silent.

"But you weren't," I went on. "You couldn't imagine it. I wasn't your blood. I wasn't your skin. I was just your assistant. Like one of your dogs. Throw me a bone, kind sir."

"Hor," Johnny said, his voice gravelly.

"What?"

I waited. And waited. But he said nothing.

"I'm done with you, man," I said. "I don't want to see you or listen to your hacky, old white man material again. Get the fuck off my tour."

I hung up and threw my phone as far as I could.

We still had another show in L.A., and two nights each in Portland, Seattle, and San Francisco, but I went without an opener. I didn't speak to Johnny again for years.

When I returned to New York, development deals and movie offers were piling up. Lots of raunchy, brain-dead, road-trip comedies where I'd be the fourth or fifth star after three white guys and a black dude. Or supporting roles in sitcoms as the token, smart-aleck computer programmer or comic book shop owner.

"It's good money," Sarah said. "It's not Shakespeare, but I didn't know you wanted Shakespeare."

She was right, of course. I never asked Sarah to be the guardian of my artistic integrity. And years earlier, I did agree that I would not violate Coleman Client Rule One: when she called, I was supposed to say "Yes."

"When Tom Cruise was still with me, right after *Mission Impossible*, he really wanted to do *Othello*," she went on. "I

asked him why. He said he always identified with the character and he wanted to do Shakespeare. Can you imagine Tom
Cruise in fucking blackface? I called up David Miscavige to set
him straight."

"You have a direct line to the Scientologists?"

"It's Hollywood, Sirius."

"This story doesn't sound real at all."

"Life is a greenfield," she replied.

I agreed to a few ideas that seemed the easiest to do for the
biggest payout. After all, I had all of the Lee family's bad habits
to pay for. My dad was calling me every few weeks now, asking
for more and more money, and I couldn't exactly say what I
was thinking, which was that I needed to preserve cash for my
coke habit! He said that the next time I was in Los Angeles,
he wanted me to look at some commercial property between
Orange County and San Diego.

"Mr. Ngu say it's good opportunity," he said in English.

"Why is what he says so important?" I asked. "Is he that
guy in the infomercials with the yachts and women in bikinis?"

"I don't understand what you're saying," my dad said. "You
come with me. You see. You decide."

"Why don't you use the money I'm sending you to buy
Mom and Grandma a house?"

"*Hai!*" my father said, exasperated. "We don't need house.
We have so much room now that you're gone."

I was cast in *Bangkok Family Vacation*, a National Lampoon
comedy. You can skip it, even when you're old enough to see
R-rated movies. It's a giant turd. I played the annoying older
brother of the Mandopop star, Kathy Wu Ziyi. I refused to do a
Thai accent because I know nothing about Thai people or Thai
culture. After a long back-and-forth between me and Sarah,
Sarah and the director, Sarah, the director, and the producer,

and finally Sarah, the director, the producer, and a fucking roomful of studio execs, they finally relented, and the script was rewritten so that I didn't have an accent because my character had studied in America. Winning that fight was the proudest part about my participation in the film.

The male lead was Hale Joseph, from the action-comedy cable series, *Con Factory*. His character marries into this Thai family, and he and his wife go back to the motherland to visit the wacky exotic relatives, who are all either in the sex or heroin trade. Hale White Leadingman has the hots for Kathy and considers cheating on his wife, played by Michelle Tanaka. Ultimately, White Leadingman decides that his marriage is too important to him (of course), and after a few hack misunderstandings (a "deluxe" massage on a resort is mistaken for one with happy endings, and a bag of heroin is dropped into White Leadingman's backpack without his knowledge), everyone ends up one big joyous family (cue the schmaltzy piano). My character's most prominent trait was his ability to compare any situation to gay sex. No Thai people were hurt during the filming because there were none in the cast and crew.

You get the idea. It won six Razzies and was a huge hit. As were the sequels.

The shooting schedule was tighter than a new prisoner's asshole. We had twenty days of filming in Vancouver, and then we were scheduled to fly to Oahu for five more. On top of it all, I had been booked on a bunch of shows in the Pacific Northwest. I'd film my scenes in the morning, and then fly back to Seattle, Portland, or Eugene to do standup.

Never one to get a whole lot of sleep to begin with, Ambien stopped working, so I upgraded to Indiplon, which knocked me out sunrise to sunset. I worked eighteen hours a day from Tuesday through Friday, and then I'd be off Saturday through Monday. During those three days, I slept. No food, no water, just sleep. If this sounds like an ad for Indiplon, it pretty much is!

By the end of the Vancouver weeks, I was so doped up, I thought my dick was a tail. I got on stage at Oregon State and started telling a Dave Attell joke, the one about how terrorists don't blow up bus stations because "damn, someone's already done this bitch!" I even fucked up the punch line ("damn, we've already done this pitch"). Some Indian kid, who had neck tattoos and seashell bracelets, called me out for stealing Attell's joke. I said something to the effect of "shut up and sit down, you smelly motherfucker," and I got booed off stage. The club didn't pay me, and I ended up going back to the Travelodge, drinking a bottle of whiskey, and projectile-puking all over the gingham canvas tarp the Travelodge called a bedspread. I tried to get the fuck out of Corvallis so I wouldn't have to deal with the mess I'd left. I went to the airport to get the last flight to Vancouver, but I'd missed it by about six hours. I bummed around the terminal, found a bar, drank more whiskey, and returned to the gate before finally passing out.

I woke to a policeman jabbing me with the tip of his boot. He informed me that I had shit myself.

Let me repeat. I shat myself. Feces all over my pants, up my back, smeared across my belly, flecked on my double chin. I even found some in my shoe. God's vomit all over again, a million times worse. I was detained. After I got deloused, I started jonesing for my pharmas, and I had no luck convincing the police to let me have some. I began kicking the walls, rattling the bars of my holding cell, and shouting enlightened things like: "I'm a fucking movie star, you know that? Do you know who you're fucking with?" Soon, I passed out again in the fetal position and woke to the cop telling me my phone had been ringing and he had answered. Sarah had called.

"I didn't know you were in the movies," the cop said.

"That's what I've been saying for hours!"

He scratched his mustache. "You don't exactly exude credibility."

"Let me talk to her."

"That's the funny thing," the cop said. "She didn't want to talk to you."

He left and came back moments later, notebook in hand. "She said the following: 'I hate it when clients call.'"

"But she's the one who called."

"Oh, and she also said, 'Think hard about the money you're costing us. Semper Fi, Sarah.'"

"That's the Marines! She told me she was in the Army."

Luckily, the airport police got bored of me and I was released. I flew back to Vancouver, wearing oversized clothes from the tourist shop. I had missed my scenes and the director was understandably pissed. During dinner, I apologized to the cast for screwing up the shoot that day. People told me later that I was paler than Hale Joseph and my eyes were so bloodshot, they looked like rubies.

Speaking of Hale, he dropped by my trailer to inform me that, in his not-so-humble opinion, I was stealing our scenes together.

"I would've said something earlier, but I thought we might get equal billing, so I decided to be more politic about the whole thing," he said, legs figure-four, with his arm thrown over the back of the lounger. "But now it's clear you're not as committed to making this film great as I am due to your . . . scheduling issues. So for the good of the film and for the good of all of us working hard on it, I'd like to ask you to, um, turn the volume down. We're not doing slapstick here. I see this film as a smart, witty comedy. Something Barry Levinson might have made in the eighties."

"Barry Levinson would have me saying lines like 'Ah, Bangkok, the city of sore asses'?" I asked.

He looked hurt. "I didn't come in here using that type of language. I don't see why you need to get antagonistic."

I demonstrated several different volume and enthusiasm levels of that line and asked which one he preferred. Disgusted, he left my trailer and didn't speak to me off-camera for the rest of the filming.

The night before the team left for Oahu, I got medical clearance to fly, but the doctor sat me down in my trailer and told me that the studio should have ordered my physical sooner per the contract, because they'd have fired me due to my liver health, which was that of someone three times my age. I learned that I was a chronic carrier of hepatitis B. He said it appeared that I'd never been vaccinated for it and I should have been because more Asians have the disease than non-Asians. He put me on antivirals and recommended the Country Boy Breakfast of drug abuse treatment programs: detox, rehab, and a sober house.

I told him my schedule wouldn't allow it.

"You need to make your health a priority," the doctor said. "You need to stop drinking immediately. Make no mistake, your life is at stake."

"Hey, that rhymes."

The doctor frowned.

"I'm planning a vacation," I lied. "I'll check-in then. I swear on Joe Smith's translation of the Bible."

"I'm not Mormon," the doctor said. I informed him he bore a strong resemblance to Donny Osmond.

It had been ten years since I'd left home. I'd never vacationed. When I heard of fellow *LOA* cast members flitting off to exotic locales between seasons, it sounded like something grown-ups did.

Instead, I went from *Bangkok Family Vacation* to the set of *The Weighting Game: Celebrity Edition*. Lyon Maelstrom, the very expensive physical trainer to the stars, was my coach. In our first session at his Midtown gym, I weighed in at 280. If you ever want to try four-star humiliation, hire a high-end personal trainer. Lyon told me to take off my clothes and stand in front of a full-length, 360-degree mirror for half an hour while being filmed. Longest thirty minutes of my life. I had a six-pack of man tits.

Runs around Central Park. Bike rides to Chelsea Piers. A chef who delivered healthy meals daily. No drugs. Drinking in moderation. I began to lose the weight and feel healthy again. Sure, I was fucking hungry for roast duck and cookies-and-cream soft serve all the goddamn time, but you know what? When I walked the streets of Manhattan, it was pretty nice not to feel like my organs were in my throat.

The network filmed every meal I had for four months. It was my job to make jokes about healthy foods like hummus (that high-protein terrorist spread) and celery sticks (an under-rated sluice for cocaine). The network flew me out to L.A. to start workouts with the other celebrities on the show (Kirstie Alley and I got drunk and made out one night). They ran me on the beaches of Santa Monica, up the Hollywood hills, not far from the Razzmatazz villa where Veronica's mom still lived—long and hard until I puked. They filmed me and fellow comics having dinner at a nice restaurant in Hollywood and zoomed in on yours truly ignoring my salad, slack-jawed while everyone else gorged on course after course of fried chicken, pork belly, and mac and cheese.

"Can't do it anymore," I said, during the confessional in my hotel suite. "So hungry. So—" I ripped off my mic, broke out of the room, ran to the nearest Ralphs, and cleared the shelves of Ho Hos and other Hostess product placements. The camerapeople galloped after me like they were filming an episode of *Cheaters*. I scarfed a basket of sweets and spent the night doped up on sugar, unable to sleep, with a rock in my belly that would eventually become explosive diarrhea.

I lost 150 pounds. The show interviewed my parents outside their apartment complex after they were presented the new me.

"He got so fat," my mom said in English. "He always have many pimple, too."

"Big belly boy!" exclaimed my dad.

"Now, he too skinny," my mom said.

"But he's much healthier now," the host said.

"Too skinny," my dad agreed.

"Are you proud of how hard he's worked?"

"*Prow?*" my mom said. "What that mean?"

"Do you feel good that he's been working so hard?" the host asked.

"Everyone work hard," my mom said.

"In China, you don't get big award every time you work hard." My dad laughed long and loud until he snorted.

The camera panned to the host. He was speechless.

KILLING SIRIUS

Sarah wanted me to do an accent. She said she had a feeling this show was going to run for years.

"You'll never have to go on the road again if you don't want to," she said. "I wouldn't ask if I didn't think this was the wise thing to do."

I told her I didn't need more money. Of course, that wasn't true. I always needed more money!

"I'm not doing any fucking accent."

The show was *2 Broke Girls*. I would have been Han, the diner owner who was too short to be a jockey. That sitcom à l'racism somehow ran for six seasons.

I've never regretted that decision, but Sarah was so upset she didn't call for months.

The Plunger. The Meat Shtick. The movies got shittier and shittier. You know the worst part about doing a movie you hate? Promoting one. Premiere parties. Radio shows. Television interviews. Press junkets. Time and time again you had to tell smiling lies about how much you admired the script and enjoyed working with the actors. How you would absolutely, positively, unequivocally work with the same people again.

After the first week of events for *The Meat Shtick*, I was putting the country of Columbia up my nose.

For the premiere, I went with Sarah as my date. By the after-party, I was blitzkrieg drunk. Sarah and the real Kristin Wiig were having wine beside a swimming pool overlooking the lights of Hollywood when I walked up and began blathering about how we used to steal Kristen Wiig's sketches.

"You did Target Lady for the first time on Saturday, and by next Sunday, Annie Gemellino would be Walmart Lady," I said. "Did you notice that? Isn't that *hilarious*?" I was teetering like the ground was the deck of a capsizing ship. Sarah was holding me up by an armpit.

"I don't think Kristen needs to—"

"What a shitshow, right?!" I shouted.

I leaned forward too far and fell over, dragging Sarah down with me. She scrambled to her feet while I rolled around on the cement, laughing. Kristin Wiig turned and left.

"Goddamnit, man!" Sarah said, straightening her tie. "She wanted to cast you in her new movie!"

The movie was *Bridesmaids*.

That night, I went to take a shit and afterward my toilet bowl looked like a war zone. In the emergency room, the doctor again warned me about my liver health. I had been noticing dark urine and the yellowing of my eye whites. She again prescribed antivirals and urged me to take them.

I walked out of that office and called Sarah.

"I can't believe I'm taking this call after last night," she said.

I did what I do best: apologize.

"Is this a recording?"

"Very clever," I said. "I called to ask if you knew anything about rehab centers?"

Sarah fell quiet.

"Hello?" I said.

She sniffled. "Oh, good God, finally!" she exclaimed, her voice wet and cracking. "I've been waiting so long to hear you say those words."

Sarah booked me into the most-frequented and highly recommended rehab facility of her clients. I had no one to notify. No Razzmatazzes. No Lee Council. It was just me and my duffel bag, waiting in front of the creaky gates of a treatment center on Long Island.

(I warned you, M, that my life story was going to be some dark sauce. I'd like to tell you that I didn't know what I was doing and that the drugs and alcohol brought out the worst in me, and blah, blah, blah. But I knew damn well what I was doing was wrong, and I just thought: *Why not? Who's watching? Who cares? My so-called family? My alleged friends? My millions of fans who wouldn't recognize me if I stopped them on the street?* My life had amounted to nothing. None of my accomplishments made me feel better about myself. I'd achieved all of my dreams only to find that inside, I was still no good, very bad Hor from Alhambra.)

My roommate was a black guy named Clarence who was addicted to heroin. He was the fattest smackhead I'd ever met; he was pushing 400. The food in rehab was average at best (and Clarence had no front teeth), but he would eat both his meal and part of mine every night. When I asked if he was sure he was addicted to heroin and not food, he laughed.

"I like everything," he said. "I've got the like-everything gene."

"Me too," I said.

I didn't want anyone to know who I was, but Clarence seemed to recognize me. After about a week, he finally exclaimed:

"You're the guy from *The Hangover!*"

"That's Ken Jeong."

"You're Ken Jeong!"

I thought about correcting him, but everyone, myself included, adored big Clarence. He was social. He loved to laugh and he loved funny movies.

"I'm Ken Jeong," I confirmed.

"So why do you call yourself Sirius?"

"It's to throw off the paparazzi."

All week, he told people I was Ken Jeong, and the other rehabbers started calling me Mr. Chow and saying his catch-phrase "So long, bitches!"

Clarence left after the third week. A few days later, we heard he'd overdosed.

Everyone stopped calling me Mr. Chow after that.

During group work, the leader, an African American lady with the most soothing voice, asked us to name our everyday heroes—people we wanted to be or wished we were more like. We had to pick someone living, someone we knew, and someone who was not famous.

Everyone else could name a relative or a friend. I couldn't name anyone.

"You don't look up to anyone?" she asked. "Anyone in your family?"

"No one I've admired has ever wanted to be admired by me," I said.

"Who have you admired?"

"My grandfather, but he's dead," I said. "Johnny Razzmatazz, my mentor. But he's famous. Veronica Razzmatazz, my ex. She's famous too."

"I loved that show!" one of the other addicts said.

"Yeah, remember when Johnny stepped on dog shit in the living room?" said another.

The group laughed. I covered my eyes.

"Okay, everyone," the leader said. "This is Sirius's time."

"Remember they blurred out the Mexican chef?" a third addict added.

"And the Asian kid!" someone else said.

"And Janet never spoke!" said another.

"Enough!" the leader said. She waited for silence, before asking me, "What were the qualities you admired about your grandfather?"

"He was kind," I said. "Decent. Selfless."

"Do you feel like you've tried to be like him and failed?" she asked.

I laughed. "Not at all."

The leader looked surprised. "Why not?"

"I've been selfish," I said. "I've been trying to be famous. I've been trying to achieve my dreams."

"So you've been trying to be like Johnny Razzmatazz," she said. "Or Veronica. What do you admire about them?"

It hit me that they had very few admirable qualities as people, other than their success, their fame, their wealth—their whiteness. I had been trying to gain their acceptance—white acceptance—all my life. I had made fun of Asians in my act so that mostly white audiences might love me. I had cast off my parents so that Veronica and Johnny might consider me family. I had been seeking an acceptance I would never receive.

I was Hor from Alhambra, California. I will never be one of them. We will never become one of them.

By "we," I mean Eddie, Rock, Aziz, and me. We could perform in front of the biggest audiences ever, and the four faces they'd put on the Mount Rushmore of comedians would probably still be white.

By "we," I mean you and me. Because of me and the half of your mother that's Chinese, people will never quite see you as how you see yourself; they'll never see you as an American. They'll always wonder where you're *really* from. Some might have convinced themselves that race doesn't matter. But it will leak out in unexpected ways. Maybe you'll be the only Chinese person in a group of white friends or co-workers and you'll wonder: why am I the only one? Why, when whites choose the people they care about, do they choose other whites ninety-five percent of the time? Why always the Brads, Darrens, and Stephanies? You might think money or class has something to do with it. And maybe it does. But the mere truth that class cannot explain all validates that your non-whiteness means something big in America. It means something big because we don't like to talk about it. Because it means anything at all, it means too much.

You might try to find solace among your own people. I will tell you that that will give you no peace either. Because that's hiding, and hiding is no way to live. All you can do is walk tall, chin up, chest out, let the world's barbs bounce off you, and do as your great-grandpa once did.

Suffer the present for a better future.

By week five, I started seeing straight. I made my bed daily, cleaned bathrooms once a week, and cooked breakfast for my cohort every other day. I wasn't just there because I had had a scare. I was there because I wanted to be, because I wanted to help the fourteen others get clean. My new roommate was a Mexican kid my age named Joseph, who was addicted to meth. He would wake up in the middle of the night screaming that spiders were crawling all over him. I made it my mission to get him through his withdrawals. I beat back those imaginary arachnoids with my pillow. I held him when he screamed and rocked him like a baby. I joked that spider hallucinations were actually a sign of recovery and that he'd be out of rehab in no time.

I tried to be as honest as possible during our group talks. My self-loathing gradually morphed into rage: for letting myself become this cliché, for not appreciating my accomplishments, for giving up on my future, for surrendering the possibility of having you.

It was in rehab that I started calling myself Hor again. I needed to kill Sirius Lee inside me. I wasn't going to be Johnny's creation anymore.

When I got back to New York City, I returned to doing what I loved most: standup. I did a set on the early show at Comedy Cellar one night, and on my way out, I bumped into Chris Rock upstairs at the Olive Tree. I almost missed him because he was wearing a baseball cap. I blabbed that he was my favorite comedian of all time and his work had helped me escape my shitty childhood. He didn't know who I was. He thought I was just a fan, because I looked like a completely different person from my *No Good Very Bad Asian* days. I was so starstruck I forgot to mention who I was before he left.

Then I heard, "Sirius? Is that you?"

I turned and saw Archimedes Jones. We hugged.

"How are you?" he asked. From the intensity with which his eyes searched mine, I knew he had heard that I had gone to rehab.

"I think I'm okay," I said. How could anyone say how they were with certainty?

"How did your set go?"

"So-so," I said. The stage time felt wrong. I was telling the jokes too quickly and my set seemed to last forever. I noticed every crowd member who wasn't laughing. I was rusty.

"What do you plan to do now that you're back in the city?" asked Archimedes.

"Start over," I said.

One night, after a set at Village Z, I was walking and texting when a car horn pealed. I had crossed the street on a red light. The cabbie opened his window and shouted mangled, heavily accented obscenities. And he barked a few more when I looked down at my phone and saw it ringing. The taxi had startled me into button-mashing. I had accidentally called Tina McMillan. Your mother.

She was Sarah's new contracts person. We had just met that day at a meeting about how much I wanted to get paid for *Another Bangkok Family Vacation*. Her caramel-colored eyes made my insides weak. I even flirted by joking that her pants suits reminded me of my crush on my kindergarten teacher, who was, if still alive, an octogenarian. (God bless you, Mrs. J.) Your mother was in her early thirties and I was only twenty-six so I didn't think I had a chance.

She picked up my call. "Sirius?"

"Oh, hi! I must have ass-dialed you. Sorry about that."

A gaggle of college-aged barhoppers shouldered past. Wafts of pot smoke. One of the young men professed his attraction to Hasidic Jewesses. ("It's the leggings, I swear!")

"Where are you?" your mother asked.

"West Village."

"That's where I live."

"Really?" I said, as if I was about to invite myself over. Of course, I said nothing more and an awkward silence commenced.

"What street are you on?"

I told her.

"That's, like, a block away," your mother said. "Why don't you meet me? We can have a drink. Something non-alcoholic."

My breath was taken. "Where?" My voice was strangely squeaky.

She directed me uptown one block, then two to the left. "There's a Spanish place on the corner."

The restaurant was named Cordoba. Through the window, she was sitting at the bar in her pajamas, wearing slippers. Her dark hair spread in ringlets across her shoulders. I froze in the window while your mom chatted with the gray-haired bartender, who caught my eye. She followed his gaze and stared at me staring at them.

"Fuck," I said as I slunk into the restaurant.

She hugged me. Her hair smelled strongly of citrus.

"You're working late," she said.

"Yeah, that's right!" I blustered. "Tell your boss. She's always going on about me not showing up to work. I work, goddamnit! I just don't wear a tie like she does. Never learned how to tie one."

She laughed and asked what I wanted to drink. I requested ginger ale. Your mother ordered one as well. When they arrived, I thanked the bartender in Spanish, and in Spanish, he responded at length. I stared dumbly back at him.

"I'm sorry, I don't speak."

He retreated to the other end of the bar, muttering. Your mom tried unsuccessfully to stifle her laughter.

"I don't think we reached a diplomatic solution," I said.

"He doesn't speak much English."

"You fluent?"

"Si," she said. "I lived in Madrid for a few years after college."

Having never been out of the country, I felt intimidated. "How do you like working with Sarah?"

Your mother shrugged. "She's a storyteller. She likes to go on about the celebrities."

"Uh-oh."

"Yeah, I know all about you."

"I'm not that guy anymore," I said. "I can't be. Docs basically said I was committing suicide." I told myself to shut up. Don't invite her to a pity party.

Her brows canted. "Well, I'm glad you aren't."

"Coincidentally, so am I."

"'Asians are the fifth Beatle of minorities,'" she said. "That's my favorite joke of yours."

I couldn't help but smile.

"'You can tell because politicians say everybody's got a shot at the American Dream,'" she went on. "'Then they list the minorities in order of importance. Women, blacks, whites, Latinos, gays! Energy efficient cars! They mention Asians right after the service animals.'"

"Not bad," I said. "I have another bit about how there are more Hollywood movies starring dogs than Asians."

"I know what you mean," she said. "I can tell by looking at a white guy when I'm just an exotic cultural adventure that he can brag about decades later to his WASPy in-laws."

I laughed. Your mother's left cheek dimpled when she was making a point. Made her look like she knew something I didn't.

"What do you think?" she asked.

"I think you're beautiful."

Her eyes dropped. "Of my joke, I mean."

"I'm sorry," I said, growing clammy. "I didn't mean to make you uncomfortable."

"Compliments are always nice to hear."

"Not if they come from sleazy sober comedians."

She put a hand on my arm as she laughed.

After several ginger ales and an eye-widening sugar buzz, I walked your mother to her apartment building.

"I have a burning question," I said.

"Fire away."

"Was Sarah in the Army or Marines? Because she signs her emails Semper Fi but says she was in the Army."

Your mother laughed until tears came to her eyes. "She's in the Army National Guard," she said. "She does training two weeks each year."

"That doesn't fucking count!" I exclaimed. "She makes it sound like she was in Baghdad!"

"Baghdad, Texas."

We giggled for awhile before it got quiet again. I wished her a good night and turned to head for the nearest subway station.

"Sirius?" your mother said.

I pirouetted. She was small against the large door. Her keys were in hand, sparkling under the streetlamp, like she was dangling a tiny firework.

"You look great," she said. "Like, healthy."

Before I could reply, she unlocked the door, pulled it open, and disappeared inside.

Two weeks later, I waited for your mother at the end of the Comedy Cellar line that snaked onto Minetta Street. She had never been to a standup show so I had gotten us two free cover passes. I wasn't sure what was going on between us. What did she want with a degenerate like me?

When your mother arrived, she was still in her work clothes, and she told a few anecdotes about office politics within Sarah's agency. I acted politely and appropriately amused, but I wasn't winning any gold medals in listening. My brain was imprinting the way she smiled, the way her long, wavy hair made her look older than her age, way more mature and self-assured than I was. She deserved a tall, well-to-do white guy, I thought. A success-ful hedge fund douche or a heart surgeon. I always imagined a tall, well-to-do white guy as the ideal mate for a woman I was attracted to—a symptom of the zombie-eye disease.

The line turned the corner, and Dan Van Pido was milling about outside Players Theatre, wearing a shiny gray suit with no tie. He was body-scanning every woman in line. Especially the collegiates. Your mother received only a cursory glance.

I stepped in front of him.

"Are you dropping in tonight?" he asked.

I told him I was busy. Obviously.

Pidofile eyed your mother. "You have a nice smile. Are you really with this guy?"

"Tonight, I am."

"Don't put out on the first date," he said. "You're too old for that."

Your mother smirked. "Gee, thanks."

"You can do better than him though," Pidofile said.

"Maybe she doesn't want someone as old as you," I said.

Pidofile beamed at your mother as the line filed into the club. "That's never true, is it?"

In the Cellar, as your mom and I wedged into our seats to the left of the stage, she surprised me by hooking her arm through mine.

The show wasn't great. Shadrick Coleman, who was the gay best friend in *Adult Coloring Book*, that CW sitcom about a sassy Latina young woman trying to find love while working her way up at a large romance publisher, did all his material on trapped miners after three other comics had joked about trapped miners. He hadn't watched the previous performers and couldn't understand why we didn't think his jokes were funny. "So you guys are all from Middle America and don't read the news unless it's about dangerous blacks and Mexicans or white folks saving lost cats, huh?" he said. Colin Quinn, Greer Barnes, and Ali Wong did well, but I'd seen them do better. I was only paying half attention anyway since I was wondering how I was going to get to first base with your mother.

After the show, the crowd drifted to the exit, and we remained seated and waited for the room to clear.

"So what did you think?" she asked.

"I was thinking about putting my arm around you." My words melted together from another ginger-ale-induced sugar rush. But it's so tight in here, I was thinking that if I did it too fast, I'd accidentally smack you in the face."

Your mother appeared puzzled. Then she laughed. "That would be tough to explain to my co-workers."

Her eyes made her whole face sparkle. Comedy Cellar had nearly emptied.

Her hand was on my thigh. We kissed. Her tiny mouth was soft, and she smelled warm and vibrant like the inside of a greenhouse. She tasted like metal and strawberry jam. I kissed her again. I worried about crossing boundaries, so I backed away. She looked drowsy. A good sign, I thought. Unless she was just drowsy.

Bobbie Jean, the blue-haired waitress (who all the comics agreed had the best weed), stood over us, arms crossed. "What you're doing looks really fun, Sirius, but we've got to clear the room for the next show."

Your mother stood, holding my hand, and I wordlessly followed her out of the club.

The next morning, I opened a gluey eye in your mother's studio. I was lying on a thin futon. She slept on her side, turned away from me. We had walked back to her block, bought condoms at Duane Reade, and hustled up to her place where we . . . consummated our new relationship.

(See? I'm learning, M. Details minimized.)

The studio was very New York City: tiny, beat to hell, and insistent that those traits were indications of character. The old oak floors were warped everywhere and, oddly, creaked when no one was walking on them. On a wall hung a large abstract painting that made a blank canvas look like it was cracking to reveal underworld swathes of blues, yellows, and reds. There was a messy desk by the window. The kitchenette appeared unused with the exception of the coffeemaker, which sat askew on the counter with its pot half full. The edges of the linoleum curled like horns and was so soiled I couldn't tell what color it had been.

I found my boxers and got out of bed. I looked out the window down at Tenth Avenue. To my surprise, an old Asian lady toting a big bag of aluminum cans over her shoulder was staring up at me. Spooked, I moved out of her view. On your mother's desk, a stack of pages with pen edits. I skimmed what looked to be an essay about Carnivale in Rio.

"What do you think?" she said, startling me.

"Sorry, I couldn't help myself," I said. "So you write."

Your mother sat up and pulled on a T-shirt and sweats, before padding to the kitchen and emptying the coffee pot. "I did a lot of traveling around Europe and North Africa while I was in Spain. I hope to finish a book of essays."

I imagined the two of us traveling together. "I'm wondering if this is all too good to be true."

"What do you mean?"

"What happened before?" I asked.

"We went to Comedy Cellar."

"No, I mean, who were you with?"

"Would you like me to provide a sexual history?"

"No, I don't mean . . . I'm sorry," I said. "Why me?"

"Are you questioning my judgment?"

"I'm sorry," I said. "You don't have to talk about it." A few moments passed. "But yes, I am questioning your judgment."

"You're not like other Asian guys, okay?" she blurted, her back turned to me as she washed the coffee pot in the sink. "I know that sounds awful."

The sky outside was muddy, a clueless backdrop for the sharp brick edges of the building across the street. She went on to say that she had been in numerous bad relationships. Her previous boyfriend had gotten another woman pregnant.

"I can tell you won't hurt me," she said.

Boy, I wish your mother had been right.

YOUR MOTHER

Your mother and I went to movies together, ate fancy ramen, walked across the Brooklyn Bridge hand-in-hand, took selfies at the top of the Empire State Building—we were in love. Unlike Veronica, she never tried to dress me or change my diet or call me by two different names. Not only did your mother go to most of my standup shows, including ones at the crumbling Village Z, but she often brought hordes of friends (how did she have so many?) to the finger-fluttering delight of Dan Van Pido. I couldn't believe my luck.

"You better not fuck this up," Pidofile said to me, counting out large stacks of cash behind the bar.

"I thought you said she was too old for me."

"I said she was too old for *me*," he corrected. "You need someone who's more mature. You need someone who, like, knows how life works." He looked me up and down. "Look at you."

"What are you talking about?" I said. "I've got my shit together now."

He pointed to my chest. "Then what's that?"

Looking down, I saw a trail of grease spots on my unlaundered T-shirt from a recent meal gone awry.

I took a night off from doing standup to see your mom read at one of the many reading series in the city. At a bar in East Village, she shared an essay about a nameless Icelandic man she'd met on a train between Vienna and Prague. They'd talked for hours about their love of travel and family while walking the "City of a Hundred Spires" all day and night because they couldn't find an open hostel bed. The piece culminated with them kissing on the Charles Bridge at sunrise before they shuffled arm-in-arm to Hlavni Nadrazi to board separate Eurails to their respective destinations (her to Budapest, him to Milan). She proposed they exchange contact information, but The Prague Icelandic insisted that they leave contactless, so as not to spoil their perfect, romantic day. It was all very Ethan Hawke and Julie Delpy. Who the fuck was this white guy? What was it with my girlfriends and Scandinavian dudes?

"How do you know Tina?" asked Kara Davidson, one of her writer friends, after your mother had taken her seat next to the other readers. "Are you a lawyer too?"

I couldn't have looked less like a lawyer. I was wearing cuffed skinny jeans, Converses, and a green tee that read "Irish I Could Drink This Beer," because though I lived in Manhattan, I shopped in Williamsburg.

"I'm her man," I said.

She brightened. "That's great!" she said. "I didn't know she was dating again."

I'd seen this woman at other readings. She was tall and blonde, and she'd published a critically acclaimed memoir about the bad behavior of her wealthy Upper West Side family. Your mother had recommended the book so I read it and was bored shitless because duh, money makes people assholes—take, for example, me! She said Kara had just gotten a seven-figure advance for her next book about her inability to find true love because of—you guessed it—the bad behavior of her wealthy Upper West Side family.

"I'm glad she's gotten over what happened in Germany," Kara said. "That one she read last month was so powerful."

Brows raised, hackles up. "Was this about the cheating boyfriend who got another woman pregnant?"

"Not that one," she said. "This one was about the guy who devoted his life to helping Syrian refugees."

I threw up my hands in despair. How many doomed romantic relationships had your mother had? And refugees! How could I compete with saving refugees?

The more I heard your mother read, the more I noticed that all of her essays were about these romantic encounters in European countries. Finally, one morning, in her studio, I asked her about German Refugee Savior, Icelandic Ethan Hawke, The French Jackson Pollock, The Romanian Gold Medal Gymnast, and all the other essays I'd heard her read.

"The only Euro country you don't have a guy in is Belarus," I pointed out while making us coffee.

Your mother laughed as she sat at her desk and began marking up her manuscript. "It's all for the book, and the book is set in the past," she said. "What we have right now is right here and real."

I walked over and stood between her and the window to keep her attention. "I don't want to seem needy," I said. "But I've been happy for like five to ten minutes total in my entire life outside of a comedy club. I know I have a past that's pretty gnarly, but that was then and this is now and I'm really serious about you so I hope you're serious about me." My face was flushed and my sinuses congested with emotions. "I guess what I'm trying to say is: I don't want to end up in one of your essays as one of your could-have-beens."

She stood and put her arms around my neck. Our fronts pressed together as one. I eyed her smooth pale cheeks and wondered if she might one day become half of me, if I could be half of her. Love is real, I thought. A two-person thing, like my grandfather had said.

"I was going to ask if you wanted to meet my family this weekend," said your mother.

Before they moved to London to be near you, your grandparents on your mom's side used to live near the Flushing-Main St. subway stop at the end of the seven line. She told me as we walked up to the house where she grew up that she used to be embarrassed by her mother's Chinese-ness in grade school, when she'd see her transporting household items she bought from street markets in canvas sacks dangling from a bamboo pole balanced on her shoulder. But now, your mother embraced her mom's Chinese-ness, returning to Flushing at least once a month to get acupuncture and cupping where her mom worked so they could have tea and dumplings together afterward.

"She's always been there for me whenever I went through one of my bad breakups," she said.

"Was she there for you in Europe?"

"Just a phone call away."

Must have been a big bill, I thought. Lots of phone calls.

Your grandpa is a son of Scots, an inscrutable, very decorated, retired NYPD detective. Your mom told me about the cases her legendary father had solved. Paul McMillan once put a serial rapist behind bars using only the surveillance video from a convenience store that displayed a hooded man's knuckle tattoo—a single pixel that none of the other detectives noticed. He was the first on the scene of a small plane crash in Queens where the NYPD stored the charred and dismembered passengers in a toy store and didn't leave the crash scene for a week. After days of sleep deprivation, he left for a cup of coffee and didn't return. His partner found him an hour later fifty feet from where she last saw him, sans coffee. Your grandpa was scrutinizing the plane engine, which dangled from a severed wing. "Bird strike," he declared. "The fan blades are damaged." Everyone else had been distracted by the carnage. Not Super-detective Paul McMillan. He was always solving the case. He figured out the cause of the crash before the FAA. He retired with a shoebox stuffed with Medals of Valor.

"He doesn't say much, so don't think that means he hates you," said your mother. "When he talks, he's usually got every-thing figured out already."

"That's like my grandfather," I said. "He's going to see right through me."

"Oh please," she said. "He's already seen everything you're in, so if you're thinking of hiding something, you're too late."

Your mother said that in high school, her dad could tell when she liked a guy before she could. "He was always paying such close attention to me," she said. "But he was quiet about it, so I wouldn't notice. He didn't want me to feel suffocated."

Needless to say, your mom's stories about her wonderful loving parents only made me more nervous as we walked up to the old red-brick McMillan house. It was on a ranch lot with manicured hedges, and there was a driveway that led to a detached garage. The handrails were made of shiny brass, and the awning was blue-and-white striped. Once your grandpar-ents opened the door, there were so many relatives inside that I thought the house was going to burst. Aunts, uncles, and cousins were crowded in the living and dining rooms. There must have been two-dozen people. Your mother acted like this was just like any other visit. She received hugs from each relative like she was the pope. One of the uncles called your mother "the big New York writer," and your grandpa turned to one of the Chinese aunts and said, "We're so proud of her."

Her mother, diminutive and short-haired like my grand-mother and dressed in black khakis and a black hoodie, told me to call her "Mommy."

"Sure, Ms. McMillan," I said.

"Mommy," she corrected.

It took me several tries before I managed to utter the word. I never even called my own mother "Mommy." And saying "Mommy" to your grandma made me feel like your mom's brother instead of her boyfriend.

"Louder," your grandma said.

"Mommy!" I exclaimed.

"Yes, good!" she said, putting an arm around my waist.

Your grandpa shook my hand with a single, hard squeeze, no excess energy wasted. He was wearing a white tracksuit, and since, as you know, he's massive (six-foot-three, 275 pounds), he looked like a hulking helmetless fencer.

"How's the rehab taking?" he said, *sotto voce* so your mom, still giving out hugs, high-pitched hi's, and cheek-kisses, couldn't hear.

"Um, good," I said. "I mean, great. Best rehab ever."

"Has your past problems affected your . . . reproductive abilities?" he asked.

Indeed, her father was a detective.

"Not to my knowledge, sir," I reported.

"You're young," he said, smileless, looking down upon me. "Twenty-five?"

"Twenty-six."

His lips parted and he appeared to draw a deep, but silent breath. Now sweating, I imagined that he would enjoy playing the bagpipes at my funeral.

"You guys don't all live in the same house, do you?" I bellowed as I was swarmed by middle-aged whites and Chinese, followed closely by a small army of teenagers and young adults.

That night, the McMillan clan dined at one of the many large Chinese restaurants in Flushing. This one was called King Kong Kitchen or KKK for short, or, as your grandma noted, when directly translated from the Chinese characters, the restaurant's name was actually Emperor Chang's Seafood Restaurant. We were so many that we took up two ten-tops, and your mom and I were split up. I could barely remember who everyone at my table was. In addition to your grandma, there was your mom's cousin on your grandpa's side, her husband and two children (boy and a girl), and your mom's cousin on your grandma's side, his wife and two boys. The children on your grandpa's side were in their early twenties, massive with ham hock arms, and double and triple bellies—bodies only made in the USA. The children on your grandma's side—the Chinese—were average-sized, but many years apart. One boy looked sixteen, judging by a cluster of whiteheads growing over his upper lip. The other was about seven. Both had buzzcuts and were dressed like clones, in pink polo shirts, khaki shorts, and white slip-on sneakers. I'm not sure why they aspired to look like retired Floridians.

"Is he actually Chinese?" your mom's cousin said in Mandarin to Ms. McMillan (a.k.a. Mommy). "I thought she only liked white guys."

Your grandma shrugged in response. I didn't know what this shrug represented, but it probably wasn't positive.

"As long as she's happy," said your mom's Chinese cousin.

"He looks like an orphan," your grandma said. "Scared in the eyes."

She wasn't wrong. I had never been around a family this large. Not to mention one that smiled and laughed and hugged together.

I avoided the grown-ups and tried to talk to the clone children. The sixteen-year-old blathered breathlessly about the SAT like it was his favorite sport, and he professed his distaste for the president, but "not because he's black." When I turned to the grown offspring, I learned that they were tellers at the same bank, and, for fun, they did "nothing much," which was fairly evident from their prodigious physiques.

"Where is your family?" your grandma asked me in English from across the table.

"Los Angeles."

"Where in Los Angeles?"

"Alhambra."

"Your mother must not like that you are so far away."

"No, I don't think she does," I said. "But that's nothing new. She doesn't like anything about me."

"Why is that?"

"I'm just not what she imagined."

"We all have our imaginings when our children are young and we are young," your grandma said. "But they don't have to become reality. Reality is usually better anyway."

I liked Mommy. Her desire to mother me was both flattering and frightening. I wasn't sure if reality was better for me and the Lees. In some ways, of course it was. In others, not. I hadn't been returning my parents' calls since rehab. I had Sarah arrange automatic bank transfers to my dad so I wouldn't have to think about *them*—my parents and the money. It was bliss not hearing their voices. My mind felt free.

"You can call Mommy anytime if you want to talk, okay?" your grandma said.

By the end of dinner, I was exhausted and wishing I was at Village Z. After the table was cleared, no one left for at least another twenty minutes because your grandpa and your mom's Chinese cousin had a tug-of-war over the bill, arguing *for* the right to pay the check as is the Chinese custom. The cousin sprinted to the register. Your grandpa chased him, grabbed his shoulders, wrestled him to the ground, and twisted an arm behind his back in a wristlock. I gasped, but the rest of the family continued to small talk like nothing was happening. The restaurant patrons also seemed indifferent, accustomed to arguments for the bill getting physical.

On the way back to the McMillan house, while your mother walked with your grandma, your grandpa shouldered his way past the filial hordes and insisted on walking beside me.

"I know you've been through a lot, Sirius," he said. "Had to grow up at a young age."

I nodded. "Still growing. Like good mold."

He squinted down at me, flat-lipped. "Tina tells me you're good-hearted," he said. "And I want to believe her."

"How much would such a belief in me cost?"

He snickered. "Do you believe in yourself?"

I wanted to tell him yes, but I didn't want to be presumptuous either. "I'm going to try to follow your daughter's lead," I said. "And the lead of people I admire, like my late grandfather, who was kind, gentle, and decent. That's the best I can do right now. I can't promise you anything. And I wouldn't want to, because I don't want to disappoint you."

Your grandpa chuckled. "Disappoint me, huh? That's a nice thought, Sirius. But you haven't been around long enough for that."

Superdetective Paul McMillan looked down at me with a satisfied expression, like he had closed The Case of Sirius Lee.

As your mother and I headed toward the seven line back to the city, I could barely speak. I'd had enough family time for a year. I just didn't have that gene, the part of me that could be genuinely open-hearted to so many people who seemed so open-hearted to each other. Standup is a solo sport, like golf or tennis, as Johnny had pointed out. I had never been the best team player.

Your mother took my hand. "So what do you think?"

"I think your family is amazing and what family should be all about."

"Thanks!" your mother said. "I'm lucky. They brought me up well."

I stopped. "I'm just not sure I'm wired that way," I said. "To be good, like them. Like you. What you guys feel for each other, I'm not sure I can feel."

Your mother squeezed my palm. "Oh, Sirius," she said. "You don't have to. We don't have expectations of you like your family. All we have is love."

Your mother's many friends became my friends. Her girl-friends all had husbands who suddenly became my Rat Pack. And gasp, they were all Asian from Flushing! It was as if I had moved back to Alhambra.

They were like me, on the surface—American-born sons of immigrants. But they all did what their parents wanted. Doctors, lawyers, and maybe one day, CEOs! They married high school or college sweethearts and settled into financially comfortable, hardworking existences. They were older than me, in their late thirties, so we had to schedule months ahead to take in a Mets game or do a fantasy baseball draft.

Once, I agreed to meet them at Spice Market for Saturday brunch in the Meatpacking District. On my walk from the subway stop, the gutters of the cobblestone streets still wafted of clubber puke from the night before, and I got flashbacks of those dark mornings out with Archimedes sitting and drinking on the curb when I was on *LOA*. Seven years had passed; it was another life that someone else had led. Foggy with reverie, I passed the restaurant's entrance several times without noticing it. But then I saw my friends sitting straight-backed like dark-haired Legos in the far corner of the outside seating area.

It was a few minutes after noon, and the restaurant was packed and squawking with tourists. I circled back to the entrance and walked through the dining room expensively designed to resemble a poorly funded Buddhist temple. Squeezing past the crowded bar, I bumped into a waiter whose high-collared uniform looked borrowed from a massage parlor. As I took a seat next to Leon (Kim), he and Edmond (Yu), both equity traders, were having an animated-to-the-point-of-musicality discussion about something called flow derivatives. Herman (Kawakami), the pediatric physician, asked for free stock advice.

"Don't be afraid to go insider," Edmond joked.

Leon and Edmond laughed. "Just give me the list of stocks you're interested in, and I'll see what intel the firm has," Leon said.

"Are you serious?" Herman asked.

"Of course not! I don't want to go to jail."

"Nah," said Edmond, whose straight wiry hair formed a rhombus on his scalp. "Unless you're in one of the two cases on the news each year, you can't get caught."

"Your fantasy baseball team sucked," Herman said to me. "And you have no excuse. You don't even have kids or a day job like us." Herman was most likely to remember the names of everyone's children. He lived on a modified ranch way out in the North Shore of Long Island in a town called Old Westbury. His household was Ark-like: he had two daughters, three sons, eight or nine dogs and cats, and his parents had separate bedrooms. I couldn't remember if he had two boys and a girl or two girls and a boy or three boys or three girls.

Edmond laughed. "The Whore Luckily's are always bringing up the rear."

"Who picked this place?" Herman asked. "The food here sucks. It's no Flushing."

"I have to be close to home, alright?" Leon said, glancing at his phone. "I have to walk the dog soon."

He delicately smoothed his heavily pomaded, center-parted hair that stuck up a little in the back. "You should do a show at our church," he said. "A lot of us work in finance and love food and money and family. FYI, so you can pick your material."

"So . . . no jokes about priests and altar boys?"

"We're Presbyterian," Leon pointed out. "My wife and mom might actually like jokes about Catholics."

"Should have never let my mother move in with us," Herman said, apropos of nothing.

Leon and Herman graduated from Harvard, Edmond from Yale. All of us were sober. They were genuinely nice people, occasionally funny. But I couldn't help but look down on them. They were the boring math-major raisin dicks I used to make fun of. They were passionless, dreamless. If they'd had any such impulse, it had been beaten out of them either by their upbringing or a world that told them early on exactly who they could and couldn't be. I tried to be empathetic and see them as just people doing their best, but that's the whole point: I was trying. I was faking it and feeling terrible about faking it.

"Do you feel like equity trading is what you were put on this earth for? Like is it your dream?" I asked.

Leon shrugged. "I'm getting tired of it," he said. "It's a younger man's game."

"I want to work for a bank at some point," said Edmond. "The hours are better."

"I just bought my wife a Mercedes for her birthday," Herman said. "I mean, who does that?"

"Apparently you do," Leon said.

I laughed for the first time since sitting down. Herman acknowledged that he had been gotten good.

"What do you get up in the morning for?" I asked. My friends were quiet, exchanging glances.

"I get up in the morning because I have to," Leon said.

"Other people seem to respect me," Herman said.

"My parents are proud," Edmond said. "What I do is a long way from being a postal worker like my dad."

The waiter came to take our order. He had a mustache so perfectly trimmed that it could have competed in a dog show. Herman dropped a gold American Express corporate card on the table.

"We haven't ordered anything yet," I said.

"It's my turn."

"Big spender," Edmond said.

"Insider!" Leon exclaimed.

My friends laughed.

Herman took his card off the table. "You're right," he said. "I should check with my mom and wife first." He told the waiter we weren't ready.

"What's with the questions?" Leon asked me. "Are you, like, gathering material or something?"

"You're going to make fun of us!" Edmond said. "Like you did on your HBO special to those poor Japanese tourists."

"No," I lied.

"When's your new special coming out?" asked Herman.

There was no new special. My new material had been spotty at best.

"Don't you feel bad about becoming famous by bagging on Asians?" Edmond asked.

I sipped water, feeling suddenly parched for a double whiskey like the old days. In fact, throw in some cocaine, please! The glass was unsteady in my hands.

"Yes, sometimes, because I'm one of you," I said. "But no, sometimes, because we deserve it."

So if I was going to love your mother, I was going to have to love everything about her, and that included her friends and family. And I didn't know if I could do it. But I put in my strongest effort. I sold my loft in SoHo and we moved into a Cobble Hill brownstone. On the weekends, we'd shop for housewares, slipcovered used furniture, armoires, bookshelves, sofas, and dining tables to fill our new home with a bourgeois warmth and comfort that your mother had grown up with. It made me happy to see her happy when she found an object she liked. It made me happy to be able to buy what she wanted, though I had no feeling for material things, having grown up with so little.

In the mornings, we'd go to Café Pedlar, around the corner from our place, and over espresso, she'd work on her manuscript before going into work while I'd write new jokes. During those mornings, with her tapping away on her laptop, with one foot on her chair, hugging a bent knee, her hazel eyes flickering from the light on her screen and the latticed glow from the coffee shop's windows, I loved your mother most.

"Hey," I'd interrupt her. Then I'd look her in the eye and kiss the air, and she'd smile the same smile that'd I'd see you smile from the crib soon after you were born.

"Now let me get my work done," your mother'd say. "You've achieved your dream. It's my turn."

MY BIG FAT
CHINESE WEDDING

After about a year and a half of dating, I couldn't visualize a life without your mother. When I imagined her in pain, I felt like I was staring down over a massive cliff with one foot over the edge. I was ready to commit. It was time to prove that I could be a better husband than my dad or Johnny.

I waited for your mother outside her office on the southeast corner of Fifty-Third Street and Sixth Avenue, where I braved the long lines at the famed halal cart for two orders of the chicken and rice platter. The food truck was our favorite and we often ate there on weekends.

Her engagement ring was in my pocket.

She strode toward me, looking sharp and angular in her pants suit. I was in a jersey tee and cargo shorts and toted a yellow plastic bag with our food; I looked like her delivery boy. I handed over her platter and waited until she got really into the eating and the white sauce was all around her lips. Then I got down on a knee and took the ring out of my pocket. I glimpsed people rushing off to their jobs, to their tourist destinations. Anonymous. Invisible. Just as we were to them. No one even looked at us. Like marriage proposals happened every day in Midtown Manhattan.

"Will you marry me?" I asked.

She began to choke on her food. I got up and ran to the halal cart and purchased a bottle of water. I rushed back, she sipped, composed herself, and blinked away the tears of her near-asphyxiation.

"You're such a piece of shit," she said with a smirk.

"So what do you say?"

She said yes. Your mother and I kissed and she brushed her wind-blown hair out of her face. White sauce streaked her bangs. I pinched a napkin and wiped her clean.

She stared down at her half-finished platter. "I've always been a messy eater."

Like I intended to do for the rest of my life, I agreed.

To my chagrin, your mother wanted our wedding to be held at the good ol' KKK in Flushing, and she couldn't wait to wear a traditional Chinese *qipao* with the high collar and short sleeves, while I had to wear a black silk vest embroidered with a golden dragon, over a jacket and pants that looked like fancy pajamas to me—all choices that pleased Mommy to no end. The McMillans were the most Chinese half-white family I'd ever seen. While we were fitted at the tailor for our absurd outfits, I asked your grandpa why they didn't observe more Scottish rituals.

He shrugged. "I like Chinese food better."

"How do we get you to like haggis more?" I quipped.

Neither of your grandparents laughed. Your mother told me to shut the fuck up.

"You sure you don't want to just do this at City Hall?" I asked her later when we were alone and at home.

"If I had no family, I'd probably do that, yes," your mother said.

In her words, I couldn't help but hear "If I had no family (like you)."

Out of 450 invitees, I invited my parents and grandmother, Archimedes, and Dan Van Pido. Your mother had ten bridesmaids. I added Leon, Edmond, and Herman as groomsmen so that Archimedes, as the best man, wouldn't feel so alone by my side.

When my dad showed up at the restaurant, he looked me up and down in my ridiculous Sun Yat-sen get-up, and said, "Wow, many people here." His hands were on his hips like he was in charge of the proceedings. "I didn't know you so traditional." He was wearing a light blazer and penny loafers—the same outfit he wore almost fifteen years ago to Lee's Liquors. My father was grinning and scanning the restaurant. I sensed that he wasn't observing as much as he wanted someone to acknowledge him.

"We thought you guys would enjoy this," I said to my dad. Truthfully, we didn't think about my parents at all during the planning.

"What kind of wine did you get?" he asked.

No port. "The fuck-up kind?"

He appeared unimpressed.

A twelve-piece band appeared, blaring horn instruments and marching around the restaurant while little kids did a papier-mache dragon dance. The first course of raw oysters was brought out by tuxedo-wearing waiters carrying giant platters smoking with dry ice.

"Does the rest of the Rose Bowl Parade come through before people get to eat?" I joked to your mom.

She and I stood for photos with guests in front of a yellow vinyl backdrop like Mickey and Minnie Mouse. A line ran out the door of the restaurant and down the block. Two at a time, guests flanked us. We did the one-two-three-smile over and over again. My cheeks grew tired.

"Just power through," your mother said, between photos.

"Should have made cardboard cutouts," I said.

I should add that your mother was absolutely stunning in her red *qipao*, her hair bunned up, her gold hydrangea flower earrings dangling. And yet, I found her beautiful in an untouchable way, like I was observing a sculpture in a museum. I felt like an imposter; I simply couldn't believe that, of all people, she loved me.

I'd never seen my mother so happy. She was clapping along with the band, smiling and talking to people. I hardly recognized her. She wore makeup, a fuchsia evening gown, hosiery, and new shoes. I glimpsed my mom's younger self for the first time.

Just off to the side of the photo backdrop, Ms. McMillan greeted my mother loudly in Mandarin, like they were about to adopt a child together.

"Your boy has so much talent," Ms. McMillan said.

"*Talent?*" my mom shrieked. "He can't even speak Mandarin."

"He makes my daughter happy," Ms. McMillan said.

"She's still young," my mom said. "Plenty of time to be unhappy." She laughed, while Ms. McMillan blanched.

"We treat him like our son," Ms. McMillan said, glancing at me with maternal concern.

My mom eyed me while I wrapped my arm once again around your mother's waist and smiled for the camera, for a picture with people I didn't know. My mom's expression seemed to grow angrier the longer she eyed me. Her pouchy eyes moistened as she said, "He is my son," sounding like she was talking to herself.

After your mother and I were finally done with the photos, I leaned against a wall in a quiet corner while she disappeared to change into her second outfit. Archimedes and Dan Van Pido came up to me, both smirking.

"We figured out the title of your next album," Archimedes said. "Wait for it!"

"WOMP," Pidofile said. "Wedding of My Peoples."

The two of them cackled while I groaned. "That is some hacky shit," I said.

"How do you know your groomsmen?" asked Archimedes.

"They're the husbands of Tina's bridesmaids."

"Too old for me," Pidofile blurted.

We looked at him, puzzled.

"I meant the bridesmaids," he clarified.

Archimedes looked around at the hundreds of dark-haired guests. "Think of all the crowd work you can do here," he said to me. "You could spend an hour insulting each table."

During dinner, Superdetective Paul McMillan rose and delivered a stunning speech. In fluent Mandarin. From what I could understand of it—his vocabulary was so large that I only understood about half—he said that his one hope for his daughter, after all the broken relationships that she'd had, was that she'd find a man interested in starting a large family, someone who had a lot of love to give—a selfless and serious man.

"Little did I know that he would actually be named Sirius," he said in English to laughter.

Guess I wasn't the only comedian in the family.

After the wedding, your mother quit her job at Sarah's agency, and we honeymooned for four months, touring parts of Asia, South America, and Africa.

Our first stop was Cambodia. When we got to Angkor Wat and climbed the steps of the giant temple originally built to elevate a boy-king to heaven, I felt the presence of something spiritual for the first time. I witnessed the sunset with hundreds of other people, and I got tears in my eyes at the possibility of a common, human intuition existing, in everywhere and everything, guiding my life, like a constant wind, like a sturdy current. I just had to be clearheaded enough to see it, feel it, and follow it. There had been so much noise in my life. What I wanted versus what someone else wanted. My addict brain versus my non-addict brain. If I could close my eyes, sit in the quiet, and try to hear the voice of the good side of me for once, instead of letting my impulses dictate all, maybe I'd have a chance to live long, stay sober—become a grown-up. I felt this upwelling of hope that I hadn't felt before. I could imagine myself not giving two shits about whether I was famous or funny or acting in stupid movies. I could even imagine myself raising a gaggle of children, loving them, believing in them more than my parents had believed in me. *I wanted that. All I wanted at that moment was to be a good father and husband. I wanted to share this amazing world with your mom and eventually, you. I wanted you to see what I saw in the sunset and the horizon and the temples, and I wanted you to feel that wind and that current, and I wanted you to grow-up to go well beyond anything your mother and I could ever show you. No matter what happened between your mother and I, you would be our continuation.*

In the afterglow of marriage, I was actually confident that everything I wanted could happen.

Your mother perched on one of the stones and began jotting in her notebook. She glanced up and saw me standing there, tears in my eyes, staring at the reddening sky beyond the many temples.

"What's wrong?" she asked.

I sat beside her and held her hand. I kissed her forehead and said that for the first time, nothing was wrong.

In Buenos Aires, we had a tour guide who was openly bitter about her lot in life.

"Where are you two from?" she asked, while Tina took photos of favelas.

"Los Angeles, originally," I said. "I live in New York now."

"You know I can never go there," she said. "I cannot travel. No money. Three children. Always hungry. I cannot travel."

"It's hard for us too," I lied. "We have to save money."

"Even if I save, not possible," she said, shaking her head and smiling. "My world small. Your world big."

She was right. Our world was big. We were lucky. We saw people dangling from the roofs of buses because they were so full, families living in huts on stilts, naked babies playing on the side of a dirt road where traffic stopped when cattle and chickens crossed. If they're lucky, their babies grew up to give bloated, whining rich people English-language tours. They didn't get educated to go to a top college or become a CEO. They got educated to serve us.

And I whine about bad movie scripts and how my mom and dad aren't proud of me?

This is what I want you to remember, M. Yeah, our family isn't what we had hoped. But you're still lucky. Even though bad luck things will happen, Master Sirius predicts that every year can be a good luck year for you.

In Fes, we walked through Talaa Kebira Street, watching camels deliver goods in Coca-Cola crates to the covered souks. We stopped by a small kisseria and got matching henna tattoos on the backs of our hands. We put our wrists together side-by-side and had a black-and-white photo taken, and it was framed in our apartment over your crib.

Whenever things were strained between me and your mom, I went into your room and eyed that photo and remembered when we both wanted the same things, and then I'd look down at you sleeping and remind myself of the best thing that we had done together.

When we returned to New York City, I started thinking through an idea for a sketch show named *Chopstuck!* If you take in any entertainment or read the news, you'd think America is divided into twos. Red and blue. Urban and rural. Black and white. Rich and poor. Republican and Democrat. Left chopstick, right chopstick. There is no third place. That's the question that inspired the show: is America chopstuck?

I recruited the guys I'd started with at *LOA*. Archimedes, Frye Johns, and Jesus Iglesias. We were going to do the show we'd always wanted to do. No one was going to marginalize us. We believed we were like most Americans: tired of categories. We didn't want to segregate laughter. I hated comedy tours with names like *Gay-larious* or *Getting Oriented* or *The Black Pack*. Why should we have to laugh in separate rooms, at our own separate comics? Shouldn't laughter bring people together?

Comedy Central gave us a season, which meant I didn't have to work on the road as much and I could spend more time with your mother. We were trying to get pregnant with you.

My favorite early *Chopstuck!* sketch was the one where four apartment neighbors (a white guy, a black lady, an Asian lady, and a Latino) get in an elevator and they all get out their phones and start posting insults about each other on text and social media.

The black lady types: *judging by his mustache, standing next to Trump supporter, haha.*

The Asian lady texts her husband: *i'm in the elevator with the woman having loud sex next door. Should I tell her to stop?*

The white guy posts on Reddit: *in the elevator in my apartment bldg in nyc. Smells like antifa in here.*

The Latino texts a friend: *should I ask him out?*

The elevator bell dings and before the white guy gets out, he says, "Y'all have a good one."

The other three smile really wide. The Latino waves and says "You, too!" as the elevator door shuts. The people of color exchange glances and the Asian lady says, "oh, he's definitely MAGA."

That's America. Talking our trash behind each other's backs and pretending not to hate one another. I hope and even sometimes pray (yes, that's right!) that you won't grow up in that Chopstuck America. I hope you'll grow up in a country where we can actually look each other in the eye and say what we truly think . . . before we decide that we're hopeless.

Tina put the finishing touches on her book and started querying literary agents. At first, she was optimistic, saying she wanted this book published before she got pregnant so she could experience in full what it was like to be an author. "I don't want to go on a book tour looking huge!" she exclaimed.

She became dogged when the first set of rejections came. "It'll find a home," she assured me (and herself). "Maybe I just need to tweak the cover letter."

After a full year of rejections, she had lunch with Kara Davidson's editor, and the lady gave her the feedback she dreaded.

"We've seen stuff like this before," she said. "The *Eat, Pray, Love* thing is over."

I told Tina it was just one person's opinion and that she should keep sending it out.

"I guess I just need to rethink it," she said, looking concussed. I wasn't sure if she was hearing me.

Slowly, she just stopped talking about the book.

Meanwhile, I was finally becoming the grown-up I wanted to be. I was happy at home and happy in comedy. I was proud. How many people can say that they're successful at doing what they genuinely care about? How many can say that they've accomplished something that people will remember them for? I guarantee you: not that many. You can't tell me that bankers out there truly care about moving money around. Lots of successful doctors and businessmen don't give a shit about anything other than paying off their massive student loans and buying sports cars. To me, that's why the world is as fucked up as it is. It's not that people can't get their American Dream. It's that most don't dream at all.

I was ready to become one of those blobby middle-aged comics who only got stage time during the summer when the kids were away at camp. I was ready to be a stroller-pushing sad sack who appeared on podcasts and never worked clubs anymore and took jobs as the sixth supporting actor with three unfunny lines in a Will Ferrell or Adam Sandler shitpile. I was okay with this, I fucking swear.

Your mother became super anxious that she was too old to be having a child even though women her age (thirty-four) were having kids all the time. We saw fertility experts and made backup plans for IVF and adoption from Africa even though doctors were telling her she was completely healthy and my sperm was up to snuff. Honestly, the last thing I wanted to do was bring an African baby into America, given our country's track record. Sure it's better than starving or being barefoot in an orphanage in a country run by a despot, but I didn't want my kid brought up thinking he was part of a club only to find out that he wasn't and that no one would ever give him a straight answer about it. I kept these opinions to myself though . . . and saved it for a bit I did on *The Late Show*, in which instead of adopting an African baby, I wanted to be adopted as a dad, even if the family already had one. I could be like a sixth man in basketball. *Need to go out on a bender with the boys? Put me in coach. I can be an African dad for a night.*

Then you came into the world. I had expected a new part of me to emerge, like a fifth chamber of the heart, where I could be protective and loving of you in a way that fatherhood demanded. Having you felt instead like I grew a second heart, Siamesed with my first, sloshing with profound waves of new emotions. Every time you discovered a new sound or a new way to use your fingers (and you seemed to discover something new about yourself every thirty minutes), I was overwhelmed with joy. Every time you wanted something you didn't know how to ask for and began crying, I felt fear so desperate I had to tell myself to breathe. For months, I had nightmares that, just as suddenly as you had come into our lives, you'd be taken away by some unforeseen catastrophe.

Soon, we became more accustomed to raising you, and I remember your first year as a time when I did a decent job of maintaining a relatively peaceful home with your mother.

But it was work. There's a downside to trying to survive marriage via constant retreat: when we had you, your mother began wanting it all, even the contradictions. She'd want me to wake with her during feedings, but wouldn't let me help in any way. Then when I would nod off, bored from inactivity, she'd rail at me for my lack of engagement. She'd say she needed a break from taking care of you twenty-four-seven, but then she'd rarely leave the house, even when I offered to take you for a few hours so she could get coffee, see a friend, or take a yoga class. I felt like I was in a factory making Good Dad Widgets twenty hours a day and your mom was examining each widget and flipping it into the trash.

I became afraid of going out in public with her because I was never sure that she wouldn't explode at some dog owner whose lab was getting too close to the stroller or an elderly woman who dared to take up the last two-top in a coffee shop. I was at a drugstore formerly named Rite Aid, formerly named Walgreens, currently named Duane Reade, and I glimpsed a *Marie Claire* magazine headline about postpartum depression. After reading the article, I began to suspect that your mother might have suffered from it. She was not the same person that I had met and fallen in love with. One night, I, very tactfully, brought up the possibility of her seeing a therapist.

"What are you talking about?" she said, holding you to her chest while you napped.

"I'm just saying it never hurts to talk to someone," I said. "I needed it. In rehab, if I didn't talk it out, I wouldn't have gotten out alive."

Your mother laughed. "Come on, you were an addict and an alcoholic," she said. "That's different. I just had a wonderful baby." She smiled at you. "I feel fine. I feel great, in fact. Mentally. Physically, I'm a little beat up."

"I've noticed you have more of a temper now."

"It's because I've had my vagina ripped open by a friggin' baby," Tina said. "My breasts feel like gas pumps on the busiest highway in New Jersey. I'm sorry I'm not cheerful and zen enough for you."

After your second birthday, your mother went back to work, getting a job at a big law firm, and I became the stay-at-home dad. She became vegan so I became a vegan cook. We had cauliflower casserole every fucking week for two years because she loved it. (As mentioned earlier, I've never been sold on the purported benefits of fruits and vegetables. *How can we trust food guidelines written by that powerful kale lobby in Washington?*) I dropped you off and picked you up from day care and preschool. On the walls of our foyer, I put up framed photos of the places in the world your mother and I had been: the Taj Majal, Machu Picchu, the pyramids in Egypt. Right beside the photos of you, smiling, mouth open, all your poses making us gush.

Hadn't we achieved happiness—at least, an adult, some-where-between-contemplative-and-ecstatic version of it?

Hadn't I, at minimum, checked all the boxes of a B-minus husband and father?

Weren't we, at minimum, just another set of parents doing our best?

This was what family was all about, right? Feeling like you were doing your best when you were actually doing the minimum?

I began to savor time away from our shrinking brown-stone in a neighborhood where every man looked like Mr.

Keaton from *Family Ties* and wore two-decade-old baggy cargo shorts and unironed medium-sized tees horribly shrunken in the wash. I practically ejaculated every time I was sent out to buy diapers. Perhaps those percolating feelings should have served as an early warning that happily-ever-after was more of a never-gonna-happen.

I started doing drop-ins again on MacDougal Street. I told your mother I was working on a new hour, and we got sitters almost every weeknight when she had to stay late at work. Dan Van Pido invited me to headline the 8:00 p.m. "industry showcase" (read: an audition arranged by a group of amateur comics as a bringer show). I showed up early at the open mic like I did when I first moved to New York.

Outside, there was a sandwich board that read "Comudy Mic" in shaky chalk-written script. The room downstairs smelled of cat urine. About thirty comics sat quietly, scattered around the room. Separated from the rest of the performers, a man hunched alone at a round table beside a mic stand. He counted bills and placed them in an envelope that had a list of names written on the back. He was in his late thirties, meat-cheeked with a prematurely gray mustache. He wore thin-rimmed glasses and a tightly tucked plaid shirt, a combination that made him look like a domestic terrorist. He asked me for the five-dollar fee.

"I'm Sirius Lee, dude."

"Okay," he said. "Five bucks."

Sigh. It had been seven years since *No Good Very Bad Asian*. If Aziz (brown), Chapelle (black), or Sarah Silverman (white) walked into an open mic, they'd be mobbed. But the famous yellow guy? In-fucking-visible.

I paid and my name was added to the back of the envelope. I perched on a barstool with a ripped cushion cover. A man wearing pajamas and flip-flops was first up.

"I've been so depressed lately," he said. "My doctor tells me I need to keep taking my meds, but I don't think they're working. I want to commit suicide, but I'm too lazy."

No one laughed. The man then diatribed about his ingrown toenail, a story I easily verified by looking down at his feet. He continued talking, not telling any jokes, spewing into a silent void.

The next twenty comics came to the stage. One read from a wire-bound notebook, doing a seemingly endless bit about the lengths she went to stalk her boyfriend on social media. A woman did thirty jokes without pausing, all about the humiliation of working at IHOP. A man from Zimbabwe showed off an upper arm tattoo of his wife's name "Dana," then joked that he could still have the "a" removed if he wanted to switch teams. The other seventeen comics did Donald Trump or Hillary Clinton jokes. When my turn finally came, I got up in front of the six gruff-looking comics that remained.

I decided not to do any old material, just the jokes I'd written that day. The mic grill smelled like rank spit.

"I have kids now," I said. "A three-year-old daughter. And a thirty-year-old inferiority complex."

Crickets. To my surprise, my body began to tremble. I tried to stay rigid but couldn't control the nerves. I could only hope that my fear wasn't noticeable.

"What else have I got?" I muttered. "I just want to be a good dad. In quantity. Not quality. Just want lots and lots of kids."

Someone in the crowd laughed. I squinted into the darkness and tried to acknowledge the person with a nod and a smile. Then I saw that the laughter came from the guy who joked about the tattoo of his wife's name, and he was laughing at the whispers of the comic who stalked her boyfriend on social media. I wasn't just bombing; I was inhaling souls.

"In the country Marriage, the national currency is Sex, and the economy is really bad," I said.

Several, single barks of laughter resembled the hospice worker of laughs: perfunctory and mirthless. At least the comics were trying to be kind.

"I'm going to leave you with this," I said, my mouth dry. "Why does it smell like cat urine in here?"

Big laughs. Even the man who ran the mic giggled.

After I got off stage, I felt a bone-deep exhaustion. Longest five minutes of my life. I hadn't felt so out of sorts on stage since the early days with Johnny in L.A. But I found myself reliving the cat urine laugh—the big one. It still felt good: walking the high wire without a safety net and getting to the other side. Electric. The laughter's imaginary echo filled me up somehow.

Outside, Pidofile was smoking. His eyes were wide when he saw me.

"What the fuck were you doing in there?" he managed between coughs. "Are you divorced already?"

VERONICA

You were almost four when I got a voicemail from Veronica. She had moved back to New York to work on an album and had broken up with Nils.

How was I doing? she asked. How was I doing? I wondered.

Your mother was taking photos of you riding around the living room on a Barbie Trike. I stared at you two, smiling in our classy white person's brownstone, a few months after Donald Trump was elected president. Many of us Americans were discovering new, bleaker sides of ourselves, and my bones vibrated as I stood there, feeling for the first time that I might have been playing a father and husband instead of *being* one.

Your mother asked who'd called.

"Apparently I've won another free Caribbean cruise," I said.

"Grandpa and grandma are here!" your mom said to you.

You sauntered to the foyer, expressionless.

Your grandpa greeted me with a formal nod and forklifted you in the air. "Grandpa's here!" he bellowed with a huge smile. You began batting at his gray crew cut and tried to remove his glasses until he set you down. You ran to your mother and bear-hugged her leg and started pulling on it.

"We can get you your own prosthetic," I joked.

Your grandma embraced me, longer than I liked. Dressed in all black as usual from her cardigan to her orthopedic shoes, she periscoped the apartment, took a deep breath, and said, "Mommy's here."

"Hey Mah . . . muh . . . eee," I said, still uncomfortable with her insistence on me calling her that. "M, say 'Hi' to Grandma. She came all the way from the end of the seven line, which now takes about seven hours thanks to the MTA."

You remained silent, returning to your playthings. Your grandma squatted beside you on the living room rug as you used a toy tablet to pancake a splay-legged baby doll.

"It's okay," she said. "You don't have to call me anything." Then in Mandarin, she added with a smile, "Her skin is so beautiful and white."

"Ooh, that is problematic," I falsettoed.

"We try not to say that she's beautiful, pretty, or cute, Mom," Tina said. To you, she added, "Even though you are."

"We don't want Maryann to be defined at all by her looks," I said. "We want her to feel like she can literally be anything she ever wants to be. We definitely don't want her to grow up thinking that her main life goals should be to find a mate and become a baby machine. That's some Baby Boomer Bullshit, amirite?!"

"Sirius!" Tina said.

"Oops, BS," I corrected.

Your grandparents looked at us like we were crazy, but it was the one parenting principle your mother and I agreed upon. After all the disrespect my mom and your mom endured in their relationships with men (myself included), after all the obstacles I had to hurdle almost from the day I was born, from the white kids in class always being chosen to speak, to Marsden High and Hollywood, I want you to be able to choose your own adventure and be judged only by your actions and accomplishments—and not by our zombie eyes. Maybe when you're older, you'll find our parenting suffocating in the same way I found the Lee Council suffocating. But your mother and I had our reasons, just as our parents had theirs.

Your grandpa turned to me and asked, "So when are you two having more?"

Detective McMillan wouldn't have liked the true answer. Your mother and I hadn't slept together in months. We had simply been too busy, too distant. Her with work and me with you and what was, after Comedy Central canceled *Chopstuck!*, quickly becoming a comedy career in steep decline. I felt bad about disappointing your grandpa, but before I could answer "maybe," your mother blurted, "One's plenty!"

Looking stung, he sat on the couch and inhaled deeply and rhythmically as if in a state of meditation.

"She's very quiet," your grandma said about you as you continued to smash your doll. "Like her granddad." She looked at her husband.

He smiled. "My biggest regret was not giving you a brother or sister," he said to Tina.

"*Ai-yuh*," Ms. McMillan said, shaking her head. "Stop talking nonsense and just be happy with what you have."

Your grandpa sighed. "I'm trying."

That night, in our bedroom, after your grandparents were gone and you were in bed, your mother turned off the lights and said, "Let's go somewhere far."

I sat up, excited by the prospects of an adventure. "Yeah, like where? Asia, South America, Africa again?"

"How about London or Berlin?" she said. "I could ask for a transfer."

"Oh," I said. "So, not like a vacation?"

"I'm not young anymore," she said. "I can't just quit my job and travel the world with you and Maryann."

"We have enough money," I said. "I wouldn't know what to do in London long-term. I don't know if I want to give up what I have here. I know New York and L.A."

"You're not doing anything big right now anyway."

"Yeah, but I don't want to quit," I said. "I still want Sarah to put me out there."

Your mother was quiet. With rue, she said, "You're right. You're represented. Someone who matters believes in you."

I recalled her writing, how much her failure must have hurt. Your mother might someday tell you a different story, but I'm going to tell it like I saw it: she hadn't really failed. She'd just stopped showing up.

"We should take a few months though, like we did before," I said. "We can travel. You can write."

Your mother laughed. "Oh, jeez, I'm not a writer anymore."

While you were at day care, I met Veronica for lunch at an Italian place outside her recording studio in Midtown. She was bleach blonde, wearing hot pants and heels even though it was forty degrees out. She said she'd been working with a trainer hired by the record label. She was going to collaborate with some of hip-hop's biggest producers. Maybe she'd even get to do a song with Rihanna.

"You look really good, Sirius."

I knocked on the wooden table. She called me Sirius. The ex-boyfriend. Someone she might consider hooking up with if drunk enough.

"So what happened to Paris?"

Veronica shrugged. "Nils and I just ran out of steam. He wanted to stay in France. I didn't. I have no roots there. Then the record deal happened."

"He seemed kind of old for you." From the tabloids, I knew Nils Pettersson was a gray-haired Swedish duke, seventh in line for the throne.

Veronica laughed like what I'd said was much funnier than it was. "My dad is still pissed at you for firing him." She revealed that Johnny was back with Sherry. There was even talk about a new incarnation of *The Family Razzmatazz* for Bravo.

"He's sober too," Veronica said. "He even ran a half marathon last year."

"Wow. I have a tough time imagining your dad running, period."

I apologized for how I'd behaved in the past. I told Veronica that I'd changed. Rehab had changed me. Traveling had changed me. Fatherhood had changed me. I should have said your mother had changed me.

"How's your wife?" she asked, glancing at my ring.

"Oh yeah, I answered a mail-order ad," I joked. "No, I met her through my manager. She's a lawyer."

"Oh."

"A writer, too. Essays and stuff."

I told Veronica about my travels overseas and how I was seeking a broader, longer-term view of life and how I really wanted to be a good husband and father—a better parent than mine were. Veronica's eyes glazed over. I sounded genuine. But why did I want her to melt and tell me what a good person I was being?

"Hey," she said, reaching across the table to tap the back of my hand. "You want to collaborate on my album?"

"Like how?"

"I'm thinking an intro with your standup," she said. "Or a funny song of your own. You've always been so funny, Sirius."

Your mother came home late from work, after I'd put you to bed. She heated up leftovers and asked how my day was.

"Good," I said. "Had a meeting in the city. Wrote a few jokes. What do you think of this one? 'I got married recently. Answered a mail-order ad. It was very competitive.'"

"How was Veronica Razzmatazz?"

My antennae went up. What had I told her about Veronica?

"You had lunch with her."

Your mother found out about my date with my ex like every wife should: through the *Huffington Post* celebrity page.

"Yeah, that's right, we did lunch. Didn't I tell you?"

The microwave bell dinged. She pulled out her plastic-wrapped plate and slammed the door hard enough to startle.

"It just slipped my mind."

"And your collaboration on her album?"

Shiiiiiiit. "It's no big deal."

"She thinks it's a big deal," she said. "She says she can't wait to work with her ex."

"Who told you this?"

"That's what she said to *People Magazine*!" she shouted. "I can fucking Google, you know!"

I began to sweat, waiting for the sounds of your awakening to flow down the hall. "I'm not even sure I agreed to do anything. This is fake news!"

"I get it," she said. "You still have a thing for her."

"Let's not overreact," I said. "Nothing's even happened yet."

"Yet?"

"Poor choice of words."

Your mother sat on our slipcovered couch and shoveled vegan casserole into her mouth as she steamed.

"There's nothing going on between me and her," I said. "That was a long time ago."

"Then why did you lie about it?"

"I didn't," I said. "I just chose not to mention it. If there's nothing going on, what's there to mention?"

She shook her head repeatedly. "I thought you couldn't hurt me."

"Please don't make this bigger than it is."

She got up and put her finished plate in the sink. She wiped her mouth with a napkin and without saying a word, marched to the door.

"Where are you going?" I asked.

The door clicked shut and our home was suddenly silent.

Of course, that was when you called out from your room for your mother.

She didn't come home for three days. I had no idea where she went. I told you she was on a business trip. I called and called and called to no answer. None of her friends would tell me where she was. The McMillans wouldn't return my calls, and when I went by their house, no one was home. It was one of the scarier things I'd ever been through. I imagined every horrific scenario happening to her. For those three days, I felt like I had stepped off a cliff and was falling and falling for hours and hours.

When she came back, she refused to explain herself.

"Maybe I went out and had a fuck-fest," she snarled.

Ms. McMillan would later tell me that she and your grandpa took your distraught mother upstate to Hudson for the weekend. A few weeks after our blow-up, I met Veronica in her recording studio and immediately saw, when she let me in, that there was no producer in attendance. She took my face in her hands and kissed me and I kissed her back and lay down right there on that parquet, acoustic-friendly floor.

Because she was my first love.

Because I'm a bad person.

Oh God, M, I'm such an awful husband and father. *Je suis désolé.*

I never told your mother about the affair.

Veronica was back and forth between New York and Los Angeles when she wasn't touring. We never did collaborate on anything other than lovemaking in the same city.

"You're not a bad person," she said as we lay in bed in a Midtown hotel room. "You're one of my oldest friends. I don't know bad people."

I stared at the fire sprinkler head, wishing it would go off and flush us clean and out of our urban sin cave.

"We all want to think that," I said. "Those who think that most often are usually the worst people."

"There are those who will never leave," she said. "And then there are the ones you deserve."

I knew which category she put me in, but I still hoped the girl I'd known since I was fourteen would think of me as more than a category. There we were, sharing a bed, and she was still wearing makeup. Deep down, I knew I'd never truly know her.

"It's unfair," I said.

She took my hand and placed it over her chest so I could feel her imperfect heart beating. "What we have is special."

"Like Special Olympics."

She tossed my hand aside and turned her back to me. "Hor, your family will never find out, okay? I'm not going *Fatal Attraction* on you."

Of course, she wouldn't. What would her four million Twitter followers think? I'd read the trolls. *He looks like a potato. He reminds me of a fish. He's soooooo ugly. My dog is better-looking than him. What is she thinking?* Trending: #veronicarazzmatazz and her rumored #Asian #boyfriend #cheating #married.

I loved your mother, I swear to God. I swear on your life. I loved her with all my heart.

I know this will hurt you to read, but I loved Veronica, too. Because I love pain.

All my life, I've been filled with the capacity to love and be loved. I'd like to think that my capacity is larger than that of most people. That's why it hurt so much when my parents wouldn't love me the way I needed. That's why it hurt so much when Johnny never saw me as a son. That's why it hurt so much when Veronica left me the first time. If you love without restraint, you will experience bottomless loss at some point. And you might experience a ceilingless joy that others will never glimpse.

I've been lucky enough to have experienced both. Who would I have been had I not chosen not to walk out to Skeet-shooting Johnny that day at the Razzmatazz villa, looking for a hero, looking for someone to love? Would I ever have taken the stage? Would I have gotten to experience the joy of making others laugh for a living?

I know that you'll grow up to be better than me, and I know you probably won't want to resemble your old man in any way. But I hope that you'll be someone who plunges headlong into life and love. I hope you'll grow up to be a person of passion, a dreamer, a romantic. I hope you'll get to feel the highs that I've felt, even if it means you'll feel the most intense of lows.

Your mother's job took her out-of-town more and more. When she was home, I'd cook dinner for you two, and we'd have a quiet night as a family like I was the head of my own Lee Council. Slowly, I noticed that all we talked about was you. How you were doing socially. Whether you should take dancing lessons or tee-ball. You were best friends with a boy and a girl your age, and we wondered whether you were old enough to have romantic feelings for one or the other. Your mother's and my goals had vanished. I was getting nowhere on my new hour. I could no longer imagine your mother joking about how white guys wanted to date her for the exotic adventure. She never joked about anything anymore, at least not around me. Our marriage began to feel like we were running out the clock until your eighteenth birthday.

When your mother was away, sometimes, I'd take you with me to my late night gigs, even though a comedy show was no place for kids. One night, I took you with me to my friend and fellow comic Neil Turnelle's Paradise Lounge show. On the way there, Veronica texted "In NYC. U?"

I told her where to meet me.

The Paradise Lounge was a dive bar with a back room behind a musty, red curtain. Our ears were subjected to an aural bludgeoning of white-boy rap metal (was that Limp Biskit?). A round-backed Latino fellow on a stool checked IDs. I asked if it was okay to bring you in.

"She's a really short twenty-two-year-old," I said.

He returned my card and waved us on without even glancing at you.

Behind the curtain, there was a crowd of about fifty. The room was filled with plush couches, loveseats, and armchairs. There was only space for us on the L-shaped sofa, where Turnelle sat. He was a skinny, plaid-wearing white guy with a fat, collar-hanging beard and dark-rimmed glasses. He wore jeans cuffed white up to his knees. Why would a six-foot-tall guy buy jeans for someone six-foot-seven? He also had heavily inked forearms. Lots of teeth in the body art. Smiling gnomes, laughing ghouls, chomping animals, and the like. I asked him to roll down his sleeves for you.

"What's she doing here?"

"She's my biggest fan."

"Has she paid the cover?"

I laughed. Turnelle's eyes widened. He was wondering what was so funny.

I paid the ten-dollar cover for you.

Turnelle covered his forearms. He pointed out the co-producers of the show: Nestor and his wife Ina. Both morbidly obese, they occupied every bit of space on a loveseat. Ina had a laptop open on her thighs. Turnelle said Nestor would emcee.

Nestor looked at you, then me. "Yours?"

I nodded.

He gripped his knees and rocked back and forth, mustering the momentum to unwedge himself. When Nestor finally stood, he fished a handful of assorted misshapen sweets from his pocket and shoved a full paw at you.

"I'm Nestor. Want candy?"

"Yes!" you said.

"No!" I stepped between the two of you. "I just want to show M here what Daddy does for a living."

Nestor swallowed and averted my gaze. "Listen, just to be clear in case Neil wasn't, we're only paying ten bucks a spot."

"Wow," I said. My career was truly in the toilet. Out of the corner of my eye, I saw Veronica, waiting in the shadows. "I'll be right back," I told you and Nestor, like she was saying the words for me.

Ponytailed Veronica was wearing a cheerleading skirt, a sleeveless top, and knee-high white platform boots. (Brace yourself, my love.) In the tiny bathroom, she rode me in a rush, with her eyes closed, lights off, while she whispered "Sirius, Sirius, Sirius."

When I waddled back to the show, Nestor was on the stage, which was not much larger than a home satellite dish; he looked like he was balancing on a saucer. He was doing a bit about how he used to be a Catholic priest with a side business as a candy distributor, and he had no idea why parents were so protective of their children around him. The crowd tittered uncomfortably and Ina rolled her eyes. I looked around for you, but you were nowhere to be found. I asked her where you went.

Ina said nothing, remaining motionless. Was she breathing? Maybe when she was rolling her eyes at Nestor, she was actually having some sort of aneurysm. Nestor announced that the first comic was a very funny guy who performed all around the city. I waved in front of Ina's frozen eyes.

She slapped my hand away. "What the fuck are you doing?"

I released a soft, frightened yelp as Nestor said, "You've seen him in movies like *The Plunger* and National Lampoon's *Bangkok Family Vacation*, put your hands together for the one and only Sirius Lee!"

Apparently, Turnelle didn't tell Nestor I was the headliner.

Nestor stepped down and handed me the mic. "Candy!" he shouted for reasons unknown.

I got up under the lights. "Big candy enthusiast, that Nestor," I said. "And I don't mean John Candy, if you know what I mean."

No one knew what I meant.

"I have kids," I said. "A four-year-old daughter. And an inferiority complex that's thirty-one."

From the invisible silence, I heard, "Meaty okra, Daddy."

The crowd laughed. You were standing next to the stage. "Mommy said you're meaty okra!" You were trying to say "mediocre."

"You're killing, M!" I said. "That's my daughter Maryann, everyone! She thinks this is my roast."

"What's with your transgender beard?" someone in back shouted.

I hadn't shaved in a couple of weeks. "Talk to Nestor if you want stage time, buddy," I said. "I think you need to bring like twenty people if you're not a real comic like me."

The crowd oohed.

"Opening at a bar show seems pretty pathetic to me," retorted the heckler.

"Do you want to do my set for me?" I held out the mic. "You sound like a comedy expert. Why don't you step on up here and kill? Come on!"

He staggered out of the shadows and in front of the stage. He was tall and white with a curt, Hitler-esque mustache; he appeared college-age. His eyes were pink from drink. I waited for Nestor or Ina to step in, but they were making out. The loveseat shuddered from their moving heft. You were watching them.

"Why don't you tell your daughter that you just fucked another guy's girl?" the heckler said.

Ugh. I looked around for Veronica. Of course, she was gone. "I'm not who you think I am," I said. "Must be another Asian comic. You probably think we all look alike."

He pounced, and before I could get my arms up, I was falling backwards onto the stack of speakers and chairs behind the stage. Tall Hitler was on top of me, hitting me repeatedly in the face. "I know who you fucking are!" he kept shouting, spraying me with boozy fumes and spittle.

I curled into a ball and heard you wailing and Nestor asking you again if you wanted candy. Tall Hitler lost interest once he realized I wasn't fighting back. "You were funnier when you were fat," he said, dismounting me.

I uncovered, dazed. You were up in Nestor's arms. He apologized to Veronica's boyfriend and said that it was Turnelle's idea to put me up because I used to be famous.

"Hey, I'm still famous!" I said, getting to my feet.

To the audience filing out of the room, Nestor announced, "Let's take five. Everyone grab a drink. Then we'll start the show for real." He reluctantly put you down.

"Daddy, you're bleeding," you blubbered.

I tasted my split lip. "I know, M, don't cry." I scanned the room again for Veronica. I saw her being dragged out by Tall Hitler. "Sorry dude," she texted the next day.

Speaking of texts, your mother had texted and called a dozen times. To my chagrin, she was home. She had just gone to D.C. for the day. For some reason (perhaps wishful thinking?), I had thought she was staying the night there.

When we got back, your mother was waiting in the living room, hands on hips, wearing her sleeping outfit: a faded, over-sized half marathon T-shirt and chocolate yoga pants. Her hair flowed down to her elbows and I ached inside. I'd always thought she was most beautiful with her hair down. She was also most beautiful when I was fucking up.

"What the hell?" she said, wide-eyed and flushed at the sight of you curled up in my arms and asleep. "Where have you been? Why are you ignoring my calls and texts? What happened to your face?"

I told her I had been in a fight at a comedy show.

"You took her to a comedy show?" she exclaimed. "Are you drinking again?"

"I did not drink. There was some drunk heckler—"

"He said Dad bucked some other guy's girl!" you woke to say.

Your mom gasped. Her face became redder and redder. I put you down and you ran into her arms.

"She's just repeating one of the jokes she heard," I said.

"You might as well start drinking again." Her voice was strangely calm. She held your hand and led you to bed. I stood there, alone, heart racing, staring at my unusually small feet and the fucking worthless steps forward I took everyday to end up the same asshole I was born to be.

Parched and numb, I left. I simply couldn't imagine being there in the morning, looking you in the eye and pretending everything was okay when I had been cheating on your mother. I had failed so fucking badly. I desperately wanted a drink. I felt like I was floating, guided by an unseen, silent force—perhaps my former self. I felt like I did when my father slapped me when I was a kid. Lost. Ignored. Inadequate. Dissolving.

I got on the two train headed back toward Village Z, where I planned to drop-in for the midnight show. Going from car to car was a man in a dusty winter coat and ill-fitting jeans slung low on his hips, ragged at the hems. He was white, in his mid-to-late twenties. The train was filled with blacks and Dominicans; many of them were high schoolers out late. The guy held a trash bag with snag holes that exposed briefs and other clothing inside.

"Please everybody, could you please give me some change, something to eat, a candy bar, a granola bar, trail mix, anything," he asked. "I'm so hungry. I lost my job two years ago and now I'm homeless. Please! I've been up and down this line all day and night and I have about a dollar! Please! Could someone give me something? Anything!"

He went to each passenger, trying to look the person in the eye. *I'm a young man who lost his job. I used to work in customer care for a bank. I'm college-educated.* Not one person gave. I started pulling out my wallet. I was going to hand him a hundred. But he walked right past me, onto the next car like I wasn't even there.

That night, I laid a horse blanket on stage and slept at Village Z.

I didn't know then that I would never live with you and your mother again.

RELAX, I'M HILARIOUS

O n the day I discovered your mother cheating on me, I dropped by the apartment while you were at school to get some clothes because I'd been staying at an Airbnb. In the living room, there was a tall male figure framed by the light of the windows facing our yard. His back was turned. His shoulders were sloped. He appeared armless. Your mother spoke softly, incomprehensibly, in a singsong voice I'd only heard in the middle of the night years ago, when she was nursing you.

When I said her name, she wriggled free of her lover, whose hulking upper body was mummified in a tee that bore the message: "Relax, I'm Hilarious." Your mother's hair was tousled and moist and her face was flushed. They'd just gotten out of a long shower, judging from the backdraft of soapy fumes hanging over them.

"You can't be surprised," she explained while her new man stared at the floor, his crossed pale forearms rippling and shining like the rods of a rotisserie. "You still want Veronica. Even if you're not fucking her already, God knows Twitter thinks you are. We're not good enough for each other anymore."

In your mother's version of first-person plural, she was not included. She went on to detail my inability to take seriously her "adult ambitions," which included becoming partner at her

law firm and paying for private schooling for you and a larger
house in New Jersey or Long Island. Her paramour was named
Gunther. They had met ten years ago on a Eurail to Prague. Yup,
you guessed it. The Prague Icelandic with whom she walked
day and night before finally kissing on the Charles Bridge at
sunrise. He was now a European patent attorney, working for a
multinational in the city, your mom informed me.

"I'm making a transition to computer programmer," he
corrected. "I want to develop apps."

"I need an app where I can erase this from my story in less
than twenty-four hours," I said.

Your mother said that she had never stopped loving him.

"How long has this been happening?" I asked. "Before or
after we went vegan? Because I want all that time back."

"Isn't that a metaphysical question for both of us?"

She was right, of course. What did it matter whether I
cheated first or she did? Either way, our marriage was Hiro-
shima. I lowered myself onto the sofa and felt the currents of
my grandfather and my father course through my body as your
mother went on to whale away at who I failed to be, for her,
for you. I was my grandpa sitting quietly reading a newspaper
while my grandma called him useless. I was John Hak Kay Soy
Lee sipping port and looking around the dining table at a life he
didn't want, getting ready to make that night walk to the South
Pasadena light rail station to eye those trainless tracks and wonder
if tonight was the night he'd have the courage to give up.

"I'm not grinding out the rest of my days in misery, so
Maryann can have a better life," she said. "Gunther makes me
feel like it's not absurd to want things other than another twenty
minutes at Village Z."

Gunther shook his head slowly as if to say, "Damn, I didn't
know things were that bad!" My head felt pressured like I
was deep in the ocean. I recalled the sound of your wailing

in Prospect Park that time your helium-filled balloon tragically floated out of your hand and into the sky.

"Nothing?" your mother said. "I'm pouring my heart out and nothing?"

"I thought this might be happiness," I said. "The grown-up version."

She walked to the front door and swung it wide open.

"What happened to our dreams?" I asked.

She remained stone-faced, refusing to look me in the eye. "We grew up," she said.

First-person plural.

I moved into a new apartment in SoHo, which looked much like the loft Johnny and I had lived in when we first moved to New York City. One morning, I woke cheek-down, my head inside the television stand, the rest of my body prostrated on the floor. My whiskey tumbler was on its side, just out of reach, adjacent a braid of power cords. How the glass and I had gotten where we were, I had no recollection.

A fire shived the bladder. I hurried to the bathroom, kicking over a near-empty bottle of Maker's Mark. I skated besocked across tiles, barely managing to undo my zipper before casting a thick, wayward rope of brassy urine that smacked the toilet rim and splattered the ground.

I loosed a madman's cackle at the mess I'd made before my bowels started barking. I lifted the wet toilet seat and plopped down, groaning as my insides compressed like an accordion's bellows. Only after I'd finished did I realize that I was also weeping. Because I'd lost your mother, I'd lost you, and I'd lost my sobriety.

A month later, I was in the Brooklyn Heights office of Cecilia Fabregas, Tina's divorce attorney. Cecilia was a thin older woman who resembled Barbara Billingsley. (Look her up.) She wore a navy blue business suit, and her fingers-only handshake felt like a bag of loose candies. Your mother and I had begun splitting time with you. She was late for our cleaving.

"Do you have any questions for me?" Cecilia asked.

"Can you recommend any good time travel agents?"

She didn't even smile. "If the desire for divorce is mutual and uncontested, the work ahead can be fairly straightforward." When I didn't respond, she added, "Implicitly, I'm asking a question."

She wanted to know whether I would contest Tina's filing, whether I planned to hire my own attorney. I wanted to look your mother in the eye once more to see if there was anything left between us, whether we could leave our mistakes in the past and give it one more try for your sake. Veronica was on a world tour, opening for Katy Perry, and I hadn't heard from her in six months. I told myself we were over, even though I wasn't sure if that was true. I had been leaving messages for your mother telling her not to throw away our four years together. I wanted to know if she'd realized—now that we were about to sign the papers, now that it was pretty much too late—that our family meant something more and transcended our own selfish desires. I tried to think of what I could offer in the way of improving the husband I'd become. All I could think of was 1) not cheating and 2) taking cooking lessons or Pilates together.

"I'd like to speak with Tina before I make any decisions."

"That's what I recommend as well," Cecilia said. "I'd like to reiterate how easy it can be to get a fresh start in the state of New York, even with young children. It's quite amazing how sophisticated kids have become in navigating divorced parents. Just the other day, I read in the *Times* that children call the D train the Divorce train."

"My daughter is too young to be taking the subway unsupervised," I pointed out, impressed at how responsible I sounded.

"You can turn back the clock on your unhappiness." She opened a bony hand and swept it in a counterclockwise semicircle. She began the motion again.

"If you don't mind, I'd just like to wait quietly for my wife, thanks." I crossed my legs and folded hands over knees. There were many, many framed family pictures on Cecilia's desk. She appeared to have at least ten children and twenty grandchildren, or five children and about twenty-five nieces and nephews. And her husband was either one-armed, or his second arm was permanently hidden behind a beaming Cecilia.

"Some of my clients tell me I talk too much and lack empathy," she said, moving papers from one stack to another.

I neither responded nor disagreed.

Your mother finally appeared, twenty minutes late, her hair still wet, and one of the cuffs on her blouse was unbuttoned. "I'm so sorry," she said, tugging on the hem of her pencil skirt.

"Pumpkin!" Cecilia cried out. She got up and hugged Tina, pecking both cheeks.

"I've missed you so!" your mother said, smiling as she sat next to me.

I looked at her, then Cecilia. "Guess I'd better get my own lawyer," I said.

"I told you that would be best for both of us," your mom said.

"It would be my recommendation that you get your own attorney as well, Mr. Lee, if you decide to contest," Cecilia said.

"You can call me Sirius," I said. "No one calls me Mr. Lee. Not even a jury duty clerk."

"An equitable distribution could be difficult to ascertain, Sirius," Cecilia said. "You don't have a prenup, and you have numerous income streams from your movies, your comedy special, and your TV work in syndication."

"Trust me, I'm fine if you don't want to get a lawyer," your mother said. "It'll be less complicated and cheaper for both of us."

"You know what would have been cheaper, too? Not sleeping with the MMA fighter."

Cecilia failed to suppress a chortle. Your mother glared at her. "So you want to contest?" she said to me.

Weight settled in my chest. All this grown-up and legal talk bored the shit out of me. This was not how it was supposed to be. Your mother was supposed to walk in, and I was supposed to tell her I was sorry. I was supposed to say I understood why she cheated on me. I was even supposed to admit that I'd cheated on her. My lips parted, and I could feel the right words rising in my throat, but that was where my taking of the high road stalled. Your mother's eyes were unflinching. We'd been married for five years, I realized. Not four. I had miscounted. She hadn't corrected me.

I told your mother I didn't want her boyfriend sleeping over at her apartment on the nights you were there.

"You don't have a say in how I conduct myself."

"I do when it's about Maryann."

"Gunther doesn't spend the night," she said to Cecilia.

"Premature ejaculator, huh?"

"Lasts forever compared to you."

Cecilia waited for us to finish, her gaze distant, like she'd heard this conversation many times before during other client meetings.

"You're the one leaving," I said. "You get to make all the decisions too?"

"Funny that you're all of a sudden interested in making parenting decisions," she said. "You were pretty happy with being the logistics guy before."

I was so angry I couldn't even manage a "fuck you."

"I'm not trying to make this personal," your mother said. "I just want what's fair financially for me and Maryann according to the laws of the state of New York. We have plenty of money for private school, and I'm not saying you'll never get to see her. If I left the decision-making to you, it'd be okay for Maryann to be a high school dropout."

"I don't want her to become a fucking boring materialist drone like your friends."

Tina inhaled deeply through her nose with shut eyes. When she opened them, she shook her head at Cecilia. "He thinks I gave up on my dreams," she said. "He thinks you can only have one. I traveled. I wrote. I didn't publish a book, but that's okay. I want other things now. I have new dreams. Like having Maryann was one of my dreams. Apparently, that wasn't one on his list."

Cecilia turned to me and waited for a response.

"I'll get a lawyer and we'll fight," I said through clenched teeth. "Five years and we rarely fought. Yeah, that's right. Five. Not four. Maybe Mr. Iceland can develop an app to help you keep track of how long we've been married."

Cecilia giggled. "He's funny," she said to your mother, who was dull-eyed, seemingly unimpressed.

"I am a comedian," I said.

"Your tax returns say 'actor.'"

"Doesn't say 'good one,'" your mother said.

I snorted. "I'm not the only comedian in the family."

It was raining out when I picked you up from school. I had forgotten an umbrella. We had a long walk to the subway and you started crying.

"What's wrong?" I asked.

"My shoes are wet," you said.

"Getting wet is not something you cry about," I said. "I shat my pants in class when I was your age, and I didn't cry."

You just blubbered louder.

I was high. I had done some coke on the way over. Just a little. Like back when I was on *LOA*. Just enough to get through the anxiety of seeing you. I was sweaty and itchy and nauseous, and every sound seemed amplified. I also had an inexplicable craving for Flour Shop's signature Rainbow Cake.

"Maryann, I'm warning you," I said. "I'm going to leave you here if you don't stop fucking crying."

You tried. But it wasn't good enough for me. I took off toward the subway stop and left you on the street. I was so angry it scared me. I screamed into the air like a crazy person. Then I ran into the nearest bodega and bought myself a bomber of beer and downed it right there in the store to calm down, only to feel panicked when I was clear enough to realize that I had abandoned you on a busy street. I ran back to where you were, and you were standing where I'd left you, still wailing.

I hugged you and apologized and thought you'd hate me and remember that incident forever.

Do you?

You and I played checkers on the floor of my barely furnished apartment while you asphyxiated a stuffed rhinoceros with both hands.

"You're letting me win," you said.

Of course, I was. "It's not your fault that Mom and I are having problems, okay?"

You fixed your gaze on the checkerboard, refusing me relief. Who's blaming me, your body language seemed to imply?

"Do you like being home with Daddy?"

"What's the difference?"

"What do you mean 'what's the difference?'"

You planted a finger atop one of your pieces. "You aren't my Daddy anymore."

You might as well have stabbed me. "I will always be your Daddy."

"Mom says you're naïve."

"Do you even know what that means?"

"It means you don't see what I see."

"What do you see?"

"We're disappointing."

"Mom says you're disappointing?"

You looked at me. You have my round face. "*You* are."

I wanted to start weeping right there in front of you. Instead, I jumped three of your pieces and earned a king. "That's what you get for talking checkers trash!"

"Daddy?"

"Yeah, M?"

"There's a glass behind the TV."

You hopped on the couch and aimed your rhino's horn down into the space behind the television stand. My whiskey tumbler. Another empty bottle of Maker's Mark wedged between DVDs of *Moana* and *Minions*.

How had I spiraled into this dim place?

"Don't bounce on the couch," I said. "And don't tell Mom about the glass, okay?"

HAPPY NOW IS ENOUGH

While the divorce was getting finalized, I decided to take you to see your grandparents on my side for the first time. I wanted you to know where I came from.

I hadn't been back to the apartment since the *No Good Very Bad Asian* tour almost ten years ago when I gave my dad those tickets that he never used. My parents never came out to visit after you were born, claiming my grandmother couldn't travel and that my father had to work, and I had no showbiz reasons to be in L.A.

"What a mess!" my mom cried out over the phone with such immediacy that I wondered if she thought my divorce was her mess to clean. "Can you believe this? Hor got *dee-vorce!*" she said to my dad.

I couldn't hear his response, but I could imagine him shrugging. I was a shrug now, as in the shrug Chinese parents offer when forced to discuss the failures of their children.

In Alhambra, you and I exited the I-10 East onto Garfield Avenue. On one side of the street was a hospital. On the other, there were buildings with physician's offices and dozens of signs displaying the Chinese names of doctors and dentists and the dubious English equivalents of those names, such as Lung Chang, Dong K. Kong and Sugar Kao. Further down Garfield, there was one strip mall after another, home to Chinese super-markets, bubble tea cafes, video stores, noodle houses, and nail and hair salons.

"Are we still in America?" you asked.

At a stoplight, after you complained of carsickness, I cracked open the passenger-side window. On the street corner, an older woman introduced her son, daughter, and several grandchildren to another Chinese family. She referred to her offspring name-lessly, by title. Oldest son. Second daughter. But she called her grandchildren by name and achievement. Grace, an excellent violin player. Eric, top of his class in algebra. This is the way Chinese parents are. Their children are a means to an end. And the end is the grandchild.

You are the prize.

Parked in front of the old apartment complex, I actually felt a pang of nostalgia for the rust-stained balconies, landscaping that was either dead, unkempt, or both, and the palm trees with brown, sagging fronds that shadowed the murky green exterior. We climbed two flights of stairs to the apartment with the purple, chipped door and the soiled, red welcome doormat with four yellow Chinese characters. Almost nothing had changed. Everything just looked older and smaller. Like me. So much had happened since I'd left, I could barely remember why I left in the first place. I pressed the buzzer.

Inside, my mother shouted in Mandarin, "Who is it?"

"Say Grandma," I said to you. "Say it in Mandarin. *Nai-nai.*"

When you did, the door opened, unleashing a thick musk of oyster sauce and sesame oil. My mother shrieked with joy and scooped you up in her arms. She smiled in a way I had never seen. I entered, wiping my feet on the doormat and taking off my shoes like I'd done thousands of times before. But you found the smell overpowering and suppressed a gag.

To my surprise, a gray-haired man in a dark suit edged out of the kitchen. His scalp was shaved in front and a Manchu queue extended down to his waist. It was Master Ming! I didn't know whether to be starstruck or pissed for my dad or both or neither—I found myself indifferent. What my mother did for companionship (if that was indeed what she was doing) was her business.

"So please to meet you," he said, nodding.

"Master Ming is just here for my monthly appointment," my mother said.

"Let me guess," I said. "It's a bad luck time."

My mother smiled and blushed at Master Ming, then you. "No, *ai-yuh!*" she said, bouncing you in her arms. In English, she added, "It is good luck time! We are so lucky-lucky, right?"

You didn't reply. After a few moments of awkward silence, Master Ming edged around us for the door and said he'd see my mother later. Because surely he would. My mother bade him farewell, licking her lips, an act I found endlessly disturbing.

The creased gray leather sofa where I'd slept still occupied most of the living room. The small desk where my grandfather used to sit was wedged between the sofa and the wall, the chair permanently stuffed beneath the desktop. The bookshelves were crowded with unused electronics like transistor radios, toy robot dogs, and a half-dozen calculators of mixed variety and size. A snowy layer of dust covered every surface. Facing the sofa, on a rolling cart, there was the DVD player, VCR, and TV combo where I'd started watching comedy. Near the kitchen, there was an end table with an incense stick holder and a bowl bearing grapefruits and oranges. On the wall hung a black-and-white photograph of a gaunt and unsmiling man—your great-grandpa. In the kitchen, there was barely room for a person to move because boxes were piled floor to ceiling. Laundry detergent, dishwashing liquid, soy sauce, canola oil, and port wine.

"Please sit," she said to me with you in her arms. Your grandma had never said "please" to me before. She was dressed up (presumably for Master Ming): a cream-colored collared shirt with dark khakis and trouser socks. Her gray hair was tied back in a ponytail.

I handed her a red envelope with $500 inside. She didn't thank me, instead she insisted that I didn't have to give her anything and that they had plenty to live on. I sat on the sofa. The cushions were so old and airy that they were hardly there. My mom put you down and unstacked a plastic stool for herself. You climbed onto my lap.

"You both look very skinny," my mother said to me. "Are you eating enough?" She got up and stared down at my face. "Your lip color isn't good. Open your mouth. Let me see your tongue."

I held up a hand between my mother's face and mine. "Enough," I said. "Where's Dad?"

My mother sighed and wiped her brow with a forearm. "He said he had to work. You know him: he never listens to me. I told him you were coming, but he didn't care. What did you do to your wife?"

"Nothing."

"That's what you do," she said, spittle on the lips. "Nothing." To you, she said, "You are Chinese, understand?" You buried your face in my shoulder. My mother shot me a disapproving glance. "She doesn't speak Chinese? She should go to Chinese school. You have the money. We didn't have the money, otherwise we would have sent you to Chinese school."

"She likes to ride around on her trike. She likes to bounce on her pogo stick. Right, M?"

You nodded, flat-lipped.

"She wears expensive dress," she said. "Expensive dress instead of Chinese school."

"She speaks to Maryann a little at home."

"What you mean 'she?'" my mother asked in English. "Where's 'she?' I don't see 'she.'"

"Very funny, Mom."

"Why don't you shave? Your face looks like a piece of tape that's not sticky anymore."

"Where are you from, Grandma?" you asked in Mandarin.

Her face lit up again. All my life, I'd known next to nothing about my parents. Why didn't they tell me more? Why didn't they want me to know them as people? I assumed there was trauma they didn't want to share, but once you asked, my mother opened up like you were her biographer. I wasn't sure you'd understand it all, but I didn't stop her. I wanted to hear her story for myself.

She had emigrated from Chaoshan, in Guangdong Province. She missed the homeland terribly and hoped to take you back to China one day. To Changle, because we had extended family there. It had become a well-off city in recent decades. Even richer than L.A., she claimed. She had met my dad in school.

"He was so confident and I was foggy all the time back then," she said. "He said 'I'm going to escape China and become rich and you should follow me' and I believed him! Your dad always had crazy dreams. *See-too-pid.*"

Was my dad any more stupid than I was to chase my dream?

They had walked along the coast of the South China Sea for three weeks with very little food in search of the relatives who would smuggle them in a fishing junk headed for Hong Kong in 1971.

"I had to leave my parents," she said. "We were in a re-education camp just because they taught Western classical music." She looked at me. "I never saw my mommy and daddy again. When we escaped, your father and I had to eat out of the trash. I carried him on my back for thirty miles on muddy roads and in freezing winds. He was so skinny and weak then." She shrugged and chuckled. "We were separated for a month because we had lost each other at a checkpoint. It was a miracle we met again in Shenzhen. I ran into him at a street market. I thought I'd have to leave China without him. We had such good luck."

You began to fall asleep. My mother's story was boring you. But I was transfixed; I wouldn't have known any of it if you hadn't been there. I asked why she never told me about her youth.

She made disappointed cluckings, like my question was dumb. "If we showed weakness, then you wouldn't respect us," she said. "But you didn't respect us anyway. Because you left and never came back."

Your grandmother has a way of being very accurate.

Your great-grandmother, tiny with thinning gray curls, emerged from her bedroom. "Who are they?" she asked my mom.

"It's me, Grandma," I said. "Hor."

She nodded, but I wasn't sure she actually recognized me. I took her by the elbow and led her to the sofa. "This is Maryann," I said in mangled Mandarin. "My daughter."

She smiled at you. I'd never seen her smile, either. She looked up at me and said, "You used to be so fat and healthy!"

Yup, she recognized me.

"But now too skinny," my mother said.

"You never come home," my grandmother said. "Why?"

My mother postulated that I moved so far away because I didn't drink enough milk as a kid. She went on to opine that I had married poorly, because mixed-race women left their husbands when they didn't get impregnated regularly. Then she said I should move back to Los Angeles and take care of the family like a good son.

"I'm taking care of you guys now," I said.

"How?"

"I send money to Dad."

She harrumphed, taking the red envelope out of her pocket and flipping it onto an end table. "Just money. You owe us that."

I shook my head and felt anger rising. She, of course, didn't know that I was sending hundreds of thousands of dollars to my father each year. "I just want you to be proud of me a little," I said in English. "Not even a lot. Just a little."

Her face puckered as if my words were sour medicine. But then she glanced at you and her expression softened. Toward you, she felt pure love that she must have felt about me when I was your age. When she looked at me again, there was barely a trace of that love left.

"You are happy now and that is enough," she said.

It would have to be, because it was all I'd get. Without you, I wouldn't even have gotten that.

For that small victory, thank you, M.

In the Little Saigon part of Westminster, I pulled into Ngu Thanh Dat Hoang Deli's parking lot. I only knew where we were from the deli's address in Google; the shop had no sign. Just four screw holes where it used to be. The store windows were tinted and the parking lot was full.

Inside, Vietnamese songs played, the vocals nasal and female. There was a large bulletin board filled with posters related to community activities. A teen table tennis tourney in Garden Grove. A concert featuring Chinese pop stars. There was a bakery display case that was empty save the unexplained presence of a car battery. Several large screen TVs showed Vietnamese soaps and soccer matches. Men were gathered at tables, smoking and drinking Vietnamese coffee, playing pai gow or Chinese poker or mahjong or baccarat. There were four occupied arcade machines in the back—Keno. You scrunched your nose at the smoke and flitted away flies. Some men stared at us. Others continued to play, chat, and laugh. They were uniformly sun-darkened and leather-skinned. Many were missing teeth.

You held my hand. You only did that when you were afraid. Not knowing what else to do, I called out in English, "I'm looking for John Hak Kay Soy Lee!"

The men kept playing their games.

I repeated my dad's name, this time in Mandarin with the last name first, omitting "John." One of the men barked Vietnamese at the open door to the back room.

My father came out, wearing a brown blazer, flanked by two high-heeled Asian women wearing pasties and a thong. I shielded your eyes for a moment, but it was pointless. Your grandfather asked what was going on in Vietnamese without acknowledging me. The women wobbled around the deli, collecting empty coffee containers.

His hair, formerly gray, was dyed a lustrous black, and there were deep lines on his tanned face that looked like Sharpie marks. He stepped behind the counter, retrieved a bottle of port wine, and began unscrewing it. His fingernails were caked with dirt. Fabric pilled his blazer. His light-colored dress shirt was threadbare to the point of translucence. In Mandarin, he looked down at you and asked, "What you want, little girl?"

"Classy place, Dad," I said. His smile faded. He reached down, pulled out two baguettes, and laid them on the gritty counter. To me, he asked in English: "What you want? Banh mi? You want pork? You want Vietnam *sah-lah-mee*? You want pâté? You want head *chee*? You so skinny. You look no so healthy."

I told him we'd just ate. I was itching for a nip from my whiskey flask. It had been hours.

Your grandpa grunted. He deserted the baguettes and walked back around the counter with his bottle of port and a stack of Dixie Cups in hand. We sat at an empty four-top.

He poured a cup and offered it to me. Maybe Dad was reading my mind. "Drink," he said in English. I sipped the port and tried to savor it, but it was no time before I was pouring myself another. Your grandfather looked at you and cracked a brown-toothed smile. "You are my granddaughter now! So beautiful! Boys are going to like you."

"Dad, come on," I said. "We want her to grow up valuing her intelligence and not her looks. And we definitely don't want her to care what . . . boys think." I almost said, "what assholes like the two of us think."

My father stared at me blankly, mouth agape, uncomprehending. He turned to you and said, "Call me *Yeh-yeh!*"

You did as asked. One more time than I ever did.

My father studied your face. He sipped his wine and then asked you, "What do you think? Are you Chinese?"

"I'm American!" you said.

My father shook his head, downed his cup of port, belched, and refilled. I wanted to tell him I was sorry for how I'd treated him when I was a kid. I wanted to say I was ashamed of my behavior and that I was young and immature and acted like my upbringing was beneath me. That would have been the grown-up thing to do. But I just sat there and watched him drink, like I did when I was fourteen. You looked at us, wondering why the hell we were looking at you. I couldn't remember the last time my father called me by name. In so many ways, I had been born an orphan.

I hope you'll never feel that way, even though I won't be there for you. Whatever you become in the future, please know that you are deeply loved, by many people, especially my parents. They filled with joy from the moment they met you, just from looking at your face, your flawless face.

"I can rest easy now," my dad said to me. "My work is finally done."

What work he was referring to other than "drinking condensed milk," I wasn't sure.

"You must study hard and be smart girl," he said to you in English. "Be doctor. Be lawyer. Be C-E-O!" He sipped wine and his smile went away. He stared into his cup. "Don't be like me." Then he glanced at me and said in Mandarin, "That joke you told about me was wrong."

Joke? Had he seen my standup?

"The one about us thinking coming to America was a mistake," he said. "My friend showed it to me. America is not a mistake. America saved my life."

The joke was: my parents came to America for a better life and now that China's better than us at everything, they realize they made a big mistake.

"It was just a joke," I said.

"I get it," he said. "Funny. But wrong. I have your DVD here in back. I watch all your movie. They're good! The women are very beautiful."

I couldn't believe it. All these years, he had been following me.

"Thanks, Dad," I said in Mandarin. To my surprise, I teared up, swallowing away a lump in my throat. "That means a lot to me."

In my mind, my pronunciation was perfect.

RED JUSTICE

On your sixth birthday, I got my dream acting role.

I was in Sarah's office on a conference call with Sony Pictures. We were discussing *Red Justice*, a biopic about a real-life Chinese American detective who helped bring down one of the deadliest gangs in Chinatown. The screenplay was written by a guy from San Francisco named Stanford Pong, and it was an action-comedy in the vein of *Lethal Weapon*. It was going to be directed by Corey Lin of the hit cars, guns, and ten-dudes-and-one-chick *Muscles and Cars* series. I was going to get top billing. My part was funny and dark, and I didn't even know if I'd have the acting chops to pull it off. But I wasn't going to tell Sarah or Sony Pictures that!

"There is a, um, substance abuse clause in the, um, contract," the producer said. "We don't have to talk about it now. You can read it over and let me know if you have any questions."

Sarah wasn't aware that I had fallen off the wagon. "Not a problem," she said. "Sirius has been dry for almost, what? Eight years." She looked to me to chime in. Everything about Sarah was so clean. No dirt beneath the nails. Teeth so white. Eyebrows plucked to a perfect toppled crescent. She'd just turned fifty and had nary a wrinkle around the eyes and her hair was still jet-black. She seemed to have a perfect family (at least according to Facebook: pretty Japanese wife, two high-school-age boys, summers on Long Island). I felt bad for even thinking about letting her down after she had stuck with me for almost fifteen years and put up with an extraordinary amount of my shit (real and otherwise).

"Seven years, eight months," I said. "It's my daughter's sixth birthday, and I met my wife, about thirteen months before she was born, and about seven months before that was when I went into rehab."

"We don't need to know," said the producer.

"He's excellent at math!" exclaimed Sarah.

When we hung up, she released a long sigh. "You won't believe how many handies I had to perform to put you in the running for that," she said. "You only got the role because Chow Yun-Fat's too old and John Cho said he couldn't fake his way through the Mandarin."

"Thank you, Sarah," I said, "for believing in me."

She smiled, her eyes cast down upon her desk. "I told you if you kept showing up, you'd be one of the ones left standing."

I thought about the others who believed in me, the many who selflessly lifted me up, to help make my dreams come true. Dan Van Pido, the people at HBO, and most of all Johnny. He had begun to appear in my dreams. In them, we were skeet-shooting and drinking together, touring shitty clubs, laughing in bars, one-upping each other with jokes about midgets. I missed him. I wanted to call, but pride or fear always held me back.

What had I done for others in my life? Had I helped anyone like Johnny had helped me? I never mentored young comics. I was all about myself, my career, my marriage, my needs. Raising you was the only redeeming thing I'd ever done for another person and now I didn't even have full custody.

I decided I needed to be better.

The shooting for *Red Justice* started right away in Los Angeles so I flew out and surprised my parents by buying them a modest Spanish-style house in Boyle Heights. I landed in the afternoon, and by that night, I had signed the papers and was on my way to Alhambra with a few unassembled packing boxes beneath my arm.

"I bought you a house," I said, when my mother let me in.

"*Hah??*" she said, incredulous.

"The movers will be here tomorrow afternoon."

"Are you crazy? Where is this place?" asked my dad.

"You didn't even let us look at the house!" my mom said.

"It's called a gift," I said. "You'll like it. It's got three bedrooms, two baths, and two-thousand square feet."

My mom looked around the apartment and shook her head. "Too much work."

"You should have talked to us first," my dad said.

"What's happening?" my grandmother, who had been planted on the sofa, said.

"He bought us a house," my dad said.

"Finally!" my grandmother cried out. "I want a bigger bed!"

My dad allowed himself a smile.

"This is a thank you," I said, putting a hand on my mom's shoulder. "For having me. Okay?"

She sighed, still frowning. "I don't know why you think you need to thank us."

"Well, I did, so can we shut up about it now?"

"I don't understand what you're saying," she said.

Shaking my head, I began to unfold the boxes. "Let's please start packing."

When I told your mother that I'd be away from you for four months for the *Red Justice* shoot, she was apoplectic.

"You're either in or you're out," she said.

"That's not fair," I said. "I'm happy to take her with me." I had hoped she would react well to that idea. Enough time had passed for us to occasionally look upon the good times in our marriage in a positive and even nostalgic light. Even Superdetective Paul McMillan sent me a Christmas card that year with a handwritten message inside that read, "I don't forget the cold cases, but at least we can start growing our family again. I hope you find peace."

"What about school?" your mother asked. "I know it doesn't matter to you because you've got a seventh grade education, but that's not what I want for Maryann."

"Easy," I said. I asked if she'd be up for letting you spend the summer with me. And that's when she said I'd be hearing from Cecilia Fabregas again. I got an email from her office a few days later saying that your mother had decided to file for sole custody. I had to start filming so I couldn't wait for a resolution. A month later, your mom texted that she was moving to London for a new job. I'd later find out that she'd dumped Gunther for Yevgeny Yukhurov, the Russian oil magnate who purchased the law firm she worked at. Not incidentally, she had also been recently named partner. I was in the middle of the shoot and couldn't get away. You two were gone by the time I got back to New York City.

Oh, and that dream role didn't turn out to be so dreamy. Corey Lin dropped out after a week to film *Muscles and Cars 8: Manila Night Moves*. Five writers showed up on set to tinker with the original screenplay. Hale Joseph was added to the cast as the lead, along with six other supporting male actors (one black, three white guys named Brad), and a Latina. Somehow the biopic about this Chinese guy's decorated career morphed into a film about Hale Joseph's quest to take down an organized crime syndicate in Koreatown. My part was reduced to almost nothing. Most of my lines became variations of "Come look at this, Chief." On the billboards, my head was visible over one of

the Brads' shoulders, but my name was left off the poster altogether. Meanwhile, *Crazy Rich Asians* became a huge, feel good
hit, and I might have been the only Asian actor in the world
who had no idea the damn movie was happening.

My father wanted me to meet him in Westminster to spend
an afternoon with him and a friend. His name was Thanh Ngu.
Mr. Poker Deli himself. When I got there, they were waiting in
Mr. Ngu's Audi SUV. I got into the back seat and we headed
south. Mr. Ngu was in his sixties, like my dad, and he also had
hair so obviously dyed that I swear I saw Just For Men stains
on the back of his neck. I asked where we were going. Instead
of answering, Mr. Ngu spoke passionately about how Asian
people understood what family truly meant. He explained that
American parents respect their children too much.

"The children must earn the elders' respect by returning to
help the whole family be prosperous," he said to my dad.

Even though my dad was nodding, it seemed like Mr. Ngu
was actually addressing me because I knew that my dad saw
the guy almost every day. It was obvious from watching my
father gaze upon this guy like a Chinese Vietnamese Jesus that
he yearned to be as successful and respected as Mr. Ngu.

Two hours later, we pulled into the parking lot of an abandoned, dilapidated commercial center. And when we got out of
the car, to my shock, I saw that my dad was holding a gun, the
same handgun he had shown me at Lee's Liquors when I was
fourteen. What the fuck were we going to do here?

As we walked around the outside of the store spaces, my
dad explained that he wanted the three of us to enter into a loan
for this commercial space that they planned to develop into a
100,000 square-foot casino. Pai gow. Chinese poker. Blackjack.
The project he'd mentioned years before.

"You have money," my dad said. "We could even take out second mortgage on new house."

Mr. Ngu said he wanted me to co-sign a $5 million loan.

I lied and said I'd think about it. "I have to consult with my manager," I said.

"Okay," he said, smiling and baring a gold bicuspid. "But no trust the whites. Never. Okay?"

When we got back to the deli parking lot in Westminster, I stormed to my rental car, and my dad followed. I got behind the wheel, and my dad sat in the passenger seat and asked why I didn't just agree to Mr. Ngu's proposition. I told him in no uncertain terms that I would not be investing with them.

"And what are you doing with that gun? What is he making you do?"

My dad sighed. "Nothing. I just stand there while he has meetings."

I shook my head in disbelief.

My dad laughed. "You just don't want to help. You never want to help me."

"I just bought you a house!"

"I did not ask for house," he said. "You always been ashame of us. Even though we love you so much. We risk our lives for you."

"You risked your lives for yourselves, too!"

"We work so hard only because of you."

"That makes no sense," I said. "Would you have sat on your ass for decades if you were childless? That's just an excuse for you to make me owe you for the rest of my life."

"I don't understand you."

"I don't understand you people either!"

"You want the money to buy drugs for yourself."

"No."

"Yes."

Well, yes, on occasion. "You're at that deli playing cards with half-naked women all around you, and you're telling me how I should live my life?"

My father shrugged. "Your mother doesn't like sex."

With my eyes closed, I rapped my forehead softly against the steering wheel repeatedly. "I'm going to send you a small monthly allowance from now on," I said. "Nothing more. No more Mr. Ngu."

"A son should help his father," he said in Mandarin. "Now that you are successful."

I laughed. "Now I'm successful? You've never believed in me."

"Of course not!" My father laughed. "How can you blame us? You were fifteen! If a little fat boy with pimples came to you and told you he want to be movie star, would you believe?"

"But I'm your son."

My father continued to laugh.

After I left him, his words just kept eating away at me, chirping and buzzing in my brain, knotting up my craw. That day, I missed my shoot. I checked into a hotel room and smoked a huge bowl and drank half a bottle of Jameson's while I waited for my coke dealer to arrive. If you weren't Sancho with a Long Beach fucking area code, I wasn't answering your call. My parents still weren't ready to forgive me. I could have paid them every cent I earned, and I still wouldn't have lived down that I chose the Razzmatazzes over the Lees almost twenty years ago. All I ever wanted was for them to have some level of faith in me, a scintilla of respect for what I'd accomplished. I don't think I was asking for too much.

By the time Sancho got to the hotel, I was already incomprehensible, laughing uncontrollably at a marathon of *Fixer Upper*.

The eight ball went up my nose and I was finally where I wanted to be. I think I popped some downers too. I don't remember much after a certain point. What I do know from the police report is this:

I was stumbling down the middle of Coronado Street in Pasadena, alternately screaming and cackling. I was barefoot, shirtless, and wearing board shorts with an open fly (no underwear). I was playing air guitar, singing "Interstate Love Song" by Stone Temple Pilots, and berating drivers who were honking as they weaved around me. When a policeman appeared, I decided it would be a good idea to run. I sprinted down the street, bowling over mothers and strollers like I was a tailback not to be denied. Eventually, I was tackled, tasered, and arrested. If I were black, without a doubt, I'd have been shot dead.

Needless to say, Sarah was not happy that I landed in the hospital with a broken collarbone. On FaceTime, she looked at me with disgust.

"You don't know what it's like," I told her. "Being Asian."

Sarah shrugged. "You're right, I don't," she said. "But I don't have to. You're not entitled to understanding. I've never asked for permission to be who I am. I've never asked to be recognized or acknowledged or represented. All of that is waste-of-time talk. I'm only interested in action."

I don't know why I expected her to be a shoulder to cry on. She had never been. "Is that what they tell you in the National Guard?"

"My service is a privilege and an honor," Sarah said. "So I tell you stories. So what? You know what's one hundred percent true? I didn't drop out on you. I didn't quit. I've always seen myself in you, because we're both different. So I'm still here, unlike the rest of the people in your sadass existence. So I need you to listen to me when I say: 'you need to grow the fuck up!'"

"I've been grown-up for too fucking long!" I shouted. "I just want to be taken care of!" I began weeping. But I should have saved my tears for when the doctor showed up.

She would not look at me as she said my X-ray had shown a dark spot in my chest that needed further testing immediately. By the end of the week, I had been diagnosed with stage four hepatocellular carcinoma, a lethal form of liver cancer. Tumors had spread to my kidneys and metastasized in the bone. The cancer was caused by the hepatitis that I had ignored. I never did take those drugs the doctor prescribed years ago, thinking, hoping (dumbly) that my getting clean would erase the disease. *Natürlich*, I didn't stay clean.

I was given three months, maybe six, if I was lucky.

REGRETS, I'VE HAD A FEW

I confess that my delete key isn't broken. It's on purpose that I haven't turned back while writing this letter. I totally understand now when people say they don't want to live in the past because it drives them crazy. Everything I've done to myself has added up. Every cigarette, every double whiskey, every eight ball. In rehab, we all told ourselves we had escaped the worst of consequences, and if we followed the magical Twelve Steps, we'd get a second chance at life. But the clock starts ticking on Day One. And for years, I had been taking a sledgehammer to that clock.

I've decided not to tell your grandparents I'm dying. I've been selfish all my life, and now I finally feel justified in being so. I want to spend the rest of my days as happily as possible. I don't have another second to be a disappointment or to be disappointed in them.

I've thought about telling your mother and getting the two of you to fly back to New York City to see me one last time. But I've decided against it. I don't want your lasting memory of me to be one of my diminishment. I'd prefer that you see me through my words and in your imagination—standing tall, live and uncensored.

I have tried to be many things in life. A comic. A boyfriend. A husband. A father. An actor. But I was always Asian first. An Asian comic. An Asian actor. A Chinese husband to a half-Chinese wife. An Asian dad to a girl who looked almost white. I was not qualified to be one of the greatest comics ever. Nor was I qualified to be just another celebrity boyfriend or a Hollywood leading man. I couldn't be the surrogate son of my mentor. Or a good son to my own parents. I never once asked to be Asian.

You know when race doesn't matter?

When you're dying.

The nurses wake you up at 5:00 a.m. to take your vitals just like they do to the whites. They collect your urine samples in a cup and stool from the plastic hat just like every other dying person.

Here, in a hospital bed, near the end, I am finally free.

Sarah called to say that I'd been invited to appear on *Kid Star Rehab with Dr. Liam*, which was filming in Connecticut. The producers wanted me to visit Veronica and offer a supporting presence as she tried to get clean.

"They're paying really well," Sarah said. "Like, crazy well."

Veronica would be there for the next four months. During our affair, I knew she had a pill problem. She had this cocktail that would kill a horse. She carried it in a cloth mini-purse with fancy embroidery and intricate buttons. She couldn't open it easily because she had these super long French nails. She'd have such bad withdrawal that her hands would shake and she'd be sick for days. I saw her try to open a packet of Chiclets once, and it was like watching someone with cerebral palsy knit.

"Why don't you use a normal pill box?" I once asked.

"But my bag is so pretty!"

That was my Veronica in a nutshell. She had so much trouble dealing with her pill bag that she rarely went farther than two blocks from her Park Avenue apartment. Sarah sent me a cut of the first episode of the show, and in her second scene, Veronica insisted that she have a personal nurse dedicated to helping her take selfies for her social media followers.

After getting cleared to visit Veronica by my doctors, I was driven several hours outside the city up winding roads into the remotest parts of rural Connecticut to the Greenest Pastures Recovery Center. As I ascended, the trees were all the autumn colors, and the rolling hills stretched to the horizon, and it made me think: I never want to leave this Earth. The facilities were visible down a steeply sloped driveway, at the end of which was a sprawling two-story mansion partially obscured by trees. I arrived at a large white iron gate and a very prominent security camera mounted on a post. After introducing myself to an intercom box, I was driven through. There were only two other cars in the lot: a dirt-caked Subaru Forrester and a large production coach with tinted windows and thick dark power lines running from the vehicle to the main house. Beyond was a shady meadow, where two women in bikinis sunbathed on towels. Rehab never looked more relaxing. The place was way nicer than the one I went to.

Inside, I told the middle-aged woman behind the front desk that I was there to see Veronica Razzmatazz. The woman was dressed in medical scrubs and wore a Red Sox baseball cap sideways over tight side curls that resembled a male Hasidic Jew. She introduced herself as "Resident Technician."

"Let me see if Ms. Razzmatazz is still doing work," she said.

I followed Resident Technician out of the building, onto a patio, where there was a very short African American man doing a downward dog on a mat. The butt of his yoga pants read, "I ain't your Monkey Tom!" He was Anthony Godwin, the former child star of *JooJoo Beans in Milk*, a sitcom from the nineties about a rich, white woman adopting five black children. "I ain't your Monkey Tom!" was Godwin's catchphrase. I used to love that show.

I was led down a red brick walkway to a cottage, where I saw the first signs of filming. On the porch, a young, bleach blonde woman in short shorts sat cross-legged facing three cameras. Several men struggled with a large scrim. Nearby, two large television trailers were parked beside each other. There was a tent covering a snacks table stocked with chips, energy bars, and soft drinks. A waterfall flowed audibly and birds trilled.

"Looks like she's doing her testimonial," Resident Technician said. "Perhaps you should wait in the guest's lounge."

We returned to the main building, and I waited in a room with uncomfortable chairs and brass-framed photos of pastel flowers in vases that look borrowed from the set of *The Golden Girls*. I pinched a flimsy paper cup from the cooler and sipped some water. I skimmed a tri-fold brochure that featured a multi-chevron diagram detailing the "One Day At A Time" process, literature I was quite familiar with. Outside, a man shouted obscenities while a woman keened. I peered out into the meadow. The sunbathers had disappeared.

"I didn't touch you!" the man shouted.

"Leave me alone!" a woman said.

The shouting came from the opposite direction of Veronica's cottage. Walking uphill to a clearing, I discovered another cottage, two cameramen, a boom operator, and the argument. It was Colin Mays and Jennifer Distefano, formerly well-known child stars who dated in the early aughts. They starred together in several straight-to-video actioners. The years had not been kind to either rehabber. Mays looked like a pregnant man, and Distefano had undergone so much plastic surgery that the quadrants of her face shifted like tectonic plates as she yelled. A broad-shouldered fellow, who had the chipped face of a boxer, stood near the confrontation, but out of camera shot. His tight, dark T-shirt read "STAFF." Once Distefano shoved Mays, STAFF stepped between the two. A gray-haired, monocled man wearing a white lab coat loped in from the woods. He was Dr. Liam, the celebrity physician and daytime talk show host.

"What's going on here?" he intoned.

Behind me, Resident Technician said, "Veronica will see you now."

The former child stars continued to scream at each other. Dr. Liam padded toward the camera and dispassionately explained that the two celebrities needed to "learn to deal with their disease in a healthy way." He expressed pessimism that the former couple could "adequately avoid the triggers of their desires to use in each other's presence," which failed to explain why they had decided to be cast on the same reality show.

"Ms. Razzmatazz has been very emotional," Resident Technician said. "I understand you two are close friends."

"We dated for a short time. Twice."

Her glance was a puzzled one. "That wasn't in the synopsis her people sent me."

At the cottage, the porch was abandoned. The cameras were still staged, and the scrims leaned unmanned against the railing.

"Big chair is for Ms. Razzmatazz," she said. "Stool, for you."

Resident Technician clipped a lavalier mic to my collar and left without a word.

I edged past the wires and cameras and waited. I peeked into the cottage and saw the sheen of finished hardwood floors. No furniture inside. Another fifteen minutes or so passed, and six or seven men filed out of the trailers and took their places behind the equipment. A scrim was hoisted. LEDs on stands were lit. A man wearing a baseball cap backwards flopped into Veronica's chair, pretending to be her for lighting purposes. A short, scrawny fellow with a crucifix tattooed on the side of his neck introduced himself as The Producer Not Just The Cameraman.

"We just did a dry run," he said. "This is going to be great. So dramatic. So real."

The Producer Not Just The Cameraman peered through the viewfinder. He gave a thumbs-up, and the man in the seat got up and hopped over the railing.

"It'll be another few seconds," said the producer.

Many thousands of seconds and three or four crew cigarettes later, Veronica emerged from her trailer. Her hair was freshly curled, and she wore so much makeup her face reminded me of a birthday cake. She was dressed in Daisy Duke shorts, platform heels, and a gold sequined tank top that bulged at the small of her back where the wireless mic was strapped. Diamond bracelets glinted from her wrists. Platinum hoop earrings and those big blonde Shirley Temple curls made her face look small.

She smiled when she saw me, but not so widely as to disturb the meticulous and voluminous labors of her stylist. "Sirius," Veronica said. Yes, Sirius.

We hugged and she pecked me on each cheek. "I'm a mess," she said.

I couldn't tell if she was fishing for a compliment, describing her situation, or both.

"Hold on," the producer said. "We're not filming yet." He told the scrim guys to move two steps to the right, then two steps to the left, perfect.

Veronica sat, crossed her legs, and smiled into the camera. "Ready?"

"Now we are, yes," the producer said.

"Thanks for visiting," Veronica said to me. "You've always been such a good friend. One of my best, really."

She sounded like she was reciting from a script. What were my lines supposed to be?

"It's good to see you," I said. "We lost touch after the world tour. And I just hope you're okay. Did you overdose?"

"Cut!" The producer glared at me. "We don't need your backstory. And don't mention the overdose. Jesus Christ, haven't you been briefed?"

"Not at all," I said.

"It's okay," Veronica said. "I'm okay. I can deal with this. I'm ready to. Really, I am. Really."

The producer asked if Veronica was sure. Her eyes moistened, and she fanned herself with those absurdly long French-tipped nails. Her blinking sped, and her artificial lashes, tipped with glitter, were so long that I became dizzy looking at her.

Veronica closed her eyes, inhaled through her nose, and took quick breaths through pursed and rounded lips. She said she was ready, and the producer disappeared again behind the camera.

"Am I supposed to say something?" I asked.

"Tell her you care for her as a friend and you want to see her healthy," said the exasperated producer.

I did as told.

"I just need this time to be Veronica, you know?" she said. "Not Veronica Razzmatazz."

"I know what you mean," I said. "You need to get back in touch with what's important in your life." I leaned forward and reached for her hands, but Veronica recoiled, and the producer again yelled, "Cut!"

"What did I do?"

"No touching," he said. "This isn't your romantic comedy, okay?"

"You're my childhood friend, Hor," Veronica said.

Ah, so that was my character.

"Okay, dude," the producer said to me. "You're going to say: 'You've always been a person who's so good at caring for other people, but not so good at caring for yourself.'"

"And then I'm going to cry," Veronica said.

Anger flushed my face. In the past, I found her irresistible, but now, she looked like a circus performer to me. I wasn't going to do this. Life was too short. I shouldn't have come. "I'm leaving. This is bullshit."

"What's bullshit?" Veronica asked.

"You're not good at caring for other people," I pointed out.

Veronica began to tear up. "What?"

The producer decided to start filming.

"You've been selfish since I met you," I said.

"Because of her disease." Dr. Liam sidled past me into the frame. He leaned against the railing and looked down upon Veronica with shortened brows and crossed arms.

"I can't believe Sirius would say that," Veronica said to the camera. "He's always been like a brother to me."

"A brother you liked to fuck," I said.

Veronica eyed the producer and waited. "You're going to cut that, right?"

"Sure, sure," he said. "Keep going!"

"We were like family," Veronica said to the camera.

Dr. Liam nodded with soft eyes, monocle affixed—a rehearsed empathy. "Of course, he was."

I glanced at Dr. Liam and then Veronica.

"You've always been ashamed of me," I said.

She stared hard at Dr. Liam and waited. He faced the woods and began to hum tunelessly.

"We have an approved set of topics Veronica is willing to talk about," the producer said, letting the camera roll. "Whatever you had with her isn't on the list."

"I'm not ashamed," insisted Veronica.

"You don't need to say more," the producer said.

She began to sob and softly repeat "why does he want to hurt me?"

I waited for her to complete her display of emotion, which was probably for her acting reel.

"Okay," the producer said. "That's a wrap. I think we got enough for that segment."

"Hor, are you staying for dinner?" Veronica asked, suddenly smiling and dry-eyed. "I've got a new album dropping next month. The same week as the *Kid Star Rehab* premiere. I'm performing later today for the patients if you want to stay, film it, put it on your feeds. The first single is entitled, 'Inspiration.'"

"It will be truly inspirational," confirmed Dr. Liam.

"My driver is waiting to take me back to the city," I said.

"You look tired, Hor," Veronica said. "What's wrong?"

"You're in rehab, that's what's wrong," I said. "You should focus on that." I stepped down from the porch and began heading back to the main house.

"Yeah, you're right, Hor," Veronica said. "We'll see each other soon?"

I'd likely be dead by the time she got out. "Sure," I said.

"One of the goals of Veronica's treatment is to get her comfortable with not having to be Veronica Razzmatazz all the time," Dr. Liam said into the camera. "In order to recover, Veronica needs to be happy with being Veronica McCloughan again. She has made significant steps today to deal with her tendency to be too good at caring for other people and not good enough at caring for herself. I'm confident that if she stays on this path and continues to be honest about her feelings regarding what it was like to grow up a reality star, she can begin her long journey to recovery."

As I passed the meadow, I stopped in my tracks, stunned by the sight of Johnny outside the house, talking on his cell phone. He was shaved bald and silver-bearded. He wore yellow Bulgari sunglasses, basketball warm-up pants, and a tight white T-shirt bearing the message "I'm a recycled teenager." When he hung up, our eyes met, and he slowly recognized me.

"Hor?" Johnny said, hiking his sunglasses to make sure he was indeed seeing who he thought he saw. He went for a hug, I went for a handshake, and we ended up in a tepid one-armed embrace.

I asked what Veronica was being treated for.

"Vicodin. Xanax. Pot addiction. That's the short list." He looked down at his sneakers. "It's all my fault."

I didn't know what to say to that. Our life together, the three of us as an almost-family, seemed so long past. When I think back on when I felt most complete and at peace, it was when I was walking through Chicago alone in the freezing cold trying to find our hotel. With Johnny, I had become a man. Should I have apologized for firing him from my tour? That was ten years ago. Should I have told him I was grateful that he took a chance on me when I was so young? What was the point now?

He filled the silence by saying that the show wanted him to film a segment telling Veronica that her life was at stake and that he knew best, because his life was at stake before he became sober.

"I'm supposed to be the recovered addict on this show, believe it or not," he said, with a chuckle. "Travel Channel wants V and I to go around the world together after this is over. *The Razzmatazzes Abroad.*" He scanned me head to toe. "What about you? Are you clean?"

"I'm free."

Johnny nodded and smiled. He seemed relieved. He squeezed my shoulder.

"Glad to hear that, little buddy," he said. "Really glad."

Johnny's voice was surprisingly soft, no longer raspy. He must have quit smoking, too. His green gaze receded, and the longer we stared at each other, the emptier it became.

The producer called his name. "We're ready for you," he said.

I stepped back from Johnny. "Your turn."

He smiled weakly, before lowering his sunglasses and facing the producer.

"Why 'ello 'ello," he said, as he walked toward him.

My living will leaves half to you and half to my parents. I'm worth $10 million. My mom and dad will finally get what they've wanted out of me. I hope they're satisfied.

As for your half of my fortune, get the business card Sarah has included in the envelope carrying this manuscript. You can trust her. Give the card to your mother. Tell her to call Sarah. She'll know what to do next.

I'm home now. My doctor says there's not much left to do other than to manage the pain. I get fevers and rashes. Some days, I can't even get to the bathroom because I'm so fatigued. I have a lovely Puerto Rican caretaker named Basilisa. She can't tell when I'm joking so she laughs every time I stop talking. She tells me about Puerto Rico a lot and how much she loves it there. Then what the hell is she doing in America?

I told her my parents came to America for a better life. Then China became the richest country in the world. What a mistake they made.

As usual, Basilisa laughs.

On days that I feel up to it, I put on a khaki windbreaker and pack a backpack with my meds, a bottle of water, a Ziploc of trail mix, and that day's *New York Times*. I drop-in and tell Dan Van Pido that I'd like to do ten minutes. I promise I won't run the light. I don't want to take time from the younger comics. A huge influx of Chinese nationals has hit the city now that they can afford to travel. There have been nights at Village Z when at least half the crowd is made up of Chinese mainlanders, which used to be a comedy goldmine for me. But I don't do that sort of thing anymore. As I've gotten older, it's become less fun to make fun of people who can't defend themselves.

Always punch up or sideways in comedy, I like to tell the amateur comics. Never punch down. *Natürlich*, I haven't followed my own rules.

I lurk in the shadows until the host says that the crowd is in for a real treat because they've seen me in movies like *Bangkok Family Vacation* and *The Plunger* so everyone please give a warm welcome to the very funny . . . then I step into the spotlight and take the microphone as I've done so many times before.

At Village Z last night, Pidofile looked at me with concern and asked if I was eating.

"*Natürlich*," I said. "I've got the like-everything gene. Always hungry. Always hungry for more life."

He got moist in the eyes. I tried not to look at him. He knew.

"You're the real deal, Sirius," he said.

I thanked him. "You can call me Hor. That's my real name."

My mom once said that when I became old, I'd realize what a waste of time living for myself was. She said I'd understand how alone I'd be.

Who doesn't hate it when his mother is right?

I hope you'll eventually forgive me for not being there to watch you grow up. I know at some point you'll be angry and confused because I was never there for you. You'll probably act out and hurt yourself and others. That reality hurts me more than the tumors.

I just hope that these pages help you see me more clearly than your memories will allow. I hope my words might eventually provide you some kind of peace on the unfortunate topic of me. Even though my life's work was the quest to be heard and seen, I feel like I've been invisible to you. Erased. And that's just not an outcome I can bear.

My biggest regret in life isn't all the terrible shit I've done. It's that I could never make you laugh. After going a lifetime without a hug from my parents, I barely remember what it feels like to hug you.

I suspect I'll keep seeing you everywhere until I'm gone. You'll be playing soccer and pitching Little League with the boys. You'll be on the subway, texting your friends. You'll be rocking a business suit like your mother. You'll be dressed for your wedding. You'll be right here at my bedside.

Be selfish.

Be disobedient.

Be free to fail.

Keep a high standard.

If you think small, your life will be small.

Don't allow others to make you small.

Never just be good enough.

Love must be between two people, like it is between you and me.

I don't know you and I don't know what you're going to be, but I don't need to in order to do the one thing required of me as a parent beyond ensuring your well-being.

My dear Maryann, when I think of you, I am so proud.

SIRIUS LEE, ACTOR AND COMEDIAN, DIES AT 33

Sirius Lee, the actor and standup comedian who was best known for his comedy special "No Good Very Bad Asian," died Sunday afternoon at his home following a brief battle with cancer, his management announced in a statement. Mr. Lee was 33.

Mr. Lee was born on May 7, 1986, in the predominantly Chinese immigrant suburb of Alhambra, California to John Hak Kay Soy Lee and Jane Dongmei Lee. Sirius's estrangement from them was a topic featured prominently on his live album "No Good Very Bad Asian" (2009).

The success of the album's HBO special and North American tour helped launch Mr. Lee's Hollywood film career. He appeared in the hit comedies "Bangkok Family Vacation" (2010), "Canadian Beach Party" (2011), "The Meat Shtick" (2012), "Another Bangkok Family Vacation: A Killer Hmong Us" (2013), "The Cock Brothers For President" (2014), "Bangkok Family Vacation 3: Apocalypse Tao" (2015), and the upcoming action-comedy "Red Justice."

Dan Van Pido, owner of Village Z Comedy Club on MacDougal Street, said that Mr. Lee had just performed last night. "I can't believe it," Mr. Van Pido said. "I hope he's finally at peace."

Actors and comedians expressed shock at Mr. Lee's death on Twitter. Hale Joseph, who starred with Mr. Lee in four films, wrote, "The best sidekick a superhero could have. Miss you, little man." Johnny Razzmatazz, who discovered Sirius Lee when he was just 15, tweeted: "SL was almost a son to me. Heaven just got a funny fortune-teller."

Mr. Lee is survived by his daughter Maryann, his ex-wife Tina, and his mother and father, none of whom could be reached for comment.

ACKNOWLEDGMENTS

Like many folks in the early part of this decade, I became a bit obsessed with standup comedy. I'd long been a lover of comedy in general, but after listening to all that *WTF with Marc Maron, The Nerdist,* and watching all that *Louie* (before its star became...problematic), I thought I'm good at voice, I'm funny, this novel will be easy! Boy, was I wrong. Eight years later, including a three-year detour to do standup in New York for research, somehow this small book, which had many different permutations long and short was made.

This book owes many debts to some of the great standup memoirs including Steve Martin's *Born Standing Up,* Lenny Bruce's *How to Talk Dirty and Influence People,* and perhaps most influentially, the surprisingly poignant *Too Fat to Fish* by Artie Lange. I also must thank the Al Martin-owned comedy clubs (Broadway Comedy Club, New York Comedy Club, and Greenwich Village Comedy Club) in New York City, where I floated on the periphery earlier this decade. And to the comedy buddies I made along the way: Jesus Chavez, Cindee Weiss, Angela Cobb, Wilson McDermut, Tony Jackson, Bobbie Jean Daniel, Rob Santos, Altai Kalatschinow, the late great Mike Jacobs, and many others, all of whom made me laugh so hard and so often. We keep saying we should meet up and do a mic, and then we remember how horrible open mics are. I hope I've captured the against-all-odds nature of a standup's life.

Thanks to Andrew Sullivan, John Gosslee, and Mandi Manns for their work at C&R Press on this book. And to my agents Annie Hwang and Erin Harris for their unceasing enthusiasm in the life of Sirius Lee. Thanks to the many dedicated people who administer the artist residencies at The MacDowell Colony, Djerassi Resident Artists Program, Caldera, Hawthornden Castle in Scotland, and Willapa Bay AiR—specifically Anza Jarschke, Rewa Bush, Maesie Speer, and Hamish Robinson.

To the writers and authors I have the privilege of knowing; they are always so inspiring and took the time to read pieces or all of this book: my writing group in New York named The Exiles (Laura Catherine Brown, who also designed the cover, Rachel Stolzman Gullo, Jennifer Sears, Anne Hellman White, Jael Humphrey, Emmeline Chang, Kate Baldus, and others), Hasanthika Sirisena, Kirsten Chen, Cheryl Tan, Ed Lin, Jimin Han, and Nami Mun.

And most importantly to my wife Jess and my brother Larry, the two most important people in my life. I'm just their sidekick in our adventures.

ABOUT THE AUTHOR

Leland Cheuk is the author of the story collection *Letters from Dinosaurs* (2016) and the novel *The Misadventures of Sulliver Pong* (2015), which was published in translation in China (2018). His work has appeared in publications such as *Salon*, *Catapult*, and *Joyland Magazine*, among other outlets. He has been awarded fellowships and artist residencies at The MacDowell Colony, Hawthornden Castle, Djerassi Resident Artists Program, Caldera, I-Park Foundation, and Brush Creek Foundation for the Arts. He is the founder of the indie press 7.13 Books. He lives in Brooklyn and teaches at the Sarah Lawrence College Writing Institute. You can follow him on Twitter @lcheuk and at lelandcheuk.com.

C&R PRESS TITLES

NONFICTION

Women in the Literary Landscape by Doris Weatherford, et al
Credo: An Anthology of Manifestos & Sourcebook for Creative
Writing by Rita Banerjee and Diana Norma Szokolyai

FICTION

Last Tower to Heaven by Jacob Paul
No Good, Very Bad Asian by Lelund Cheuk
Surrendering Appomattox by Jacob M. Appel
Made by Mary by Laura Catherine Brown
Ivy vs. Dogg by Brian Leung
While You Were Gone by Sybil Baker
Cloud Diary by Steve Mitchell
Spectrum by Martin Ott
That Man in Our Lives by Xu Xi

SHORT FICTION

Notes From the Mother Tongue by An Tran
The Protester Has Been Released by Janet Sarbanes

ESSAY AND CREATIVE NONFICTION

In the Room of Persistent Sorry by Kristina Marie Darling
the Internet is for real by Chris Campanioni
Immigration Essays by Sybil Baker
Je suis l'autre: Essays and Interrogations
by Kristina Marie Darling
Death of Art by Chris Campanioni

POETRY

CPSIA information can be obtained
at www.ICGtesting.com
Printed in the USA
FSHW010634260919
62361FS

9 781936 196999